UNCAGED

UNCAGED

PAUL McKELLIPS

NEW YORK

FIRST EDITION: July 2011

Published by Vantage Point Books
Vantage Press, Inc.
419 Park Avenue South
New York, NY 10016
www.vantagepointbooks.com

Manufactured in the United States of America
ISBN: 978-1-936467-09-9 (pbk)
ISBN: 978-1-936467-06-8 (hc)

Library of Congress Cataloging-in-Publication data are on file.
0987654321

Cover design by Matthew Wenger

This is a work of fiction. But there's nothing make-believe about the diseases, illnesses and injuries that attack and afflict millions of people around the globe each year. This book is dedicated to all of the biomedical researchers, scientists and physicians who work in our universities, medical schools, veterinary schools, teaching hospitals, pharmaceutical, bio-tech and medical device companies; to the men and women who work in our government agencies and wear the uniform of our Armed Services and fight for our health; thank you for all that you do in your endless quest to find cures and treatments for the diseases and conditions that affect all people and all ages. This book is also dedicated to Frankie Trull and the late Dr. Michael E. DeBakey, both of whom championed the cause, and possibilities, of biomedical research for more than 30 years.

UNCAGED

PROLOGUE

A simple, brown-wrapped package from UPS was sitting on her desk as she turned the light on. The package was unopened.

Phyllis Mayweather was an overweight, fifty-one-year-old single mother of two. Tom was a junior at the University of Washington, and Tori would soon be a freshman at Puget Sound University. Private tuition scared Phyllis to death. But she wasn't nervous about tuition right now.

She had never done anything like *this* before.

She had placed the order on the Internet just two days prior. It was actually pretty easy to do.

Just like they said it would be.

She stopped unwrapping the small, cigar box-sized package long enough to get up and shut the door since the hallways were starting to come to life with morning arrivals and coffee runs.

The blue-and-white packaging looked quite professional

and modern. *ANGEL EYE: Keep the Eye on What You Care.* The fragmented promotional slogan from a company called China Vision seemed to be authentic broken English.

The JS 308 was the mini digital video recorder and the JS 618 the mini button camera. The video screen was half the footprint of a credit card and about as thick as a slab of butter. Play. Rewind. Fast forward. It even had a USB port with connection cord for easy uploading to the hidden Web site portal.

She opened the recorder and inserted a one gigabyte mini SD card into the unit, along with the Sony-Ericsson mobile phone battery that was included. At 640 x 480 pixel resolution she could easily record fifty-five minutes of full motion video. Five seconds after she connected the three-foot camera cord she pressed the power button and, presto, she was already recording.

Angel Eye provided a package of eleven different button styles to choose from. Phyllis unbuttoned her blouse and stuck the recorder in her bra and snapped the camera into the second button from the top of her blouse.

Getting up from her desk she took in a deep breath and let it out slowly. She thought about her phone call with Ms. Ballinger. "Get us what we want and its $50,000. No questions asked and your identity always remains anonymous."

She walked out into the hall and headed down to her job in the lab at the Continental Primate Research Center where she worked with pigtailed macaques on AIDS research.

LOS ANGELES

Fletcher swiped his key card, pressed the button, and the elevator dropped three floors down below the lobby level.

His new graduate student, Tracy Lin, didn't even know the floor existed.

The doors slid open, and she was hit with noxious aromas. "Smells like Pet Smart on steroids down here."

Fletcher smiled and reached for his lab coat as Tracy geared up in her smock, mask, hat and gloves.

Her paper booties pulled up off the tacky mat with a sticking, sucking sound as Fletcher pressed the button to open the vapor-locked door. Once inside the vivarium, animal food, urine and dander were obvious smells.

"You'll get used to it," Fletcher said as he led her through a maze of hallways. There were no windows on the walls, and only a few doors had signs.

WILLIAM D. FLETCHER, PHD—
NEUROSCIENCE LABORATORY.

Fletcher extended another smart card from the retractable lanyard loop collection fastened to his belt. He swiped it and entered his secret four-digit code.

"Last time we won the national championship," he said. "But that was so long ago no one would know my PIN number now."

They walked into the lab. The cages came to life with non-human primates. The monkeys were interested in their human visitors.

"Shared," Tracy said, talking about the NCAA football championship Fletcher had alluded to.

Fletcher turned on his computer and punched in his password.

"Huh?"

"One, nine, five, four—your PIN. Didn't we actually

share the championship with Ohio State and Woody Hayes in 1954?"

An energy and smile came over Fletcher's face.

"This is good. Gretchen is showing signs of being able to reject the drugs; at least the addiction markers are diminished."

"Gretchen?"

"Rhesus. Cage three. Go on over and give her a biscuit before I dose her."

She activated the iPod shuffle she had just received from China Vision and walked out of Fletcher's lab office toward the rhesus monkey cages.

"You're not going to be entertaining her with music, Tracy. Just give her a biscuit," he called out while studying the most recent data-dump.

"Don't worry. I've got the Monkees Greatest Hits on this playlist. Maybe she can relate."

Gretchen was sitting alone, facing the back wall and her eyes were transfixed. Tracy tapped at the Plexiglas wall between them. "Hey, sweetie. Want a treat?"

Gretchen turned her head slightly but never made eye contact. She resumed her stare.

"She eating?"

Tracy adjusted her iPod shuffle.

"Not yet."

STORRS, CONNECTICUT

The leaves along the parkway were spectacular in color. It was shaping up to be a gorgeous New England autumn.

A rusted-out Dodge Rambler pulled into a parking place

as Jason Schmidt took the last possible drag on a Winston before he flicked it out the window. Pulling his rearview mirror down slightly, he checked out the gel-inspired faux-hawk and the earring loop, and then carefully fixed the second button down on his oxford shirt to make sure that the China Vision button camera was in place.

He reached for his Starbucks double-shot mocha, pulled on a red Swiss Army backpack from the passenger seat and went off to his new job.

"Good morning, Jason. Big day."

"Thanks, Sheila."

He smocked up; put on his booties, gloves and mask; and went into the lab.

"There he is. Congratulations, Mr. Schmidt."

Four researchers looked up and offered nods and waves. Dr. Masdan applauded though the noise was muffled by his purple latex gloves.

"This is the natural progression of things, Jason. Your first six months on the job in shipping and receiving have earned you this promotion."

"Thank you, Dr. Masdan."

"Being a veterinary technician is serious work, young man. We'll rely on you to make sure these rodents are well-taken care of, fed, watered, cages cleaned and lives enriched whenever possible."

Masdan removed an athymic mouse by the tail from its cage and put it in Jason's cupped hands.

"It's a naked mouse or what we call an athymic mouse."

"Athymic?"

"The thymus is knocked out in breeding, impacts their immune system. This type of mouse is incredibly valuable to research because it accepts many different kinds of tissue and tumor grafts without rejection because it does not mount an immune response."

"It doesn't have any hair."

"That's the naked part."

Jason held the mouse close to his smock and studied it closely.

"What's this? Looks like it has a huge growth on its butt."

"It's called the flank. They all do, in fact. It's human breast cancer. We grow human breast cancer in them and then see how they respond to new chemotherapies and other drugs."

"So they die from human breast cancer?"

The three other researchers snickered and walked off.

"No, they don't even feel a thing. But these *are* terminal studies. At the appropriate time we'll need to examine tissue samples and various cells to see what impact the drugs had on the cancer. Every day we get a little bit closer to another answer."

Masdan walked away as Jason moved the mouse closer to his chest.

"How do you know?"

Masdan turned back. "I know because tens of thousands of biomedical researchers are at work in their labs right now all across the world. We all contribute to the emerging body of knowledge that is cancer research."

"Not what I meant. How do you know they don't feel a thing?"

Masdan's eyes caught the concerned glances from the other scientists. He walked over to Jason and took the mouse from his hands and placed it back in its cage.

"Looks like you have a small rip in the middle of your

smock. Better get a new one and then Margaret will walk you through your daily tasks."

Desiree unbuttoned his top two buttons and slipped her hand down onto his chest. She was half his age, if that. She kissed his neck as he answered the office phone.

"Erol Meisberger."

"Dr. Meisberger, this is Chad Rasnor with USDA."

He motioned to Desiree to knock it off. She pouted and took a seat at the small conference table and kicked her leather and fur UGG boots up on the mahogany.

"Hi, Chad. What can I do for you?"

"Just a routine follow-up call after our last inspection of your animal facility."

"Right. Is there a problem?"

"No, not really. Just wanted to verify that you have replaced the two HEPA filters and six overhead light bulbs that were cited in the report?"

He winked at Desiree, who was now listening to music through her iPhone buds.

"Yes, in fact it's all done. I'll have my assistant fax over our compliance report in the morning."

Meisberger hung up the phone and put on his lab coat. Desiree was still lost somewhere in *Five for Fighting*. He tapped her on the boot. No response. He stepped behind the table and draped his arms around Desiree as she sat in the chair. His hands slipped under her cotton sweater and up to her breasts, unfettered in all of their glory. She didn't respond. He gently removed one of her ear buds.

"Can I help you?" she said, warming up to his advances.

"How about we take this show down to a dark, remote part of the lab and do some more anatomical research?"

"And then dinner? I'm starving. How 'bout Chinese?"

"Sure. But I need to get home by eleven."

"Your wife?"

"Not now. We have some serious work to finish. And I've got something I want you to see."

Meisberger walked over to his utility closet and pulled out a six-pack of light bulbs.

"I thought you promised a dark, remote place?"

"I did. But I also promised 'USDA Chad' some lights. Come on, let's go."

The two walked into the animal facility as most students and researchers were leaving for the day. Desiree was plugged into her iPhone as Meisberger started replacing light bulbs. The last light was replaced over a stainless steel surgical table in a quad suite of small rooms. He turned the light on as Desiree took a seat.

"Be right back."

He came back carrying a small cage with three rats inside. Each rat was maybe nine-inches long from nose to tail with brown and tan fur. He pulled one out of the cage and put it on the table.

"Good God, that thing is gross. That's what you wanted me to see?"

Meisberger rubbed his hands together like an excited little boy. He pulled a syringe out of the drawer and then a vial of liquid. He filled the syringe, then opened an alcohol rubbing pad. He vigorously washed an area of the tail next to the rat's hind quarters.

"That, my darling, is a rat's ass. His name is Beauregard."

"Not that I give a rat's ass, but what are you going to stick up Beau's butt?"

"In the tail—not the ass—I'm injecting a solution that will put the little guy to sleep."

"Forever?"

"No, just a few hours."

The rat went limp and Meisberger turned on his new light bulb. He removed a small razor from the top drawer and shaved an area in the center of the rat's back. After another bath of alcohol rubs, he removed a scalpel from the sealed surgical tool wrap. He made a half-inch incision in the center of the back and pulled the top and bottom flaps of skin back ever so slightly with sterilized spacers. Desiree moved in closer now and took the ear buds out. She held the iPhone in front of her in a mesmerized, almost catatonic state.

Meisberger reached in for a small pair of surgical scissors.

"What the hell are you doing?"

"I'm going to cut the nerves to his spine."

"What? Why?"

Meisberger, held the scissors up in front of Desiree's face, opening and closing them quickly. He hunched his back and let out a ghoulish laugh.

"Because I can. I am the mad scientist Doctor Erol von Meisberger, vivisectionist and ruler of the animal world!" He bellowed in laughter at his own silliness.

He reached the tip of the scissors into the area around the rat's spine. The bone was narrow and white, almost yellow. There wasn't much blood, but he dabbed it up anyway. He found the spot he wanted and isolated the tip of the scissors with precision.

Snip.

The sound of the tiny bone and nerves being severed seemed like deafening madness to Desiree. She screamed and ran out of the suite of rooms into the hallway. Her body slid down the cinder block wall of the university's sub-basement animal facility called a vivarium.

"Desiree? Dezy? Are you okay?" Meisberger called out.

There was no answer.

"Are you alright, baby?"

He walked out into the hallway as Desiree was coming to.

"I think you fainted. You okay?"

She started crying. He tried to comfort her, but she pushed him away.

"Okay, okay. I've got to give him an injection of the good stuff now, dress the wound and put him back in his cage. You'll feel better in a few minutes, then we can go grab some Chinese in Laguna."

Meisberger got out another vial and made the injection of experimental mouse embryo stem cells next to the rat's injured spine. Four little stitches and a dressing the size of a dime, and Beauregard the rat was back in his cage still sound asleep. He turned off the light and pulled the door shut and locked it.

"Okay we can—Desiree? Dezy?"

The hall was empty. She was gone.

WASHINGTON, DC

Every seat at the National Press Club luncheon in Washington was filled. C-SPAN cameras in the back of the room were locked-in as print reporters and bloggers scribbled cryptic notes next to a gaggle of radio correspondents with digital recorders in outstretched hands.

"So please welcome the new president and CEO of the American Humane Fund, Angela Sherman."

A smattering of polite applause filled the room as the former top lawyer for the Sierra Club took to the podium.

"It's a pleasure to be here with you today, and I do so appreciate your fine welcome. To my predecessor, I wish Wayne well in his bid for the U.S. Senate. Hopefully, he will have a new job after the great citizens of Connecticut head to the polls in eleven days on November 8th.

"With $150 million in annual revenues and more than $200 million in assets, the American Humane Fund is finally positioned to revolutionize the way Americans treat their animals.

"Our ballot initiatives are polling neck and neck in all twenty-four states and the District of Columbia, and we are optimistic about three referendums in New Mexico, Kentucky and Maryland as well."

The American Humane Fund, or AHF, had already deployed 200 lawyers around the nation to get out the vote on twenty-four ballot initiatives and three referendums.

"Each ballot initiative and referendum contains similar language. But let me state the four core components of each, and then I'll be happy to take your questions. First, the proposed new laws will prohibit any person or any company from owning more than 200 animals. This will protect, for example, the family farm that might have 200 head of dairy cows but will effectively stop factory farming and mega research centers that destroy millions of animals each year. Second, the new laws will prohibit the interstate transportation of any animal for agricultural or scientific research use. Animals must not be used as widgets of interstate commerce. Breed it in your state and take care of it in your state. Third, the new laws will prohibit any animal, whether covered by the Animal Welfare Act or not, from being killed at the end of any scientific research project. As many as 80 million of our animal friends are used in scientific experiments each year in the United States. It's time we started using computers, simulators and other alternatives. And finally, with the recent passage of the Great Ape Protection Act, or GAPA, which now protects chimpanzees and gorillas from medical research, it's time to prevent all invasive, cut-testing research on all monkeys. No more monkeys, folks…no more. With that, I'd be happy to answer your questions. Yes, sir."

"Jim Rundell with USA Today, Ms. Sherman. What about the hundreds of poultry houses in one state—let's say Georgia—that normally send their chickens to a processing plant in, say, Alabama. Won't that have an enormous economic burden on most poultry producers?"

"Three responses to your question, Jim: Prop 2—passed by 63 percent of the citizens of California in 2008—prohibits the confinement of certain farm animals in a manner that does not allow them to turn around freely, lie down, stand up, or extend their limbs fully. That was a good law. Some of these Georgia chicken prisons you are referring to cram up to 20,000 birds in one building. So we believe the '200-animal maximum rule' greatly improves the living conditions of these beautiful birds. By processing plants I presume you are referring to slaughterhouses. If you wish to grow your 200 chickens in Georgia, then you'll have to slaughter them in Georgia as well. The law prevents breeders, slaughterers and executioners from crossing state lines. Yes?"

"Dawn Merriman with the Associated Press, Ms. Sherman. These new laws would prohibit the termination of lab animals after biomedical research studies. Could this have a negative impact on the future of medicine in this country?"

"Absolutely not. It is well-proven that research with animals does not correlate to the human experience. Since President Nixon declared a 'war on cancer' in the 1970s, we have killed billions of mice and hamsters that were already poisoned and induced with cancer only to slaughter them in order to put their tissue under a microscope. For what? Do we still have cancer? Yes. The animal experience does not translate to humans. There are far more sophisticated and modern methods of research. It is time that an educated society, such as America, stop these Dark Ages practices of old, white-guy vivisectionists who conduct animal torture experiments in their dimly lit, deep, damp and dank laboratory dungeons. No terminal studies means that we now have a 'no slaughter mercy rule.' Equally as important as the no-slaughter mercy rule, scientists who choose to continue these barbaric practices must comply with the '200-animal limit rule,' and the interstate transportation rule as well."

"Follow on, please...some corporations exist solely as breeders to the research industry. Won't these new laws basically put them out of business?"

"Well, I would submit to you that companies once existed to build catapults for medieval battles. Some companies were hired to make Nazi flags. Times change, and companies must evolve. Breeders could expand to develop software simulators instead of spawning millions of little lab mice just as Chevron and Texaco should evolve to produce wind, solar and improved battery power instead of hoarding Middle Eastern oil or contaminating our coastal waterways with offshore drilling spills. This is, indeed, the logical next step in greening the planet, where all animals—human and non-human—live in harmony. Final question?"

"Yes, just a comment really. Today's entrée of chicken salad was excellent."

"Now, that's what I'm talking about. I'll bet you didn't realize that you were actually enjoying high protein, nutritious, and completely animal-friendly tofu, now did you? Thank you everybody and please support these twenty-four ballot initiatives and three referendums on November 8th."

PART
ONE

1

Lieutenant Colonel Leslie Raines entered the large conference room. Military officers and enlisted personnel alike rose to their feet. By the time they made it to their feet, the simultaneous return drop to the seats all around the Eisenhower-era table was well underway.

Raines was a stunning brunette who wore a long, slender figure well in her U.S. Army greens. She joined the Army's Veterinary Corps right after she graduated from Auburn. If it involved animals and the military, Raines had her paws all over it. She had done everything and been just about everywhere.

She was branch chief for the Navy's marine mammal program in Key West before being assigned to the same position at the Kaneohe Marine Corps Air Base in Hawaii. Raines entered the Army's Combined Laboratory Animal Residency Program in 1999 and then served as department head at the Naval Medical Research Institute in Bethesda where she earned board certification in veterinary preventive medicine and laboratory animal medicine.

Raines had deployed to both Afghanistan and Iraq on special assignments for bio-terror defense and engineering.

She joined the Defense Advanced Research Projects Agency (DARPA) in September. She wasn't a big fan of San Antonio, but the food suited her just fine.

"Good morning."

The room was filled with almost twenty men and women from various branches of the military and from posts worldwide. A placard with name, rank and general assignment was positioned in front of each attendee.

Major Kiewit was head of the Interagency Confederation for Biological Research and the National Interagency BioDefense Campus at Fort Meade in Frederick, Maryland. Kiewit studied biochemistry at Notre Dame, then earned his doctorate in veterinary medicine at Purdue. He picked up a PhD in pharma-toxicology from Duke somewhere along the way. First Sergeant Bricker was a veterinary technician at Fort Sam Houston. She staffed the Army's trauma training exercises where live pigs were anesthetized then shot with military rifles. The pigs served as battlefield training props so medics could learn to stop the bleeding, treat the wounds and evacuate the pigs while they were still alive. After the exercises, the pigs were euthanized.

"Thanks for coming. This will be an intense, two-day, classified briefing and discussion of the Infectious Disease and BioTerror Working Group out of the Tactical Technology Office. We'll muster back here every month for the next twelve months, so you'd better get used to each other. Before we get started I'd like each of you to provide—."

The conference room door sprung open as a Navy officer scampered in rather haphazardly carrying a Starbucks cup and a backpack draped over his shoulder.

"Sorry, ma'am."

The officer sat down.

"Captain Martin?"

"No, ma'am. Commander Campbell, Seabury Campbell, but please call me Camp."

"Nice of you to join us, Campbell, but you're sitting in Martin's chair."

Camp picked up the placard in front of him, spotted his name four chairs away, and promptly got up and swapped them.

"Guess that works. Looks like you already have your coffee, Commander, so we can proceed. I was just about to ask everyone to provide a little bio since this is our first working group meeting. Perhaps you would like to start?"

"Okay. Not much to tell, really, I graduated from the Naval Academy, trained as a SEAL, but I serve as a Navy doc now, got my MD from Georgetown, and spent three years in Iraq at the Balad Trauma Center. I teach at the Uniformed Services University of the Health Sciences in Bethesda, focusing on infectious diseases."

"A teaching SEAL with an MD? After three years in Balad no less? Who'd you piss off?" asked Kiewit.

Camp smiled and took a long pull from his lukewarm chai tea.

"Infectious diseases? Did you by chance read the article in today's Wall Street Journal?" Raines asked.

"Haven't gotten to that page yet," Camp responded as Raines tried to hide her subtle contempt.

"Chickens. Covert chickens to be exact. Clandestine operations out in Pennsylvania Dutch farm country to the tune of $44 million or more."

"Really? That's where I'm from," said Camp.

"I know," said Raines as she slid a folded copy of the Journal effortlessly down the table past three officers before it came to rest next to Camp's Starbucks cup.

LANCASTER, PENNSYLVANIA

The white cargo van, with no side passenger windows, slowed to a crawl behind an Amish buggy just a few miles down the Old Philadelphia Pike past Smoketown Airport. As oncoming traffic cleared, the van veered around and sped up as it passed through Bird-In-Hand, Pennsylvania. Orchard Road turned into Church, Church into Monterey, and then finally right off of Monterey onto Miller Lane. Reflective adhesive letters on the mailbox read Harvey Smith. But it was the next sign that was a bit more ominous: KEEP OUT—DISEASE CONTROL AREA.

The van turned right onto a long gravel driveway that meandered around hedges before coming to a stop in front of two steel gates. The driver reached out the window, flipped up a plastic cover, and placed his thumb on the biometric reader.

The rusted steel gates creaked open.

The van pulled up next to the farmhouse, a two-story salt box with a slanted roof. The building was probably built in the 1930s, and in desperate need of a new coat of paint and some sideboards. The sliding doors on both sides of the white cargo van opened, and four Asian men got out as the driver kept the engine running.

Walking across the old wooden porch, the four entered without knocking.

The house had been completely gutted inside. The walls between the living room, kitchen and downstairs bedroom had been removed to create one oversized room. Four steel I-beams supported the second floor even though the stairs leading up were boarded and sealed just above the third step. The room was humming with computer equipment, blinking lights, laboratory research canisters, microscopes and satellite phones.

Old Harvey Smith sat at the stainless steel table. It was in the same spot where his antique drop leaf had hosted thousands of breakfasts before. A well-weathered man of sixty-seven years, he wore coveralls, a flannel shirt and a stained denim jacket. An old John Deere tractor cap sat tilted on his head as he pushed his glasses up on the bridge of his nose to watch the men as they took their seats.

"Mr. Smith, this is Mr. Lee and his associates from South Korea," said the young technician who was assigned to take care of Harvey but now stood in respectful reverence behind him. "They will finalize the transaction with you."

Mr. Lee pulled out his smart phone.

"I presume you still bank with Susquehanna Bank on Manheim Pike?"

"Yes, sir…been with them pretty near forty-five years, or so."

Lee handed him the phone as it was ringing.

"Tell them your account number and ask for your current balance."

"Good morning, Susquehanna Bank. May I help you?"

"Yes, Harvey Smith from up on Miller Lane here. I wanted to check the balance on my account, please."

"Certainly, Mr. Smith. Checking or savings?"

Harvey looked over to Mr. Lee for guidance, but Lee was busy examining a folder of papers and ignoring him.

"Checking," he finally continued. "The account is 136-72-9118."

"Yes, sir, I have it right here. The wire transfer for your real estate sale did come through last night, and the funds are now verified and available. Your current account balance is 12 million, seventy-two dollars and forty-five cents. Looks like your October social security check should post today as well. Anything else I can help you with?"

Harvey lowered the phone slowly and wiped perspiration from his forehead as he ended the call.

"That should conclude the transaction," said Mr. Lee. "My driver will drop you off in Lancaster at the bank, where Mrs. Smith will be waiting for you. But first I'd like you to give my colleagues a tour of the poultry barns and explain the operations to date."

With that, the three other Koreans stood, and Harvey's handler pulled his chair back as he stood up. The $12 million shock still hadn't quite sunk in.

Harvey led them to the first barn where they entered a modern room built on the outside of the larger barn. Each one of them grabbed special hooded jumpsuits and put them on. After each had placed a paper face mask over their nose and mouth and hooked it around their ears, they stepped into a sanitizing foot bath, then passed into the big barn.

The heat, light, aroma and sound were all intense.

"Well, each hen lays an egg a day, whether it's fertilized or not. All hens do. We've been feeding these chickens a special food blend. We usually alternate between corn and millet. Gotta be real careful how much salt they get. Too much salt and it'll change the shape of their eggs, even the number laid. Next month you wanna make sure you leave the lights on longer because the days will get shorter. Light stimulates egg-laying, you know."

"How many birds are in here?" one of the men asked.

"About 10,000 chickens per barn, give or take. Six barns total. There's 1 rooster for every 15 hens."

Harvey pulled a harmonica out of his flannel shirt, and quickly blew out an entire verse of *Amazing Grace*.

"If you folks don't have mouth harps, then just pipe in some music. The birds respond to the music. Happy birds means greater yield."

The Koreans just stared at him.

"Really!" Harvey said with some desperation in his voice.

"Where's the vaccine work done?" asked another.

Harvey motioned and they followed him down the length of the long narrow barn and through a passageway of sealed doors into another steel building. The aroma from the ammonia brought tears to the eyes of the three Korean scientists. They each dipped the bottom of their shoes in another sanitizing bath before going into the vaccine barn.

"Eggs that you scramble up for breakfast and eat with toast and jelly, well, those are unfertilized eggs. The kinds used for vaccine testing need to be fertilized. Our techs work in here. They inject flu viruses into the fluid surrounding the chicken embryo. The virus multiplies inside the embryo. Then it's extracted, killed and blended into flu shots. Point of fact, I got mine last week at the K-Mart pharmacy over there off Fruitville Parkway."

The three scientists looked around for a moment, then nodded to Harvey's handler that they were finished. The fresh air outside was a welcome relief from the ammonia.

The doors on the van slid open as the men got in. Mr. Lee was already waiting.

"Are you sure you folks got enough room for me?" asked Harvey. "I can ring up my old friend Sea Bee for a ride if I need to."

Harvey's handler reassured him. "No problem. The van has an open third row. But before you go can you walk me through the power grid on the back electric panel one more time? I'm familiar with the master breaker, but I'm not clear as to which breakers control which barns."

Harvey nodded, and the two of them walked the length of the barn around to the backside near the pasture. Harvey took the opportunity to light a quick cigarette.

"Never thought I'd say it, but I'm gonna miss this place. Really...it was the only life I ever knew."

His handler only smiled.

"I guess a part of me will always be here."

The electric panels were housed in a dilapidated wooden shed out by the garbage pit. His front loader—or at least the one he just sold with the farm—was parked next to the shed.

Harvey opened the shed door just as the driver of the van stepped out of the darkness. He saw a flash of steel a second before the blade cut across his throat. His cigarette fell silently to the cold ground. Warm blood pumped out of his neck with every beat of his heart as the handler and the driver gently laid him into the lowered bucket of the front loader. Harvey noticed that they took great care to be gentle with him as they laid his head down. He tried to speak but couldn't.

The front loader started up and drove a few hundred feet out into the pasture where a new hole was already dug next to the trash dump he'd used for three decades. The bucket lifted up high. Harvey could see a few clouds in the brisk Pennsylvania sky. As the bucket came down quickly, Harvey slammed to the earth and rolled down the side of the hole as his weakening arms came to rest on the body of Mrs. Smith. He never felt the first load of dirt hit him.

The van passed through the gates and down the long driveway. The driver stopped and put two letters in the mailbox and raised the flag. The personal notes from Mrs. Smith told both of their sons that they had sold the farm and each would receive $3 million. She and Harvey were "going to Costa Rica to enjoy the warm breezes and ocean air for the remainder of their years."

Mr. Lee worked his smart phone quickly and efficiently as he wired $3 million to both of Harvey and Mildred Smith's sons. He allowed himself a slight smile just thinking about the looks on their faces the next time they used an ATM machine. Finally, he transferred the remaining $6 million out of Harvey's Susquehanna Bank checking account in Lancaster, Pennslyvania, and into Harvey's new account at the El Banco Credito Agricola in San Jose, Costa Rica, where it would sit accruing interest for the rest of eternity.

2

Eileen walked him out to the parking lot. She hooked her arm into his even though his hands were buried deep in the front pockets of his old Levi jeans. A distinct chill was in the air, and the clouds looked as though they had snow flurries to offer.

"Great seeing you again, Camp."

"You as well."

"They working you too hard in DC?"

"Actually, just got back from a quick trip to San Antonio for some meetings. So, no, it hasn't been too rugged."

"Are you staying stateside for a while?"

"Not planning on Iraq or Afghanistan anytime soon, if that's what you mean."

Eileen reached out and gently caressed his hand. She kissed him on the cheek. With a quick caress of her face, Camp got into his Land Rover, a dusty Defender 90, and pulled out over the gravel driveway of the Lightner Farms Bed and Breakfast.

The brochure said it was used as a federal hospital for wounded soldiers following the 1863 Battle of Gettysburg. Camp didn't need a brochure to tell him that he loved the place. This was his twenty-fourth stay in eight months. He loved telling Eileen that he kept coming back for her country breakfasts and blueberry muffins. He loved the sweet ham she served with eggs sunny side up on sourdough toast.

He loved room number three and stayed there each visit, guaranteed.

And he loved Eileen, more than she would ever know.

He drove slowly until he had passed through all nineteen acres of Lightner Farms and then onto the Baltimore Pike for the ninety-seven mile drive back to his townhouse in Old Town Alexandria.

ALEXANDRIA, VIRGINIA

Camp was at full speed, winding down into the last mile of his workout. The treadmill was humming at a 5:20 pace and his gray Navy t-shirt was saturated with sweat. He chose a classic rock playlist for this workout. Zeppelin. Metallica. The Who. Stones. He seemed to like the classics whenever he came back from Lightner Farms.

Refilling his water bottle from the tap he noticed two missed calls on his mobile, both from the same number. Two voice mails as well.

"Where the hell is 2-1-0?" he muttered. He played the messages.

"Commander Campbell, Lieutenant Colonel Leslie Raines in San Antonio. Please return my call at your earliest. Calling at 2050 hours on 6 November. I need you to watch—."

Delete.

What the hell did Raines want? He played the second voice mail.

"Campbell, isn't this a government-issued phone? 2110 hours. Call me."

Camp threw the phone on the kitchen table and started the shower. It had been a long weekend. Besides, it was his time, not Uncle Sam's *working group*.

The pounding on the front door was relentless, but Camp was so deep in sleep he couldn't be sure that he wasn't really back in his rack in Iraq. Had he just pulled another eighteen-hour shift in the trauma center? The Blackhawk blades were getting closer. He didn't have the stamina to go back into the OR.

The simultaneous ringing on his mobile and pounding on his front door pulled him out of the hooch thousands of miles away and halfway across the world in Balad and back to his bed in Virginia. He reached into his second dresser drawer and pulled on a pair of boxers as he went to the door where he looked through the peep hole as the pounding continued.

"What the—?" He opened the door.

"Commander Campbell, you got a problem returning phone calls?" Raines walked into his townhouse uninvited.

"Come on in, Colonel."

Dishes were stacked in the sink, and several microwave dinner packages from bygone meals were overflowing in the trash can.

"I like what you've done with the place. Obviously not married, are you, Commander."

"What freaking hurricane just walked into my house? Do you know what time it is?"

"Time to get dressed. We brief at the Pentagon in four hours, and we need to prep. I presume you watched the show?"

"What are you talking about?"

"My voice mails?"

"Oh, those, well I never got the chance to—."

"Save it. I'll make some coffee while you get ready. You have coffee, don't you, Campbell?"

"Please, cut all the Commander Campbell shit. It's Camp. And no, my coffeemaker is a barista who works in the coffee shop at the end of this block, *Les*."

"Les?"

"I presume your BFFs call you Les, don't they?"

"As a matter of fact, no, and you're not my BFF, *Camp*. I'll get the coffee. We roll in ten."

Raines was attractive but by the book. She had taken a C-130 MIL AIR from San Antonio to Andrews Air Force Base in Maryland and then a taxi over to Old Town across the Wilson Bridge. She had been summoned to Washington to brief the chairman and the Joint Staff.

After only a few minutes on the George Washington Parkway, she and Camp passed Reagan National Airport, then pulled into the south parking lot at the Pentagon where Camp parked the Defender in a visitor's spot.

"You're pretty lathered up over this TV show. Did your American Idol get kicked off, or voted out, or whatever the hell they do to the losers?"

They walked into an open conference room on the fourth floor of the E-ring. Raines got out her laptop and clicked the icon.

"ABC News aired a special election edition of *Nightline* last night. I recorded it. Some key points you need to see. I've written down time codes so we can jump ahead."

"How thoughtful…"

Raines tilted the laptop screen so both of them could watch as the familiar *Nightline* music began to play.

"It's Sunday, November 6th, and welcome to a special election edition of *Nightline*. I'm Owen Tasker."

"Who?"

Raines just rolled her eyes and ignored him.

"This Tuesday, Americans will go to the polls in all fifty states to choose their elected officials and vote on special projects. But none may have more impact on our daily lives than ballot initiatives and referendums in twenty-seven states. The American Humane Fund—the folks who help us help our abandoned and furry friends at the local animal shelters—has put together some shocking new undercover video that may forever change the way we view animals after Tuesday's election."

"That's a joke. AHF has nothing to do with local animal shelters," said Camp. "They're a lobbying group and they know it."

"Tell that to the millions of pet lovers who send them nineteen dollars every month," said Raines.

"Joining me tonight is the new president of AHF, Angela Sherman. Angela, welcome to *Nightline*."

"Thanks, Owen. A pleasure to be here."

"AHF is basically sponsoring these twenty-seven ballot initiatives and referendums, are they not?"

"Not completely. We are aligned with millions of like-minded Americans who want to see every animal treated humanely all the time."

"But it's your money and your staff out in twenty-seven states putting these issues before the voters."

"Yes. AHF has spent more than $200 million on this election cycle."

"That's a bit shocking, isn't it?"

"Well, not nearly as shocking as some of the videos that have been sent to us that we're about to see. Citizen journalists from all across America finally have the videos that will reveal just exactly what is going on behind closed medical research doors and closed barn doors. So much for being a 'civilized' society."

"Did you pay to have these videos produced in order to help your cause on Tuesday?"

"Absolutely not. The American Humane Fund does not pay any journalists for hidden camera stories."

Camp shook his head in disgust. "Clever, but she forgot to mention that AHF proxies pay bounties for these videos after AHF donates grant money to the proxies. What a crock."

"Listen," Raines snapped.

"Well, let's go to the first video montage. Set it up for us, Angela."

"The monkey's name is Gretchen, and she's a beautiful, playful, three-year-old rhesus monkey. Scientists in California have addicted this beautiful creature to cocaine. Here the citizen journalist captures Gretchen's wild mood swings as she comes down from a high and screams for more drugs."

Camp winced as he watched the monkey become hysterical and violent in her cage.

"What's the purpose of all this, Angela?"

"Money. To see if they can find miracle cures to stop people from voluntarily taking illegal drugs, all at the expense of ruining this poor creature's life. I can assure you that Gretchen did not sign up for this insanity."

"In this piece, the citizen journalist films a mouse receiving a chemotherapy dose. They call her 136047-X or something idiotic like that, but I think she looks more like a French mouse named Flibo, don't you?"

"What's that on her hip?"

"Breast cancer. They inject her with human breast cancer cells. That enormous tumor mass on her hip grows and grows until they finally gas her to death with carbon dioxide, then cut her up and take tissue samples to see if the chemotherapy did anything to cure the cancer."

"You're kidding, right?"

"I wish I was. NIH doles out $32 billion a year in taxpayer money to see if they can first, *give* 'Flibo the mouse' some human breast cancer; then second, to see if they can get rid of it. I'm sure the millions of children who have mice and rats at home in their bedrooms as pets will attest to the fact that their little furry friends don't get human breast cancer very often."

"What are we seeing here?"

"This citizen journalist indicates she is a single mom and just got tired of the abuse at a primate center. For two weeks straight she chronicles the starvation and death of a two-year-old macaque monkey named Larry. For fourteen days, Owen, the technicians forgot to feed Larry. Macaques are socialized in such a manner that they won't display their illnesses. They won't complain. Here we see Larry dead on the floor of his cage. Why? Because no one remembered to give the poor child any food."

"Give me a break. The woman holding the camera could have fed the damn monkey every day!" said Camp, growing angrier by the minute.

"I must confess, that's very difficult to look at, Angela."

"Then you'd better prepare yourself for this one. This is hard to watch but even harder to hear."

Raines leaned over to turn up the audio on the laptop.

"We must warn you, the following scenes are very graphic," Tasker said as the two watched the scenes play out.

"The journalist here is an attractive young female," Sheldon narrates. "She's also a student at the Newport Beach Institute of Spinal Cord Research. Obviously, these researchers think that torturing animals is great fun."

The iPhone video closes in on a scientist in his early fifties sitting at his desk, talking on the telephone. In the video, he assures a USDA inspector that his facility is in compliance and that he'll fax over the statement in the morning. He then gets up, removes a six-pack of light bulbs from his closet and puts on his lab coat.

The video then cuts to the university's lab, where the scientist reaches for a small pair of surgical scissors.

"What the hell are you doing?" a female voice asks.

"I'm going to cut his spine."

"What? Why?"

The scientist holds the scissors up in front of the iPhone camera, opening and closing them quickly. He hunches his back and lets out a ghoulish laugh.

"Because I can. I am the mad scientist Doctor Erol von Meisberger, vivisectionist and ruler of the animal world!"

He reaches the tip of the scissors into the area around the sleeping rat's spine. The bone is visibly narrow and white, almost yellow. There isn't much blood but he dabs it up anyway. He found the spot he wanted and isolated the tip of the scissors with precision.

Snip.

Tasker covered his eyes in discomfort.

"Oh, God, that's awful. Why? For what purpose?"

"This guy? Who knows? Pure pleasure it appears."

The camera moved in for a close-up as Tasker took the audience to the first commercial break.

"In the next segment, citizen journalists will take us behind the scenes at Fort Sam Houston in Texas and Fort Campbell in Kentucky where our United States military is seen on video shooting pigs and goats all in the name of training. And in our final segment you'll go inside an American factory farming operation where 20,000 chickens compete for food, air and water in one sizzling hot barn."

Raines started to advance the video when Camp stopped her.

"Okay, I get it. Enough. What's the fallout, and what's all this got to do with me?"

"You use animals at USUHS in your infectious disease research."

"A few. But we run a clean program. None of that shit."

"So you think these are not *clean* programs?"

"Hard to say," said Camp. "The citizen journalists, as they were, are not exactly objective. Looks like they have an ax to grind. I mean, for God sakes, the woman records a starving primate for fourteen days. She works there. She should have fed the monkey."

"Well, the next segment shows soldiers putting ten pigs to sleep, then plugging each of them with a half dozen rounds of AK-47 fire."

"That's got nothing to do with me. Go get your first sarge from Fort Sam."

"Commander, you know as well as I do that animals play an essential role in research. We use simulators whenever we can, but we need to test on living organisms," Raines pleaded.

Camp got up and grabbed his briefcase. "Maybe so, but

this is not my issue. Just leave me alone and let me do my work."

"The old man asked for you specifically."

Camp stopped.

"What old man?"

"Your former XO in Balad."

"Colonel Ferguson?"

"Brigadier General Ferguson now, he's a special assistant to the chairman, and he wants you—us—to brief him."

Thirteen highly decorated military officers were seated around the conference room table engaged in small talk as two Army Majors offered coffee to Camp and Raines. The officers were quietly complaining about the recent policy change handed down by the Secretary of Defense.

After 9/11, military personnel were allowed to wear their combat fatigues, or BDUs, while conducting their daily business at the Pentagon. But with one silent stroke of the pen, the SECDEF changed all that. All 23,000 military aides at the Pentagon packed away their camouflage and flight suits and replaced them with precision-pressed military business uniforms, complete with medals and service ribbons.

"General Ferguson," one of the majors announced.

The officers snapped to their feet with the respect of attention.

"Seats, please."

Ferguson took his seat at the head of the table with the best view of the two flat-screen monitors.

"Camp! Long time, my friend. So good to see you."

"General Ferguson, a pleasure as always, sir."

"You're at Uniformed Services now?"

"USUHS or 'useless,' as we like to refer to it. Yes, sir, infectious diseases."

"Geez, Camp…does that keep you engaged? Enough action?"

"I believe you and I got more than enough action to last a lifetime, sir."

"Indeed we did. Lieutenant Colonel Raines, thanks for making the trip on such short notice. What do we have?"

"Well, sir, last night ABC News aired a special election weekend edition of their magazine news show, *Nightline*. And in that show they allegedly showed some undercover video of our trauma training at Sam Houston and Fort Campbell."

"Nothing 'allegedly' at all, Colonel Raines. They did in fact show undercover video," one of the attending JAG legal officers piped in to the muted laughter of some. Raines smiled at her gaffe.

"Noted, sir. I meant to say that the video was allegedly authentic footage from our trauma training exercises."

"That's not alleged, either. The real deal and verified. Must've been filmed by one of our own soldiers who is now what they call 'a citizen journalist.'"

"That's unauthorized," an overly eager and recently pinned light bird chimed in.

No one gave the dignity of a response to the "Einstein" deduction.

"What's the fallout, Lieutenant Colonel?"

Raines cleared her throat and went to her first PowerPoint slide. The LCD monitors came to life.

"As you'll see in the first of the following thirty slides, the U.S. military has been using animals for more than 200 years."

The general raised his hand to cut her off. "Raines, please."

"If I may, sir?"

"Go ahead, Camp."

Raines was put out at the interruption from her once reluctant sidekick. "General Ferguson is a bottom-line guy. He hasn't sat through thirty slides total in thirty years of service," Camp said quietly.

"Fine. Enlighten us."

"Sir, this is a calculated effort by the American Humane Fund and it appears that ABC News is either intentionally, or unintentionally, complicit. With twenty-seven states voting on animal issues tomorrow, this is a brazen attempt to swing those elections. Does it matter to us? Hell, yes. If twenty-seven states pass stricter animal rights measures, then Congress feels the pressure. They conclude that this must, therefore, be the will of the people. Congress sides with the people and uses its greatest weapon—funding—to shut down factory farms and animal agriculture, stop biomedical research, and prevent the military from using live animals in trauma training."

The room went silent.

"Can we do anything about this?"

"Sir, in a word…no. Are we really going to sit here in this conference room with our mouths hanging open in shock and dismay and imply we never saw this coming? The time to act was eighteen months ago, eight years ago. Somebody somewhere saw this developing on a distant horizon and concluded it would never happen, or it's not my concern, probably some hero in this building, maybe even in this room."

The room was silent.

"Seriously…animal rights crazies have been saying this kind of crap for years. None of us are surprised. Right?"

3

A throng of local TV and radio reporters had already gathered outside the home of Dr. Erol Meisberger on Table Rock Drive in Laguna. His home was among the least expensive in the neighborhood but still carried a $5 million plus price tag.

Meisberger's wife, Susan, pulled back the kitchen curtains long enough to see the gathered crowd, which allowed her blood to return to full boil.

"Okay, brilliant scientist, now what are you going to do? You're the damned laughing stock of the entire nation and the free world this morning."

"I've already called in sick."

"Called in sick? Great strategy. That's grad-school clever, if I do say so myself. They're going to fire your ass after that display of supreme ignorance. You might as well get out of that robe because you're taking the kids to school. I'm not going to be the 'embarrassed wife' on the six o'clock news that hangs her head in shame and covers her face while she muscles her kids out of the driveway in the oversized, gas-guzzling family SUV."

"Fine. I'll take them. I'll go out there and talk to them, give 'em what they want—their token pound of flesh—and then they'll be gone. They're animals, and I do understand animals."

"How did they even know where we lived?"

"Public records. It's not brain surgery."

"No it's not. It was more like rat surgery—or mutilation—that got us here in the first place, now wasn't it, Erol?"

Meisberger grabbed his coffee mug and headed to the front door as his two children pawed aimlessly at their cereal bowls. He turned the handle and opened the door.

The press corps, lawfully gathered on the public sidewalk and in the street, snapped to attention. Cameras turned on and reporters started screaming questions. Towers on the satellite trucks buzzed with energy, and spotlights flooded the already sunlit front yard. Meisberger raised his hands to stop the questions and walked onto the grass, halfway between the house and the sidewalk.

"Folks, I've got a brief statement to make, but I'm not going to take any questions. We are conducting federally funded research at the Institute, and we follow and adhere to all federal regulations, requirements, and protocols for the treatment of our lab animals. The video captured me being silly in a casual moment, and I regret that. But let me assure you, no animal was ever mistreated. Every protocol was followed as written, and I completely stand by my research."

"Not mistreated? Dr. Meisberger, did you really cut the spine of that animal on the video?" a reporter yelled.

"That's all I'm going to say. Now if you'll please excuse me, I must take my two children to school."

"Dr. Meisberger, how does rat mutilation fall into the category of research? It looked more like animal cruelty."

He ignored the question, waved to the reporters and smiled as he walked back to the house. An overnight FedEx envelope leaning against the house next to the front door caught his eye. The FedEx label said it was shipped to him from the U.S. Department of Agriculture, 1400 Independence Avenue, Washington, DC. "Probably from Chad about his damn light bulbs," he thought.

He cradled his coffee mug between his arm and his chest as he unzipped the package while looking back out over the sea of media.

The explosion lit up the front of the house.

Reporters screamed as cameras and recorders caught it all on tape. His ceramic mug smashed on the street behind the crowd of reporters as pieces of his dismembered body showered down from the blast cloud, into his yard and driveway. The remnants of a forearm, still robed and smoking, dangled from the roof gutter above.

PENTAGON

A military aide opened the door to the briefing room and walked briskly over to General Ferguson and handed him a note. Ferguson handed the remote control to one of his coffee-pouring majors.

"Get CNN on."

Within seconds, both LCD panels showed the disturbing video from Laguna Beach.

"To recap, Dr. Erol Meisberger, the subject of an undercover video aired on the ABC News *Nightline* program last evening, has been killed this morning by what local witnesses are describing as a letter bomb that exploded outside of his Southern California home." The reporter's words trailed off as the room sat glued to the images of Meisberger's body parts still smoldering in the rubble of his front porch.

The general waved his hand, and the TV went dark.

"Looks like we might be dealing with just a bit more than simple public opinion, Camp."

4

The two-room office headquarters of the Animal Liberation Front, or ALF, were buzzing with activity. Four elderly women worked the phones as Gerald Virostek put the finishing touches on a press release. Virostek was a medical doctor but didn't have a practice or hospital that he worked out of, at least according to FBI and IRS records. His only source of income seemed to be as press officer for ALF.

Phone calls were coming in from donors all over the United States, mostly in the form of ten and twenty-dollar gifts.

ALF was an undercover movement with no employees other than Virostek and his wife. A shadowy group of activists purported to conduct direct actions against animal rights violators and vivisectionists who conducted animal tests for medical research.

The ALF web site displayed photos of masked liberators holding rescued puppies, rabbits, mink and mice.

With a final spell check Virostek hit "send" as the ALF

press release hit the inbox of several thousand media outlets around the world. It was a terse, two-line statement:

Communiqué from Animal Liberation Front Underground
Date: November 7
Institution Targeted: Newport Beach Institute of Spinal
Cord Research
                                    Posted Anonymously

It was a bit chilly this morning when at 3:00 am we arrived at Dr. Meisberger's palatial estate on Table Rock Drive in Laguna Beach to personally deliver his FedEx package. With front door service like that, we can only wonder which vivisectionist will be getting the next special delivery.

ALEXANDRIA, VIRGINIA

Camp reached for the last slice of pizza in the box as Raines cradled two new bottles of Miller Lite in one hand while shoving the last bite of pepperoni and olives into her mouth. They were watching election returns from CNN on Camp's big screen TV.

"Thanks," said Camp, his eyes transfixed on the screen as he took the beer from Raines. "They keep talking about the ballot initiatives, but they're not giving us any returns."

"Polls are still open out West."

"Right. Well, you're welcome to stay as long as you want to."

"I intend to."

Camp started to laugh and couldn't help but spew a mouthful of beer. Even Raines got a chuckle out of her comedic arrogance.

"So, I thought I should let you know that I'm officially resigning from your working group, Raines."

"Wow, before you even try to hit on me? I thought for certain that you'd wait until you got the first cold shoulder move."

"Who said anything about hitting on you?"

"You're Navy. And you're a man. Lethal combination. Regardless, you can't resign, already got it cleared," she said before taking a big pull on the longneck.

Camp reached over to his briefcase and pulled out an envelope and handed it to her.

"Read it."

Raines read through the short, two-paragraph letter in seconds. She put it down for a moment, then closed her eyes.

"Can we talk?"

"If you call me Camp."

"I just don't get you. It was General Ferguson who assigned you to our Working Group. He said you were the most incredible officer, human being—damn, legend—that he had ever had the privilege of serving with. He sent me your file. Academy graduate, trained as a SEAL. You even earned the Navy Cross for Combat Heroism in some remote Tora Bora pass in Afghanistan right after 9/11. You come back from your tour and the Navy fast-tracks you to Med School. Then off you go to Iraq and, for some unknown reason, you come and go through the better part of three years residency as a surgeon, working twenty-hour shifts in the tent-city trauma center at Balad Air Base. And after all that, you come back here, slink into a lowly, back-pew position at 'useless,' and now you show me this letter? Are you insane?"

Camp sat silent for a change, then surfed over to a different channel for election coverage.

"I'm tired of Washington. Too hectic. Frederick is a nice part of Maryland. Fort Detrick is more rural but close enough."

"Close enough to what?"

"Hunting, fishing…Pentagon if I need to."

Raines put her beer down and swung her long legs over the arm of the deep cushion chair.

"So what's your assignment?"

"Well, Detrick is a quad-services Army Medical installation. Primary missions are biomedical research and development, medical materiel management and global telecom. I'm being assigned to the NIBC."

"And that is…?"

"National Interagency BioDefense Campus."

"Sounds like another sterile university setting."

"Actually, it's like a farm. Barns and laboratories intertwined."

The onscreen graphic indicated early returns on the ballot initiatives so Camp quickly pressed the mute button again.

"Fox News is now projecting that the AHF ballot initiative will pass in twenty-one out of twenty-four states, with only Oklahoma, Arkansas and Mississippi voters rejecting the measure. Likewise, similar statewide referendums will carry easily in New Mexico, Kentucky and Maryland. Let's go to Senator Jameston of Oklahoma. Mister Senator, what will be the impact of all this on both agriculture and medical research?"

Raines got up quickly and turned the TV off. She walked over to the kitchen counter and grabbed her purse as she reached for her coat on the back of a kitchen chair.

"Can you believe that?"

Raines dug deep into her purse, looking for car keys.

"What are you going to do?"

"Not your problem anymore, Commander. Thanks for

the beer and pizza."

"By the way, Raines, what comes after the first cold shoulder move?"

Raines walked to the front door and let herself out before Camp could get another word in. "Call me!" Camp said after the door slammed in his face.

5

SEOUL, SOUTH KOREA

Mr. Lee sat patiently in the backseat of the company town car outside of Incheon International Airport baggage claim as his driver paced near the carousel waiting for luggage.

The elevator door opened on the thirty-sixth floor at the executive offices of Dokwang Pharmaceuticals, Ltd. Several female administrative assistants were already standing and bowing in front of the doors as Mr. Lee arrived. He never looked at them or even acknowledged their presence or respect.

The three scientists that had traveled with Mr. Lee were now in the hallway and followed behind him as they walked down a maze of interconnected hallways to the corner suite.

A young lady stood up from behind her desk as Lee and his entourage approached. She knocked softly on the oversized mahogany door then held her bow as Mr. Lee and the three scientists entered.

Tae Sook Yoo was a very large man with a gregarious laugh and a razor sharp tongue. His work ethic was legendary. No one dared to call it a day until the tail lights from Yoo's car had disappeared for at least five minutes. He was known to have his driver circle the block, then ride the elevator back up just to see who was following him out the door.

Yoo studied finance in college. The bank that "drafted" him out of college gave him two companies to run, both of which he turned into major successes. They believed in him so much that they invested nearly 110 billion won (95 million USD) into Dokwang even though the company had never created or even licensed one single product, let alone earned a single plugged won. But the bank board had grown impatient over time and had given Yoo just one more year to turn a profit, or else. "Or else," in Korea was a matter of honor. Face. Yoo would have to take care of the "or else" himself, and that was not a particularly appealing proposition.

One thing Dokwang, Ltd. did not lack was cash. They had plenty of it. But the days of no products, no markets, and no growth opportunities, were killing the company.

Mr. Lee was hired to change all of that.

He and the three scientists behind him bowed even as Yoo ignored their presence, just as Lee had done to the women outside the elevator. Yoo's sticks worked frantically through the rice bowl on his desk as he read a financial report on his computer screen.

"The first phase of the business plan is complete," Lee said after a brief delay.

Yoo kept eating.

NEW HAVEN, CONNECTICUT

Police, fire and ambulance first responders were everywhere. Yellow police tape stretched around the entire perimeter of the School of Medicine, Department of Psychiatry, at 300 George Street. Scientists, physicians, nurses, technicians, staff and students stood across the street trying to take cover in a light rain.

The note left in the backseat of the Metro Taxi said the bomb would detonate at 8:08 A.M.

Bomb threats weren't unusual for any university that conducted biomedical research with animals. Research involving primates was always even a bit more controversial.

Typically, these threats were called in by some local kook but occasionally by an anonymous student looking to get out of an exam, or at least that's what local authorities often surmised. But after the murder of a researcher earlier in the week out in California, the New Haven Campus Security team was taking all precautions.

The New Haven Police Department Bomb Squad and two K-9 teams trained in explosives were in place. Now that the building was cleared, they planned to wait ten minutes past the threat time before sweeping the building.

The explosion blew out every first floor window facing George Street.

The previously put-out and irritated employees who had huddled in the rain on the other side of the street, screamed and scattered. The K-9s went crazy as several officers unholstered their firearms, though not at all sure who they were aiming at or protecting themselves from.

Fire hoses started to immediately douse the flames that licked out of three first-floor windows, the apparent ground zero location of the device.

Police Chief Lewis stared at the building in disbelief.

The scanner in his white cruiser crackled as his lapel radio fired up.

The fax machine at the *New Haven Register* started to print the same press release as was being seen at several media outlets around the world. It was a brief, terse, cryptic warning:

Communiqué from Animal Liberation Front Underground
Date: November 11
Institution Targeted: New Haven School of Medicine
Posted Anonymously

The people have spoken at Tuesday's election. End all animal research, animal agriculture and the slaughtering of innocents for your evil pleasures. Another bomb goes off tomorrow...and the next day...and...

WASHINGTON, DC

The emergency closed-doors meeting of the Senate Committee on Homeland Security and Government Affairs promised to go well into the night. Not lost on any of the members was the fact that the Connecticut Senator still chaired the Committee, in spite of being reelected as an Independent once the Democrats abandoned him in the primaries. He had gotten too cozy with other moderates in the Republican Party.

But it was more than politics for the Connecticut Senator. New Haven was the institutional crown jewel of his beloved Connecticut. Domestic terrorism showed up in his backyard rather rudely and unannounced. Connecticut didn't even have a ballot initiative process and the animal rights issue hadn't been placed before voters there.

"So why Connecticut?" the Senator asked rhetorically as

his Senate colleagues shook their heads in disbelief.

"They're not targeting states; they're targeting institutions. Universities that use animals in research," Senator Hempfield said.

Connie Blanton from Missouri jumped in. "Does that mean cattle ranches, dairy farms, pork producers and poultry farms in Missouri are next? This is nuts."

"I suggest we get the DHS secretary in for a closed hearing in the morning, as well as the FBI. Perhaps the ranking member from Maine will also join me at the White House in the morning for a briefing with the president's chief of staff?"

"Yes, of course," said Senator Williamson.

Connecticut Senator Hansen was about to adjourn the meeting for a dinner break when Oklahoma senator Terry Jefferson raised his hand.

"The communiqué says another bomb will go off tomorrow. How are we going to look tomorrow if another university is bombed before we offer guidance to the public. Our statement condemning the attack may not be sufficient if Northwestern, or Cal Poly, or Oklahoma State, or Arizona State University is in flames before lunch."

The room was silent.

Hansen waved his chief of staff over from the back row of seats.

"Get the president's people on the phone. Now."

HOUSTON, TEXAS

Sitting on metal folding chairs in a hangar at Houston's George Bush Intercontinental Airport, three print reporters waited for Continental Airlines' CEO, Melvin Boyd, to take the podium. None of the five local television affiliates in Houston even bothered to show up.

LTC Leslie Raines had been instructed by General Ferguson that she was to attend this press conference. The drive from San Antonio was fine, but the event seemed like a colossal waste of time. With arms folded and a scowl on her face from the first row, she made sure everyone knew that she wasn't happy being there.

Boyd walked in from a production office in the hangar and promptly got to the point.

"Effective immediately, Continental Airlines will no longer provide shipping services to any organization that wants to transport animals for either biomedical research or lab animal breeding. We are sickened by the images we have seen from the dark basement laboratories of America's universities and research centers. We believe that with the passage of the AHF ballot initiatives in many states, the time has now come to treat our animals differently. With that, I'll take questions if you have any."

A middle-aged woman sitting alone in an audience of three stood up.

"Ruth Kastel with the *Waco Tribune-Herald.* Mr. Boyd, as you know Baylor University and the Baylor College of Medicine conduct advanced biomedical animal research on their campuses. They also have an institutional contract to fly Continental whenever possible. Are you concerned that this new policy may trigger tension between Baylor and Continental?"

"No, I'm not concerned."

"Then a follow-up, please. Your wife sits on the board of the Houston SPCA. Did that have any bearing on your decision?"

"I'm sorry, but my wife's private advocacy work does not influence decisions taken by this publicly traded corporation."

"Aren't you in the early stages of a merger? This statement feels more like posturing and appeasement than relevant policy."

Boyd gave the reporter a cold stare. "With that, thanks to each of you for coming."

MONTROSE, WISCONSIN

Kasturi Jaluria gave her husband Raja a kiss on the forehead while reaching over his shoulder to wipe a clump of apple sauce out of the corner of their fourteen-month-old daughter's mouth. Raja's in-home architectural and design business allowed him to care for Ayanna during the day while Kasturi worked at the Great Lakes Primate Research Center.

Funded by the National Institutes of Health, more than 250 of the center's scientists were conducting research in primate biology with relevance to human and animal health. The day was a bit unlike most other days in that Kasturi and the out-of-state colleagues she was collaborating with from the University of Minnesota were about to make a major announcement. They had recently identified a compound that, when applied vaginally, could prevent transmission of the primate version of HIV, called SIV.

While not a cure—the compound still had to go through human clinical trials before it could be used to prevent HIV—Kasturi believed the research was a huge step toward prevention of the devastating disease that infected 33 million people around the globe.

Signs of an early winter were all over her Volvo's windshield. It took her a few minutes to dig the scraper out of her glove box. She and Raja bought the little farm on Fritz Road hoping they could raise some alpacas, plant a huge garden, and enjoy a rural lifestyle, even though it meant a seventeen-mile commute to campus every day for her. Raja opened the front door holding Ayanna. He loved to talk, and he loved to hear Kasturi talk about her research. "So, I still don't get it. What is this 'GML' stuff you're talking about?"

"Glycerol monolaurate," she said as she scraped. "It's a natural compound that the FDA says is safe. It's widely used as an anti-microbial and anti-inflammatory agent in food and cosmetics."

"Okay. Which leads me to ask again…so what?"

"After twenty-five years, an effective vaccine for HIV is still on the distant horizon, so not only vaccines, but all research into ways to prevent the continued spread of the HIV virus remain critically important. If GML can be used as a topical microbicide that adds to prevention in these monkeys, then it could save millions of human lives."

After sexual exposure to SIV, the monkey's own natural defense system was activated by rushing immune cells (T-cells) to the scene of the infection. The virus used these T-cells as fuel to expand infection locally and spread it throughout the body.

"So, even though it sounds counter-intuitive, halting some of the body's natural defense system might actually prevent transmission and the rapid spread of the infection. That's where GML comes in."

To test her theory, Kasturi tested GML's safety through daily vaginal application of two types of a GML gel-based topical solution on infected primates. A group of nine monkeys received warming gel with GML added. The other group of three monkeys received warming gel alone as a control group.

The researchers then challenged five GML-treated and

five control animals with large doses of SIV—an infectious dose that in a tissue culture would infect 50 percent of the cells—to see if GML could prevent transmission and infection. An hour after applying GML, the two groups of monkeys were injected vaginally with a large dose of the virus. Four hours later, the monkeys were again treated with GML and then given a second dosage of SIV.

Kasturi's team monitored the animals for evidence of transmission for two weeks—infected animals would typically have hundreds of millions of viruses circulating in the blood stream. If there was no evidence of infection, the treatments and viral challenges were repeated.

Four out of the five in the control group contracted SIV, while none of the five in the GML-treated group showed any evidence of acute infection after receiving as many as four large doses of the SIV virus.

"Kas, this shit could save millions of people. Think of all the pediatric AIDS patients in Africa. This could change the world." Kasturi got into her Volvo, winked and gave Raja a smiling "thumbs up."

He finally got it.

A brief second after she started the engine, the chassis of the legendary, rock-solid Volvo was nearly fifty feet in the air and engulfed in a massive fireball. The front axle dislodged and blew through Raja, throwing Ayanna out of his arms and crushing her head against the side of the house.

6

General Ferguson and the Chairman of the Joint Chiefs were both seated in the back of the room.

The press had assembled in the East Room, the largest room in the White House, waiting for the president to step to the podium. The large room planted in the eastern corner of the White House had been used in many different ways during the first twenty decades of existence. First Lady Abigail Adams used it as a laundry room before president Thomas Jefferson carved an office and bedroom out of it for his aide, Meriwether Lewis, of Lewis and Clark fame. James Madison used it as a Cabinet Room after Jefferson, but the room wasn't completed and adorned until 1829 when Andrew Jackson finished it. Then, in 1902, President Theodore Roosevelt commissioned the East Room be restored to its original appearance, just as it was before the fire of 1814.

Funerals, weddings, press conferences, receptions and receiving lines had all had their day in the East Room. President Woodrow Wilson used it as a movie theater and First Lady Jacqueline Kennedy created a theater for the performing arts. During the Civil War, Union troops were quartered in the room, and the bodies of both Presidents Abraham Lincoln and John Kennedy lain in state in the East Room.

President Erik Norton walked up to the podium in the East Room holding the hand of a monkey on his left and a leash leading to a frisky golden retriever in his right. He was followed by the First Lady carrying a young rescue kitten, as well as Angela Sherman of AHF, who was holding a newborn pig, and Dr. Alden Mitchum, executive director for the Physicians Committee for Responsible Medicine (PCRM), who was carrying a see-through plastic cage with several playful lab mice in it.

"Today I'm joined by Spencer, a nine-year-old orangutan and frequent performer at Disney's theme parks in Orlando; my beloved Duke, as well as a shelter kitten that our First Lady just rescued this morning; an open-range baby pig from California; and some recently liberated lab animals from a local school of medicine."

"First, let me say again that this Administration strongly condemns the recent string of violence at the Newport Beach Institute for Spinal Cord Research, the New Haven School of Medicine and the Great Lakes Primate Research Center. The full investigative and prosecutorial powers of this government have been unleashed to bring these perpetrators to justice. Our thoughts and prayers remain with the victims and their families."

"Unfortunately, these threats against researchers have taken an enormous toll. Widespread 'blue flu' is being reported at more than 400 medical schools and almost 1,000 universities conducting biomedical research. There are perhaps 70-80 million animals currently on study here in the US. If the researchers, students and administrators are too frightened to go to work, then who will take care of these millions of animals? This must stop."

"The November 8th elections of a week ago have echoed through this town and the chambers of Congress with complete bipartisan clarity. As each state wrestles with how to implement these new laws, I expect the issue to be hung up in the courts for several years to come. However, innocent animals simply can't wait in limbo for the judicial process. Scientists can't fear for their lives and their jobs as this issue churns through the legal system."

"So, by Executive Order, today I am issuing a one-year moratorium that will accomplish the following three objectives while the states and courts sort this all out. First, effective today and by Executive Order, no private citizen or corporation can own or house more than 200 animals in one location. If you own more than 200 today, you will receive a grandfathered exception until your holdings fall below 200 animals. Continued herd or stock breeding to keep your holdings above 200 for commercial purposes is prohibited. Second, effective today and by Executive Order, the interstate transportation of animals for economic purposes is prohibited. And third, effective today and by Executive Order, animal research that leads to terminal studies is prohibited during this period moratorium. Alternatives such as computer modeling should be used."

"In closing, I realize that the National Institutes of Health grants billions of dollars to American universities and our brightest scientists for biomedical research each year. But there comes a point when we must ask ourselves—that we must seriously question—has our health reached the level of 'good enough?' Think of all the medicine we have available to us today. It's amazing. It's plenty. It's more than we have had available in the history of humanity. And for those of us who need medicines, surgeries, therapies and diagnostic tools—it is the sum total of all that we have available to us today. If it's good enough for those of us who need it today, then perhaps it's good enough for those who will need it tomorrow as well. Every generation has searched for the fountain of youth. But can we afford to spend more time, more money, and—frankly—more animals just to live longer? Natural selection is an uninvited guest within every family. Some of us will die old; some of us will die far too young. We cannot continue to fund the search for the fountain of youth. We must realize that certain diseases of aging—such as cancer, Alzheimer's and Parkinson's—are inevitable. Our lifestyles and nutrition are environmental factors that certainly contribute to our health. How much longer can we pretend to play the role of God in our own laboratories?"

"Today I am challenging our universities and our brightest minds to reallocate these billions of dollars from biomedical research and shift these funds over to alternative energy research. I've directed the Secretary of Energy to work with Health and Human Services to make this a seamless transition. I'm asking Congress to make a fundamental shift in the way we fund research at our universities. Let's move away from basic biomedical animal research and move that research money over to alternative fuels and energy. It is time to break our dependence on foreign oil, reverse climate change, and show the world that America is committed to the humane treatment of all our animals, both human and non-human alike. Thank you and God bless America."

The President and his entourage of animal rights advocates

and animals turned and walked out of the East Room as camera shutters clicked.

"Spencer, are you going to take any questions?" a reporter from NBC Nightly News yelled out as others laughed. The orangutan never turned around but lifted his right hand with middle digit extended before scratching his backside. The President was oblivious.

Spencer's one-finger salute was the front page photo in every newspaper around the world. Within four hours the YouTube video of it had registered more than 4 million views.

The Chairman of the Joint Chiefs smiled warmly and softly applauded as the president left the East Room.

Ferguson reached into his pocket and pulled out his phone and started to dial area code 2-1-0 in San Antonio.

"Colonel Raines..."

7

The server stopped by to top off his coffee cup for what seemed to be the tenth time. For an early Wednesday morning this Denny's Restaurant on Southeast 82nd Avenue was just about empty. The 2:00 A.M. bar rush crowd wouldn't come until the weekend, and it was still too early in the fall for any procrastinating students to come in and cram for finals while running a caffeine drip from a ceramic mug.

The server kept trying to read the stickers that were plastered all over the customer's laptop while he meticulously worked on the document.

"Are you getting good Wi-Fi strength in here?"

He stopped typing but looked annoyed.

"I'm not on the Web right now, actually."

The server sat down on the other side of the booth. She was bored.

"Is that big sticker for the subway?"

He took a sip of his hot coffee but didn't warm up to her.

"Underground. The British Underground."

"British? You don't sound like you have a British accent."

"That's because I'm not British. Listen, I really have to get—"

"Right, sorry. Are you a student?"

He ran his hands over his shaven head. She could see the tongue pierce and the neck tattoo as his patience expired.

"Second-year law student, Lewis and Clark. Now please."

She got up and left in a hurry.

The interruption caused him to lose his place. He was trying to write in code so it wasn't like writing a normal letter. He had to be creative.

"Negotiation is over. The revolution has begun. Unlock every door, free every captive, and restore the balance to Mother Earth. This is the beginning of the death of speciesism. No specie is greater than other specie. No specie has the right to own or manipulate any members of other specie kingdoms. From this day forward all species are equal and morally equivalent. Brothers and sisters, global liberators, tonight is our night. When the sun sets tonight, come out of the darkness and into the light of liberation and complete your missions. History will remember your actions tonight. The revolution has begun. All cells now twenty-four green."

He copied the file on to his flash drive, closed up the laptop and dropped a five dollar bill on the table. He was paying for booth rental as much as the coffee and ten top-offs. He put on his black trench coat and slipped out the front door with his head down.

Within minutes his 1994 Toyota Corolla was on Interstate 5 passing through downtown Portland, then over the green interstate bridge into Vancouver, Washington. The steady beat of the windshield wipers and the eclectic throb from three hours of punk rock tunes helped him stay awake until he got to Seattle.

He parked in the lot next to the Seattle Ferry Terminal and walked the three blocks up to 816 3rd Avenue. He was pleased to see that there were several people in the FedEx Kinko's. He wouldn't stand out.

He went to the front counter and asked for a computer to rent. He gave the clerk ten dollars and said he didn't have a credit card.

Sitting down at the terminal labeled Computer 4, he inserted his flash drive and logged on to his Google mail account, loaded the text, and selected his distribution list. He hit send and clenched his fist beneath the table as the revolution was triggered. By the time each region and cell recirculated his message, more than 400,000 email accounts worldwide would be activated.

After logging off he walked out of the store, not bothering to close-out or collect his change. He went back to the Corolla and went to sleep. He needed to catch a few hours before driving back to Oregon. He had an ethics class in the afternoon that he simply couldn't miss.

A computer screen at the Federal Bureau of Investigation's Counterterrorism Division in Virginia sprang to life at 8:06 A.M. and triggered a flash alert. One of the thousands of alias screen names the FBI used to infiltrate Web cells had just received an email with a 70 percent keyword match.

The on-duty agent in the strategic assessment and analysis unit transferred the message up the chain of command. Within seconds, operational support branch offices worldwide were on notice.

The branch office in Seattle was notified that the originating IP address was on 3rd Avenue in downtown Seattle. An unmarked brown sedan pulled up and two agents ran inside the FedEx Kinko's. The clerk walked them over to Computer 4 but the guy with the bald head and black trench coat had already left.

A revolution was beginning, but no one was sure just exactly what that might mean.

FORT DETRICK, MARYLAND

Camp sat staring at the computer screen he had yet to turn on. His townhouse was full of boxes sixty-nine miles away in Alexandria. He was ready to move to northern Maryland for his next assignment. It was only a ninety-minute drive to work but he didn't want to do that drive in the Defender twice a day. He needed to move. But the president's press conference the previous night seemed to change everything. What was he supposed to do now? Hell, did he even have a job anymore?

A day earlier he had taken a delivery of 1,000 rats. He hadn't even started the testing protocols that the Department of Defense wanted done on influenza vaccine research. He had a hunch—an educated guess—as to how the military would respond to the president's Executive Order. Certainly the SECDEF would have gotten an exemption based on national security if nothing else. Research universities, pharmaceutical and biotech companies would have to wrap up all of their experiments and get beneath the 200-animal threshold or move their research operations off-shore. But without tissue analysis generated from terminal studies, there was very little left to wrap up.

The rats were all housed and ready for work in Camp's small lab at Detrick. They were nestled down in their new

Tecniplast ventilated cages. These plastic cages gave the rats eighty-two square inches of floor space. Institutional Animal Care and Use Committee guidelines stated that when the rats weighed less than 100 grams then each rat was required to have seventeen-square inches of floor space. But as they grew to 200 grams, then they would need twenty-three square inches of floor space each.

The whole notion of cage population density seemed ridiculous anyway. Rats could have all the room in the world, yet they still preferred to lie on top of each other in mounds of rat and rodent body warmth. Aside from the filtered ventilation tops, Camp thought the old cages were just as functional as the new ones.

With 1,000 new rats, he would need 1,000 cages when they reached full size at more than 500 grams each. But since the rats were still so small they could be housed three to a cage, which meant that only 333 cages were needed for the time being.

The faded plastic cages had been used at Detrick for more than twenty years. Somebody could probably use them for filing trays or storage containers. He surmised that maybe the mechanical shop on base could use them for small parts, screws or bolts.

He thought about loading them up into the Defender and driving the cages over to the shop. He had nothing else to do. He was basically on hold. His one-story, ground-floor lab was fairly isolated on Detrick. He could even park his car out in front of the lab windows. But there wasn't much point in doing anything until he got his orders.

A slight knock on the lab door pulled him out of aimless, meandering thoughts.

"Commander Campbell?"

Camp got up and started to walk over as the Army Colonel came in.

"Good morning, Colonel. I was hoping to see you and get some guidance on my orders."

The Colonel was a man of few words and obviously didn't feel comfortable in a lab setting.

"Looks like you got your shipment."

"Yes, sir."

"Well, send them back." He held out a piece of paper and handed it to Camp. "Effective immediately, no new research projects will begin on any bases in any of the fifty states. Any ongoing projects will be moved to the Navy base on Diego Garcia."

"You're pulling my chain, right, sir?"

"Wish I was. Your job is easy. You just call the breeder and say come back and get them. The rest of our poor researchers have to accompany these little rat bastards back to the other side of the world."

"So what am I supposed to do at Detrick now, sir?"

"Research something, I suppose. Command will let you know when they get around to you. Hurry up and wait until then."

The Colonel turned to walk out as Camp stared down at the paper.

"How many?"

"Sir?"

"How many rats did you get?"

Camp looked over at the brand new cages teeming with rats.

"Well, I'm using just over 265 of the cages right now with three to a cage."

"Don't look very healthy if you ask me."

"Actually, we put a disease *into* them. They're fine now."

"Great. So you make them sick on purpose and then try to make them feel better? Brilliant! No wonder people hate you guys. I suppose you do that to monkeys, golden retrievers and red robins, too!"

"Blue-eyed, blond-haired human babies too, sir, but only when we can slip into daycare centers unnoticed and grab them from unsuspecting mothers."

The colonel gave Camp a cold stare.

"Seriously, sir, that's how biomedical research is done."

"Not anymore it isn't. Send these little guys back to their mommas."

"Roger that, sir. I need your signature on the order here. Just indicate that we're returning all 800."

The Colonel made the notation and walked out of the lab without turning back. Camp didn't really have a plan, and he certainly didn't have any need for rats. But 200 animals seemed to be the magic number nowadays. He grabbed 200 of the old plastic cages and stacked 100 of them on the floor and another 100 across the lab countertops. He filled each with bedding, water bottles and food hoppers.

He reached into every new cage and pulled out three rats by their tails randomly and loaded them into the old cages until he had three to a cage. The pups had all been weaned and quickly piled on to their new mates in each cage. Even though Camp was technically stealing from the federal government, he was actually much more concerned about having a cage out of compliance.

The breeder didn't ask any questions and agreed to come back and pick up the rats the following day. They were getting similar demands from all over the country. Tecniplast would send a shipper in a few days to pick-up and return the new cages. Conventional wisdom predicted that most of these lab-animal supply businesses would be out of business within a week.

"Who would they supply?" Camp reasoned with himself. Researchers at American universities had "bomb-scare flu" and the president had just slapped a one-year moratorium on medical discovery.

The Defender was squealing with Camp's 200 new "pets" beneath a green tarp as he merged onto the I-495 beltway from I-270. As he drove through Cabin John, over the Potomac River and then looped back onto the George Washington Parkway, he was keenly aware that he had just violated an Executive Order by transporting these 200 animals over state lines from Maryland to Virginia.

He laughed out loud as he programmed his AC/DC playlist. Good thing he had most of his stuff in boxes. It meant he had an empty bedroom where 200 rats could sleep.

Camp could hardly hear the ringing of his cell phone over the blaring anthem of "TNT" as his left foot pounded the steel floor of the Defender in perfect rhythm.

"Hello?"

"Commander Campbell, this is Sheriff Bud Prescott, in Lancaster, Pennsylvania."

Camp's heart sank to the pit of his stomach.

"Is something wrong with my parents?"

"Well, health-wise they're fine, but we had to arrest your father today. He's posted bail and we've taken him home already, but I thought you should know."

"Arrested my dad? What the hell?"

"He, ah, fired his shotgun in the general vicinity of some protesters."

"Protesters? Where?"

"They were—actually still are—lawfully assembled on the street at the top of his driveway to the farm. I'm not sure your dad has calmed down enough. Maybe you can give him a call and talk some sense into him. We don't want anyone to get hurt."

"Thanks for calling, sheriff. I'll be there in the morning."

LANCASTER, PENNSYLVANIA

As Camp approached his parents' farm, he saw several cars parked and leaning precariously into the drainage ditch. Eight or nine people, mostly middle-aged women and college-aged kids, were holding posters and marching in a circle in front of the driveway.

The sign slogans were unambiguous: TAIL DOCKING IS BARBARIC; BURN THE BATTERY CAGE, FREE THE CHICKEN; AND NAZI = GESTATION CRATES.

Camp tapped on his horn and the group parted and jeered at him as he pulled into the long driveway. One of the sheriff's cruisers was parked by the kitchen door.

He had walked into his kitchen a million times as a kid but usually a patrol car parked outside meant he was in trouble, not his father.

Seabury Campbell, Sr. was sitting at the kitchen table with Sheriff Prescott. Camp's mother, Ruth, was topping off their coffees as her son walked in.

"Oh, my gosh," Ruth said as she ran into Camp's arms.

"Hi, mom, looks like dad's gonna have to stay after school and write his name on the board again. Morning, sheriff."

Camp shook his hand quickly and moved his dad's loaded

shotgun leaning against the wall so he could sit down and join them at the table. A cup of steaming coffee was placed in front of him before he could even settle.

"What's going on, dad?"

"You didn't have to come all the way out here for this, son."

"What exactly is 'this,' dad?"

"Crows. Damn crows won't leave us alone. I shot at a few crows. End of story. Any law against shootin' crows in this county?"

The sheriff rearranged himself and offered a clarification. "According to your father, the crows were in the field on the other side of the protesters, which is why he fired over their heads."

"And you don't see any more crows, now do you!"

Ruth took a seat and the four of them sat in silence for a few seconds.

"So, when did all of those folks outside show up?" Camp asked.

"About ten days ago, after the election, they've been hitting all of the local farms trying to intimidate us," said his mother. "I told your father to just ignore them and they'd go away. Now his 'crow shooting' has caused more to show up and more are on their way."

"Can't you just ignore them, dad?"

"We've been farming this land for 120 years, boy. My grandfather was a doughboy who came back to this place from World War I to raise seven children and just about fed half of the county for twenty years. I came back from Korea and did the same thing. Your sisters will probably take it over and my grandkids will be running it fifty years from now. I don't need no animal rights nut job trying to tell me how to care for my dairy cows, or my chickens, or the few pigs I raise. You don't farm for 120 years if you don't know how to raise livestock."

Camp saw a side of his dad he had never seen. "The old man is pretty worked up over this," he thought to himself.

"But dad, you've got to admit that the whole tail-docking thing is pretty gruesome and probably unnecessary."

"What's tail docking?" Sheriff Prescott asked.

"Once our cows are about a year old we place a tight rubber ring on their tails. The band cuts off the blood supply and then about two weeks later we can take off the lower half of the tail. Sometimes the cows holler for a few minutes. Most times they don't even notice," said the elder Seabury.

"Why? Why do you do it?"

"Keeps their udder's clean from the manure they'd normally swish around with a full tail. Also, stops leptospirosis. Lots of farmers around here get that from their cows."

"But dad, there's just as much evidence that says tail-docking doesn't keep the cows any cleaner."

Seabury's face turned visibly red. He was growing angry.

"So it's okay not to worry about getting sick cows or contaminating the milk? Since when did you and all those geniuses out at the road decide you are experts on animal agriculture? In fact, here's a little test. Come on, sheriff. Let's go on out there and ask them how many would drink my milk if I didn't tail dock. I'll tell you that answer—none of them. Because they're all damned fegans."

"Vegans, dad."

"Whatever."

Ruth got up to get the coffee pot.

"They don't drink milk, eat beef, pork, chicken or eggs in the first place. But that doesn't matter because they're hell-bent on telling me how to do it properly anyways."

"They don't want any chickens in cages or pigs in gestation crates, just like the new law they passed in California," his mother added.

"Free range chickens aren't that bad, are they?" asked Camp.

"The hell they aren't, son. We've got 21 million egg-laying hens here in Pennsylvania. It'll cost too much to raise free range eggs. Free range hens are prone to more disease. Poultry farmers will quit the business. Are poor families really ready to pay five dollars for a dozen eggs from Pennsylvania free range chickens or four dollars a dozen for eggs shipped in from Mexico?"

"Dad…"

"Don't 'dad' me. You haven't been back to this farm since your last day of high school. What do you know! Those folks out there, they'd never eat an egg, or an Easter ham, or even have a cold glass of milk. Yet they want to dictate how I contribute to the food supply while they chew on grass? Give me a break. This isn't about animal rights. This is about an extreme *fegan* agenda."

"Vegan," Ruth chimed in.

"Whatever."

Camp hadn't a dressing down from his father since high school. He wasn't sure what to say.

"Regardless, you can't shoot them."

"I was shooting crows. I hate crows. They're probably mad at me for shooting their beloved crows. Probably thought I was going to eat them."

"Maybe you should eat just a little crow right now, dad, and this whole thing could probably go away."

Camp made eye contact with Ruth just about the time she was desperately trying to stifle a laugh. She couldn't hold it any longer. Sheriff Prescott even found the situation funny.

Seabury didn't see the humor. He kicked his chair back and stood up.

"Glad you think it's funny. But this is how my family has made a living for five generations and how we fed thousands of our neighbors. Maybe you should just head back to Washington, sit in your ivory tower and enjoy a tossed salad while the Pennsylvania Farm Bureau sells us out to these lobbyists just like they did in Ohio."

Seabury grabbed his shotgun and marched upstairs to his bedroom.

8

A three vehicle convoy of the Algerian secret service, the Departement du Renseignement et de la Securite (DRS), was on a routine patrol down Highway 12 near Zaouia when they noticed a dead carcass on the side of the road. The first vehicle only slowed, assuming that it was an animal, more likely than not a goat. On closer inspection it was clear that it was the body of a fairly young man.

The security officers started to call it in when they noticed a young shepherd boy watching them from the hills. The third vehicle cut into the desert sand and pursued the boy who ran a few hundred feet before the vehicle stopped him and three AK-47s had a direct bead on his head. With minimal persuasion the boy told the officers that the man was dropped off two days before. He was alive at the time but very ill.

"Who dropped him off?"

The boy was too frightened to say the name out loud.

"Men with Droudkal."

Abdelmalek Droudkal was a local warlord. The Algerians suspected he was also running an Al-Qaeda training camp in the cave hideouts of Tizi Ouzou Province, almost 150 kilometers east of Algiers, the capital city.

The boy said the survivors abandoned their hideout in the Yakouren forest, then dumped this guy before driving north toward the Mediterranean seaport in Bejaia Province.

"Survivors? Survivors of what?"

The boy did not know, but he did know where their camp was so the DRS put him in one of their vehicles. Droudkal was said to command more than 1,000 terrorists. He purportedly had other training camps in Morocco, Tunisia and Nigeria. He called his operation AQLIM, or Al-Qaeda in the Land of the Islamic Maghreb. In 2007, it was AQLIM that claimed responsibility for the bombing of UN headquarters in Algiers that killed 41. The three vehicles pulled into a clearing at the base of the mountains. It was clearly a camp with tables, chairs and camouflage sunscreens still in place. Several caves opened up to the camp. The DRS officers got out of their vehicles cautiously with weapons drawn.

The boy pointed over to the truck. A dilapidated five-ton truck was parked at the back of the camp. Radio equipment and two satellite phones were still on the table. The camp was fresh.

With a series of hand gestures, the agents moved into position on both sides of the truck. A mound of dirt—possibly a bunker—extended out behind the truck. On signal they burst around the sides of the truck and up over the mound of dirt. The stench dropped several of them to their knees.

The bunker was filled with bodies.

The lead officer covered his nose with his hand and kicked

over the naked body of the closest man. He had no visible gunshot wounds, no stabs or puncture marks. The dead man's groin was covered with what appeared to be boils. He had bloody sores around his neck and his armpits.

"There must be forty men in this hole," said one of the special agents. "What did they die from?"

The twelve DRS officers looked around for answers or clues.

The boy stood up in the vehicle and yelled, "Chemicals!"

The agents looked at each other, covered their noses, and sprinted for the vehicles. They kicked up a huge cloud of dust and sand as tires spun and they left the camp much faster than they had arrived.

On a mountain ridge on the other side of the valley camp two high-powered binoculars were lowered as the DRS agents stormed out of the AQLIM camp.

Someone was watching.

MCLEAN, VIRGINIA

The Langley neighborhood of McLean, Virginia, was a rare stop on the map for Camp. He was always being summoned to Walter Reed and Bethesda Naval Hospital and any number of other military bases around the world that had medical facilities. But Central Intelligence was a unique experience.

Camp was escorted to the third-floor NCS Wing of the National Clandestine Service. Three men were waiting for him.

One of the field Collection Management Officers, or CMO, had just arrived from the Mediterranean area. CMOs served with operations officers on the front lines of human intelligence (HUMINT) collection overseas. They focused on clandestinely spotting, assessing, developing, recruiting and handling individuals with access to vital foreign intelligence on the full range of national security issues.

"Commander Campbell, thanks for coming in on such short notice. I'm Special Agent Daniels, and this is my partner Bryant Jackson. Borysko here is one of our NCS field agents. We pulled him out of country to meet with you."

"Gentlemen."

"If I may draw your attention to the screens, sir, we developed some HUMINT in an Al-Qaeda training camp in the mountains of Algiers. The camp had forty-six commandos and three senior operations officers. Our indigenous source was in place for the last eight months, and we were getting actionable HUMINT. We had a perfect dry cleaning location and everything was tracking. Then, eight days ago, everything went south. Not a bullet fired but forty of these guys drop dead within seven days. Papa and his brothers abandoned the training and command OPS center and left it as a mass graveyard. Borysko took the photos you're looking at right now and cut a slab of meat off one of the deceased for lab analysis over at Quantico. A three vehicle convoy from the Algerian secret police stumbled across this site three days ago, but they have not returned since."

The room was silent as Camp analyzed the forty close-ups of the bodies.

"Looks like some kind of chemical weapon experiment gone horribly wrong—or right—depending on your intent and point of view," said Special Agent Daniels, hoping to trigger an observation from Campbell.

"One could only wish." Camp stood up and walked over to an extreme close-up of the bloody sores in the armpit of a corpse. "Unfortunately, gentlemen, those sores are not from chemicals. Those are flea bites."

Daniels and Jackson laughed nervously, then stopped short. "Commander, we didn't ask you to advise us on desert hygiene and camel fleas. We were under the impression you might have some operational experience in this area. Sorry to have wasted your time."

The two agents stood up and closed their files. Borysko watched Camp, who continued to examine the close-up.

"If you look past the sores you can see the flea bites. Now I'm not talking about your run-of-the-mill camel fleas. No sir, not these. These are infected fleas, fleas that jumped off plague-carrying black rats and onto these boys."

"Did you say plague?"

"Plague comes in a variety of servings, all of which have biblical proportions. Bubonic plague, which is spread by bites from infected rat fleas, killed 75 million people in the fourteenth century but can now be treated with basic antibiotics. Pneumonic plague is less common but more deadly. It is spread by airborne bacteria, like the flu, and can be inhaled and transmitted between humans without the involvement of animals or fleas. And you can't eliminate septicemic plague, either."

Jackson shook his head in disagreement. "With all due respect, Commander, I've had this portfolio for two years now, and I know for a fact that Algeria has been free from Black Death plague since World War II."

"You're completely correct, Special Agent Jackson. This is no random outbreak. This, my friend, is a bioterrorism experiment gone horribly wrong—or right—to coin your phrase."

"Is it contagious?"

"Highly. But with basic medical supplies and antibiotics, it may be very controllable."

"So we have nothing to worry about. Maybe these guys will just circulate the bug among themselves."

Camp picked up his briefcase and started to walk to the door.

"Maybe. But my guess is that they might have a plot a bit more sinister in mind."

"Such as?"

"Well, such as developing a bacterium that our current medicines aren't yet equipped to fight. Plague is a bacterial disease, an infection that attacks the lymphatic system. In the early stages of the disease, you get plague from flea bites. The fleas are found on rodents, rats and mice, but fleas look for other prey when their rodent hosts die. The bacteria form of the disease aggregates in the gut of infected fleas, which causes each flea to regurgitate ingested blood, blood, which of course is now infected at this point, and then into the bite site of a rodent or—in this case—a human host. Once established, the Black Death bacteria spreads to the lymph nodes and multiplies. Lymph nodes get swollen and hemorrhage, which is why you see the bloody sores around the lymph nodes in each guy's groin, armpits and neck. The bacteria can also spread to the lungs, where it becomes pneumonic plague. Cough, sneeze...and you've just gone airborne and contaminated the airplane, the stadium, a village or even New York City."

"But we have antibiotics for all of this, right?"

Camp tucked his service cap under his arm and against his dress whites.

"I realize that you are the intelligence guys, and I'm just a Navy doc who didn't like your chemical weapons theory. But I'm guessing they're trying to develop a Black Death recipe that we've never cooked before. But, hey, what do I know. You've got HUMINT, so go ask them."

9

It had the makings of a "who's who" convention of radical writers and philosophers from the animal rights blogosphere, yet it was only a simple table at Crabby Bill's Beachwalk Bar and Grill overlooking the Gulf of Mexico in Clearwater, Florida.

Candy Embrerro was an overweight New York transplant who wore more make-up than Tammy Faye Bakker during a prime time fundraiser and crying fest. Candy divorced and disappeared from New York only to resurface in Clearwater as the executive director of No More Talking, or NMT. A nefarious organization at best, Candy's laptop was her corporate headquarters, and any good WiFi signal served as her 24/7 global sales force.

Well-educated and articulate, Candy was trying to earn a living by spewing her "blogosophy" against the Animal Exploitation Complex. Any human organization that used animals for capitalism was defined as exploiters, at least according to NMT. Dairy farmers, biomedical researchers, Sea World, dog breeders, fur and leather manufacturers, the circus and Kentucky Fried Chicken were all in the same boat and classified as card-carrying members of the Animal Exploitation Complex.

Candy's blog was gaining international traction as well as FBI attention. She made no effort to conceal the fact that she was a militant, not a pacifist, activist. Pacifists negotiated and protested, making signs and banners. Militants advocate for both legal and illegal direct action, bombs, bullets, break-ins and the liberation of any animal confined against their will. Militants incite violence by simply hiding behind the notion of justifiable direct actions that "others" might feel compelled to take. A poultry house in Georgia was as much a target as were the handlers of Shamu, the killer whale that performed at Sea World. The dog confined in the backyard by a fence or walking on a leash should be liberated as much as the 10,000 mice on study at Harvard Medical School.

Candy was drinking shots with Jeremy Graves. Jeremy had travelled by Greyhound Bus on the "executive charter" all the way from Kansas City, Kansas, in order to meet with Candy. He had already pitched his corporate sleeping bag on her couch as shots of Jägermeister flowed freely, allowing them to discuss their potential business merger more effectively.

Jeremy had earned his PhD in philosophy from the University of Missouri, Kansas City. He used his brilliant mind to articulate the pitfalls of speciesism and lobby for the moral equality of non-human animals. Unlike the English judicial norm of treating animals as property, which had been embraced in the United States for more than 225 years, Jeremy advocated a pacifist resistance to the Animal

Exploitation Complex. A self-described vegan abolitionist, Jeremy saw non-human animals as morally equivalent to human animals. Jeremy's Common Sense Corner, or CSC, served as the intellectual moral compass for the animal rights movement. CSC took the cause beyond saving puppies at the pound and, in fact, made the moral argument for the CSC legal standing of animals in American courtrooms.

The judicial system was taking notice. Divorce cases were winding through the system with a new common denominator: divorced couples were waging custody battles over family pets and the losers of the custody battle were countering with scheduled visitation rights.

Mere "property" is not the beneficiary of visitation rights and privileges. A divorced ex-husband is typically not granted visitation rights to the '69 Camaro his wife gets to keep in the settlement. The Camaro is property, just like the Labrador.

Whether they knew it or not, the courts were introducing an incrementalism that was, in fact, giving non-human animals legal standing as millions of dollars in endowment donations from a former TV game show host was funding a new legion of animal rights lawyers.

Candy and Jeremy had reached a tipping point. They had a large following of readers who were growing restless. They were calling for direct action that would liberate animals everywhere. The political climate in the U.S. was perfect. Now was the time to move. There had to be a way of combining the militant advocacy platform of NMT with the pacifist platform of CSC without killing any animals. Killing people, however, was not of great concern.

That's why Candy sent Jeremy the bus ticket with a few dollars left over from her $1,200 divorce settlement.

"Here's what I'm thinking: do you remember the tainted Tylenol events back in the 1980s?"

"Changed the packaging world overnight," said Jeremy.

"It did, sort of, anyway. When's the last time you shopped for meat at the grocery store?"

"Never. Just the thought is disgusting."

"Perfect. On the way home we're stopping at Kroger's. Here's what you'll see. The refrigerated section holds various cuts of beef, pork, chicken and ground beef. The meat sits on little Styrofoam trays, and the whole thing is wrapped in clear plastic."

Jeremy took a handful of chips and chased it with some water. He shrugged his shoulders.

"What? What am I missing?"

"The meat is wrapped in clear plastic wrap. That's cellophane, Jeremy. Hundreds of containers in this Kroger's, and millions more around the country are only protected by thin plastic wrap. Millions of our slaughtered, murdered innocent animal brethren, waiting to be devoured by the capitalist greed that put them on the Styrofoam in the first place, wait in the refrigerated section for the next generation of cancer and heart patients to consume their flesh for a buck-ninety-nine a pound with a coupon."

"And the only thing standing between the slaughtered pig and the capitalist pig is plastic wrap."

A plan was starting to emerge.

"Are you saying we kill a few people to get them to stop eating meat?"

"More than that, Jeremy, and much less than that, I hope nobody dies but tough shit if they do. We make sure that enough of the meat supply in this country is poisoned. A few packages in a few stores should create the necessary widespread panic. The public health concern must get the headline. It must be perceived as being far greater than our vegan agenda."

Jeremy didn't like the word "poison." It was too radical and way outside his comfort zone.

"Can we meet in the middle?"

"Talk to me."

"Candy, I don't want to poison anyone, human or non-human. But what if we were to contaminate? Just enough to get some people sick?"

Candy got excited. "Can you meet me in the middle of that?"

"I'm listening."

"What if we contaminate? And we announce the contamination. It is our warning to all consumers that the government knows the meat supply was tainted but won't say anything because they're trying to protect the interests of big business. They won't talk about it because of capitalism and greed. We'll tell the world that the government was willing to sacrifice their public health in order to prevent a redux of Tylenol."

"So, just as poisoned meat packages are discovered in a few homes, we covertly announce why they've been poisoned just as contaminated packages start to hit grocery shelves across the country."

"*We* only need to contaminate a few batches. But *public hysteria* will contaminate every batch with fear. Same with the poison. A few packages in a couple of states would freak everyone out everywhere."

"Candy, what are you thinking for contamination?"

"I don't know, maybe *e. coli* at a packing plant would do the trick. Arsenic injected with a syringe into a few meat packages will work just fine."

"Easier said than done. You would need too much arsenic. It wouldn't work."

"What about ricin? There are plenty of castor beans around here."

"I still don't think it would work," said Jeremy, who was now growing uneasy.

"Not true. Follow my logic. She strolls into the store, purse full of a few syringes with insulin because she's a diabetic. She walks past the meat section and grabs a pound of ground beef, some top sirloins, lamb chops, a package of bacon and some salmon. She wheels down multiple aisles, striking up a few conversations with strangers along the way. Over by the paper towels she gets too warm and takes her coat off. She's not feeling well so she gives herself what looks like an injection. She reaches down into the grocery cart and nonchalantly injects the ricin into all of the various packages. After a quick change of heart since she's not feeling well, she decides to return the meat. She even offers the ground beef to a mother about to buy for her family. She pays for her paper towels in the express lane and leaves."

"What about the store's surveillance cameras?"

"They only saw a sick woman giving herself insulin injections. The outside camera observes her walking to the bus stop by the store, getting on the public bus, where *he* promptly removes his wig and wipes the make-up off."

"And underground web sites across the world warn the globe that the meat supply has been poisoned in order to protect them from the government cover-up of an *e. coli* contamination."

"Maybe they eat the meat, maybe they don't," said Candy. "But as soon as one gets poisoned or confirmation of one contamination is found in the marketplace, then BOOM."

"V-O-D…veganism-on-demand."

"You've been at this a lot longer than I have, Jeremy. Do you know of anyone sleeping and active in the meat processing industry?"

"As a matter of fact I do. I know some guys in Minnesota, Worthington and Winona, I think. How about you?"

"Maybe. I just got some photos and a posting on my wall from some lady in Monroe, North Carolina, who works at a poultry complex."

"You're kidding me. She actually called it a poultry complex?"

"I kid you not, she says they call it a 'poultry complex,' complete with a processing plant, feed mill and hatchery. She says she's had enough, not to mention she might be laid off."

"The bastards slaughter the innocent and then cut her job. Asses."

"At least they're honest about it. The Pentagon should formally rename itself the Military Industrial Complex."

Candy paid the bill and the two of them walked out of Crabby Bill's and onto the bike path next to the sand as the sun started to set over the Gulf.

"Any ideas on how to fund this direct action?"

Jeremy thought for a second or two. "I've got a colleague, a law student in Oregon. He's got access to some 'educational grant' money from PETA. How much do you think we'll need?"

"Five grand each ought to do it for a couple of peeps in Minnesota, the gal in North Carolina, and our mystery shoppers. Think he can get twenty?"

"As long as PETA gets the right of first refusal on the press release, we're golden. Oh, thanks for the drinks and chips."

"You can thank my ex. Dinner and drinks on him."

10

Leslie Raines weaved in and out as she jogged through tourists and locals out taking a stroll on the River Walk. Her gray "Property of Auburn University Athletic Department" t-shirt was soaked with the undeniable evidence of a nine-mile run. Fresco's Juice and Smoothie Bar had become the exclamation point to her weekend runs. It was her tradition, and everyone who knew Raines knew not to mess with her during her weekend conditioning.

With a strawberry-banana smoothie and a cup of raisins and almonds in hand, she landed at a small wrought iron patio table next to the Walk. Wiping the sweat from beneath her Oakleys, she was too busy cooling down to notice the guy behind the newspaper sitting near her.

He wasted no time.

"Lieutenant Colonel Leslie Raines?"

She wiped some smoothie away from her lips uncomfortably with her hand. "Who's asking?"

"Edgar Garcia with the IG's office, Defense."

"Since when did the Inspector General's boys start stalking and ambushing military officers during their personal time?"

Garcia pointed to the chair across from Raines.

"May I?"

"Knock yourself out...please!"

Garcia pulled a file out of his backpack and put it on the table. "If you ever go overseas you might want to consider mixing up your routine. Your situational awareness protocols need refreshing. You're pretty predictable and easy to find."

"You came all the way from Washington to tell me I'm predictable? Should've just called my ex-husband. He could've told you that and saved the taxpayers some airfare."

"Let me get to the point."

"Please do."

"Commander Seabury Campbell, United States Navy."

"No, I'm not sleeping with him. Not my type."

"Ma'am, are you aware that he was recently assigned to Fort Detrick in Maryland?"

"Yes, infectious disease research or something of that nature."

"Did you know that the program was terminated days after his arrival?"

"No, as a matter of fact I didn't."

Garcia removed his sunglasses and leaned in closer.

"Then you have no knowledge of Commander Campbell's unauthorized removal of thousands of dollars of federal property from that Army base?"

Raines spewed smoothie at the notion of Campbell stealing from Uncle Sam.

"What, did he take a couch to decorate his apartment?"

Garcia smiled. "I don't know. Does his apartment need redecorating?"

"I wouldn't know. What, Mr. Garcia, do you allege he stole?"

"Rats. As many as 200 research rodents were missing and unaccounted for when the breeder returned to Detrick to pick up 1,000 recently delivered rodents after the project was terminated. Hundreds of old cages were missing as well."

Raines was angry. "You've gotta be kidding me. The breeder says 200 rats are missing so you launch a federal investigation on a highly decorated Navy officer? Tell you what, how much do the rats cost? I'll write you a check."

"It's not about the money. Why would he take the animals?"

"You're assuming he took them in the first place. Maybe the breeder made a mistake. They got pissed at you for cancelling the contract, and now they want to squeeze a few more dollars out of you before the well runs dry and they're all out of business."

"Fort Detrick personnel worked with the breeder and they assert 200 are missing."

"Maybe he has a pet snake or something. I don't know. Ask Camp."

"Camp?"

"Commander Campbell," said Raines, exasperated.

Garcia pulled out a photograph and placed it on the table. "Do you recognize this vehicle?"

Raines gave it a quick glance.

"Yes, it's his Land Rover, Defender 90. He drove me to a Pentagon meeting in it."

"Here's a screen shot from the security camera at Detrick as Commander Campbell passed through the checkpoint gate. The back is covered floor to roof with a tarp."

"So?"

"Here's a screen shot from his arrival earlier that morning. No tarp."

Raines shifted uncomfortably in her chair.

"Listen, I don't know anything about this. I have no idea why he'd want to take research rodents, if in fact he did at all."

Garcia put the photos in the file and returned it to his backpack. "Tell me about his research with infectious diseases?"

"I really don't know that much. He was recommended to join a Working Group that I lead. Our paths first crossed about five weeks ago. He was assigned to Detrick and removed from my Working Group. That's all I know."

Garcia stood up. "Well, here's my card. If you think of anything we should know, please call me."

Raines studied the card for a second or two as Garcia started to leave.

"Colonel Raines, one more thing. Is there any reason why America should be concerned or afraid of Commander Campbell? Any ax to grind over Uncle Sam's head?"

Garcia never received an answer other than the "shove it up your butt" glance from Raines.

She took another swallow from the smoothie and pulled the BlackBerry out of her fanny pack. His number was now on speed dial.

"Lieutenant Colonel Leslie Raines for General Ferguson, please…"

GETTYSBURG

Eileen was waiting out in the driveway as Camp pulled in. She hurried to his door and gave him a full embrace as he kissed her gently on the forehead.

"Commander."

"Good morning, Eileen. You look gorgeous as ever."

"Keep it up and I'll serve you breakfast in bed tomorrow."

Camp grabbed a small pack from the passenger seat and Eileen hooked her hand in his arm as they walked into Lightner. Eileen went right to the kitchen and poured a mug full of freshly brewed coffee and a plate of still steaming blueberry muffins.

"Blueberry, your favorite."

A crackling fire was raging in the hearth. It took the chill out of the air where almost two inches of freshly fallen snow had blanketed Lightner Farms.

Camp sat quietly, starring at the fire. He seemed upset.

"I was so surprised by your email, Camp. Fort Detrick seemed like the perfect assignment. Close enough that I was hoping you might even move here."

Camp smiled and reached for a muffin.

"Think you could have handled me seven days a week?"

"You aren't so tough."

An awkward silence filled the room.

"So what's next? Any word yet?"

Camp got up and started to pace back in forth in front of the stone fireplace that filled an entire room. He thought of Civil War patients who sat where he was and wondered about their fate as well.

"I don't know, Eileen. I guess I wait for orders. Not enough years in to retire but more than enough years to know I'm just tired."

Eileen got up and walked over to the key tree above the front desk. There were twelve rooms at Lightner and all of them were named after Civil War soldiers, six Union soldiers in the north wing and six Confederate soldiers in the south wing.

But one key was always missing from the tree.

Eileen reached into the desk drawer and pulled out the key to room three. "The number three bedroom awaits you, Commander. You'll find fresh towels in your room. And maybe you'll even take me on a walk later this afternoon?"

Camp smiled, caressed Eileen's cheek and headed up the old wooden stairs that split on each side above the fireplace.

The white Mazda that had followed the Defender all the way from Alexandria was safely tucked away off the road leading up to Lightner Farms. A tripod was out and a camera was pointing up into the trees and away from the house.

Eileen smiled as she looked through the kitchen window above her sink where she finished the last of the dishes from lunch. An elderly couple from Biloxi were her only other guests. They had been tracing the steps of one of their ancestors, an ancestor who met an untimely death in the fields of Gettysburg.

The couple had already checked out. Eileen presumed that they, or some other passers-by, were enjoying all of the birds getting ready for winter. The branches had long ago shed their leaves and bird watching was perfect right now.

Camp finally came down just a few minutes before five. The aroma in the lodge reminded him that he was famished.

"You're baking bread."

"Southern rolls, twice-baked potatoes, and a spiked shepherd's pie that'll knock you on your butt. Consider it my patriotic duty to do my part for the good of America's finest."

"Do we have time for that walk?"

"I'm grabbing my fleece right now. Mind throwing another log on before we go?"

The two strolled arm in arm through the thin forest of birch and poplar, never letting the farmhouse out of sight.

Squirrels were busy with winter preparations. and tracks from all sorts of animals were everywhere. The snow gave way with a soft crunch at every footfall. The sun was almost completely down, but the golden glow lit the scene like a postcard.

Camp and Eileen stopped and admired the scene.

The engine from the white car started, and the headlights came on as the car did a U-turn in the road and headed back towards the Baltimore Pike.

"Neighbors?" Camp asked, breaking the silence.

"Bird watchers. They've been here a few hours. Best time of the year for some great photography."

After dinner, Eileen and Camp retreated to the two, over-sized deep leather chairs facing the fireplace. She poured him a tall, single malt whisky, neat, as she nursed a glass of her favorite red zinfandel.

A calm, relaxing silence passed as they lost themselves in the magic of a dancing fire. Eileen stirred and reached for a light blanket on the table and covered her legs and lap.

"Camp?"

He looked over and raised his eyebrows. No words needed to be said. They understood each other completely.

"How much longer? How much longer can you keep doing this? How much longer can *we* keep doing this?"

Camp didn't have an answer. He reached over and took Eileen's hand and closed his eyes.

11

Camp was reaching for his briefcase and service cap when his cell phone started to ring. He recognized the number.

"Colonel Raines, I was wondering when I was going to hear from you again."

"Good morning, Commander. Had your coffee yet?"

"Matter of fact, I am heading out the door right now and down the sidewalk to my only coffee pot."

"Perfect. I just had the barista give me two pours. I'm at the front table next to King Street, Army dress greens, can't miss me."

"Raines, I've gotta hit the road to Detrick, so I can't stay and—."

The connection went dead. Raines hung up.

Camp hustled into King Street Joe's with a schoolboy grin on his face and quickly spotted Raines a few tables away. She wasn't smiling.

"Raines, I appreciate the coffee, but I've got a meeting at

1100 hours at Detrick that I can't miss. What about pizza tonight?"

"Sit down, Commander."

The stern look on her face was sufficient to delay his early departure.

"Okay…"

Raines stared him down for a second or two with obvious contempt on her face.

"Well, I'm trying to save your ass from a probable court martial or, as Inspector General Garcia seems to suggest, a potential act of domestic terrorism."

"What in the hell are you talking about?"

"You're going to join me for a meeting at the Pentagon this morning."

"Les, I'm not in your working group anymore. Done. Remember?"

"We'll be meeting with the Inspector General's office as well as Brigadier General Ferguson—"

"What's going on?"

Raines kept talking as though she had never been interrupted. "—where you'll explain why you stole U.S. government property."

"What are you talking about?"

"And you'll account for what you did with 200 lab rats and explain why you took them."

"Oh, geez."

"After you hand them a personal check for $4,318."

"Four grand?"

"That's the bill the breeder sent to Fort Detrick for your 200 unreturned rats."

Camp rubbed his face vigorously.

"Raines, I can explain."

"Yes, trust me, you will. I'm absolutely insane for doing this."

"Doing what?"

"Bottoms up, Navy boy. Time to walk your plank."

Raines stood up and tossed her cup in the trash as Camp followed behind.

"My car is back at the apartment."

"We're not taking your car."

Camp got into the passenger seat of her white Mazda rental as Raines pulled out and headed for the Pentagon. Not a word was spoken.

Raines and Campbell sat silently in a small conference room. Raines was nervous, but Camp just seemed to be mad.

Three staffers followed Edgar Garcia into the conference room and were quickly followed by Brigadier General Ferguson and two JAG officers. Raines and Camp stood quickly as Garcia moved rapidly to start the meeting.

"Commander Campbell, in your affidavit you state the 200 rats were either dead when they arrived or died shortly thereafter. Is that correct?"

Camp looked first toward Raines, then Ferguson for guidance. He had not written an affidavit. Neither looked back at him. All eyes were fixed on Garcia.

"Yes, sir, that is correct," Camp finally said, more as a question than as a statement.

"And according to your statement and that of Lieutenant Colonel Raines, you both took the dead rodents to the countryside for disposal. Is that correct?"

Camp was shocked at his own answer. "Yes, sir, we did."

"And why did you and Lieutenant Colonel Raines ignore established protocol and procedures for the disposal and proper reporting of expired lab animals?"

"Sir, if I may?"

Garcia nodded to Raines.

"Commander Campbell and I are both animal lovers. Our professional and personal lives are intertwined with the animal kingdom. In light of last summer's drought and forecasts for a winter more harsh than normal, we felt the animals would be better utilized in the circle of life as food for predatory birds than as soot and pollution in the incinerators."

Camp bit his lip trying not to laugh hysterically in the middle of his administrative hearing with the IG. Even Ferguson had the slightest glint of a smile turning in the crease of his upper lip.

Garcia was incredulous. "Seriously, the two of you are suggesting that you took 200 dead rats out into the forest in a picnic basket and fed the falcons like pigeons in Central Park?"

"Actually, sir, we had help...and a witness."

Garcia's staff started writing furiously in their notebooks.

"Really. There's no mention of a witness in either one of your statements. Lieutenant Colonel Raines, you say you had help and a witness exists? Another officer?"

"No, sir, a civilian. She owns the Lightner Farms Bed and Breakfast in Gettysburg, Pennsylvania. She took us out into the woods where we placed the rodents on stumps for predatory birds."

The room fell deafeningly silent. Camp dropped his eyes into a cold stare at the desk in front of him. Raines never looked away from Garcia.

"Is this all true, Commander Campbell?"

Camp clenched his teeth and exhaled slowly.

"Yes, sir."

Garcia nodded his head at Brigadier General Ferguson, the two JAG lawyers and his staff.

"Very well. With restitution of $4,318 and a reprimand in your files, we'll consider the matter closed. I'll need your signatures on both affidavits and a check made out to the U.S. Army, Department of Defense."

Raines and Campbell signed their statements, and Ferguson signed each as the witness of record. Garcia and his two staffers gathered up their files. Garcia leaned down close to Camp.

"I hear you have a real ugly couch in your apartment. Be careful how you choose to remodel, Commander."

The door shut behind Garcia at about the same time Ferguson slapped his hand down on the table.

"What the hell were you thinking, Campbell?"

"Sir, I don't know, sir. I—."

"Save it. Raines just took one for the team and saved your butt from certain court martial."

"I don't know what to say, sir."

"Say nothing."

Ferguson threw an envelope on the table and it slid over to Campbell.

"Your new orders. You and Raines report to me now. No more Detrick and no more working groups with Power-Point slides and fancy coffees. You two are wheels up tomorrow morning at 0400 from Andrews."

"Sir?" Raines asked.

"Diego Garcia. You both need some time away from the IG's office before he smells a rat in all of this nonsense. You've both been assigned to a SPEC OPS research mission."

"With all due respect, General, you know my situation, sir."

Ferguson removed his glasses and softened his bark.

"Yes, Camp, I do. But I didn't ask for this mess—you did it all by yourself with the stunt you just pulled. I'm sorry, Camp, I know you've been through a hard patch, but this is final. We need six months—maybe a year—to let this storm pass. Then you can come back."

Ferguson stood up and left the room, followed by the JAGs. Raines gathered up her things and started to leave.

"How did you know about Gettysburg?"

Raines stopped but didn't look back.

"I was pretty damn well settled in San Antonio, Commander. I really didn't need to play in your sandbox just to wipe your snotty little nose."

"I'm sorry, Raines."

"Me, too. Better call your lady friend and get some help. I suspect you have a lot of falcons to feed. 0400 at Andrews. Don't be late."

12

The roar of the engines intensified as Raines and Camp strapped in for what would be a sixteen-hour flight. Raines looked irritated but rested. Camp hadn't been to bed. After a three-hour round trip drive to Gettysburg and a few hours of work with Eileen on the ground to deal with a few hundred rats, he had a million other details to take care of before he left. He stopped his mail delivery, set up automatic online rent payments for his apartment, and made sure all of his other bills were handled while he was gone.

He had no other choice but to park the Defender at Andrews for who knew how long.

Camp had called his parents from Lightner to explain that he was being sent out on a last minute mission and might be gone for a year. He could hear the anguish in his mother's voice. "Are you sure you're ready for this, Seabury?" There was nothing he could say to reassure a mother who had seen the horrors of war through her only son's silence.

His father was a bit more stoic. Duty. Honor. Country. If the military wanted his boy spur of the moment, it must be for national security, probably an Executive Order from the White House.

"Well, I hope you're back in time for harvest. You know I could use some help in the fields."

Camp hadn't helped in the fields in almost seventeen years, but that never stopped his dad from asking. Seabury Campbell, Sr. was old school, and he always believed his boy would come back some day to Lancaster, home of the Amish and Pennsylvania Dutch to take over the family farm. But everyone knew better, even Senior.

His three sisters never moved farther than ten miles away from the farm. They married local boys and were never more than a long bicycle ride away. His folks were always busy with Camp's nieces and nephews, mostly playing taxi drivers for soccer games and piano lessons. The sons-in-law did most of the farming now while old Sea Bee did most of the supervising from his front porch swing.

The neighbors called him "Sea Bee Seabury" after he returned from Korea. He was trained to build anything anywhere under any condition. Camp decided to join the Navy when he was only six years old. He wanted to be a Sea Bee just like his daddy. The officers at the Naval Academy, however, thought he was a bit more suited to becoming a SEAL.

Camp was a typical rural farm boy. He was up long before dawn every morning tending to the dairy cows, bucking hay, and finishing a seemingly never-ending list of sunrise chores. School and grades came easy for him, but football and wrestling were his escape routes away from the routines of a dairy farm with forty acres of row crops to boot.

He got into more than his fair share of fights on the football field and behind the bleachers but always managed to avoid serious trouble with the sheriff. Farm life taught him how to use his hands, guns and even a knife.

One late spring, when Camp was only twelve and his parents were away at his aunt's funeral, one of the pregnant cows got into trouble. She was trying to birth her calf, but the calf was breeched. The cow's moans and anguished hollers could be heard for miles. Camp's sisters were hysterical and called the local vet but he was thirty miles away finishing up some vaccines in the next county. He told them there was nothing they could do. "Sometimes nature won't be denied," the vet had told them.

Camp didn't like that answer because he wasn't about to lose two cows. The pregnant Holstein was lying on her side in serious trouble. Camp ran into the tool room and pulled out a sharp hunting knife and his father's pistol.

A quick shot to the skull silenced the cow and after a 20-inch incision into her lower abdomen, Camp pulled the calf out and got her breathing. He called her "Mira," which was short for miracle and then spent the next two months hand-feeding that calf ten bottles of milk every day. Most nights he slept in the hay right next to her until first light.

The calf followed Camp around the farm for the next six years no matter where the next chore took him. Most folks figured Mira just thought Camp was her momma. When old Sea Bee loaded his boy up into the Ford pick-up for the drive to the academy in Annapolis, Camp turned back to see Mira standing at the fence line.

Camp closed his eyes, stuck the ear plugs in, and grabbed the canvass mesh behind his head. Everyone's face shook and heads bobbed in unison as the C-17 Globemaster III rumbled down the airstrip trying to gain speed.

A solitary drop escaped Camp's closed eyes and rolled down his cheek, a tear that Raines happened to notice before she fell asleep.

INDIAN OCEAN

Camp had slept for nearly sixteen hours, including a refueling stop in Iceland. He woke with his body screaming from stiffness but was well-rested otherwise.

Raines had left his side and was standing near one of the round portal windows. She was gazing out at endless miles of blue water and sunshine.

"Welcome back to the land of the living, Commander."

Camp looked over her shoulder and out the window at the ocean.

"Gorgeous."

Raines smiled for one of the first times in a day or two.

"Well, thank you, Commander."

He delivered a playful forearm to her shoulder and the laugh served to break some tension.

"I don't even have an explanation, Raines."

"I'm not asking anymore."

"I guess I was just so upset that the research was cancelled. I'd been trying to get to Detrick for a year. And before my first day was done, the project was over."

"What were you going to do? Conduct bioterrorism research with your little rats on your kitchen table?"

Camp laughed. "Like I said, I really didn't have a plan. It was a stupid impulse."

"And now you're following all of your furry little friends to Diego Garcia. It'll be a homecoming for you."

"Have you ever been here before, Raines?"

"Twice actually. The first time was a quick stopover. I was just a strap hanger on a B52 bomber. The other time I was here for six weeks, working with the Brits at the Branch Medical Clinic."

"Branch of what?"

"Part of their Naval Hospital Yokosuka."

"So, are we going to like it here, or what?" asked Camp.

"As for the island, I'm telling you straight up. It's paradise. But as for the BIOT, this place is loaded with strange crap every turn you make," she said.

"BIOT?"

"British Indian Ocean Territory. We're officially governed by the Brits but it is all joint OPS with the U.S. In 2008 the British foreign minister announced that the CIA used the island for rendition when we took some jihadists off the battlefield in Afghanistan. We, of course, claimed that the CIA only refueled here."

"Did they?"

"Well, only if refueling takes six months to complete. All of the other fifty-one islands in the Chagos archipelago recognize the African Nuclear Weapons Free Zone Treaty, but Diego Garcia does not. Aerial refueling of B1Bs and B52s takes place 24/7. A couple of U.S.-guided missile subs always seem to stick around even though they are U.S. Georgia-based. Of course you know it's an alternative landing strip for the space shuttle, but did you know it's also part of the base for the U.S. Space Surveillance Program? Three mammoth GEODOSS telescopes are here, spanning the globe for bad guys. Now throw in the USS *Bob Hope* bringing in more than 250,000 research animals from the states and, well, you've got a veritable circus in paradise."

Camp took it all in as paradise passed beneath them.

"You're quite the tour guide, Raines. I'm impressed, and now I'm educated."

"Educated? Really? I figured you knew all that already, since you staged here for Afghanistan and your operations in Tora Bora. Then again, maybe you didn't get out much when you came back two months later to recover from your shrapnel wounds and a bullet to the leg over at the branch clinic. Hard to do much sightseeing when you're in and out of a coma for ten days and in critical straights for another four weeks before you can be stabilized for evacuation. Seriously, Commander, when do you start telling anyone the truth? When do you actually open up and be honest?"

"Truth? Look who's talking about truth, transparency and the American way. I don't recall trailing *you* out into the country to spy on your little life, but apparently you were okay with that."

Raines' light demeanor turned stormy.

"Listen, when the IG's office hunts me down on a morning run in Texas suggesting I might be a player in your half-baked broken arrow plot in Maryland to unleash a bioterror attack on the U.S., I just figured you could use a friend. Clearly you're a thief, but I never pegged you for being a Timothy McVeigh."

"So you trailed me out to Gettysburg?"

"Yes, that's what General Ferguson recommended. He put his career on the line to cover your ass. But forget about stealing government property. You're more concerned that your colleague trailed you and caught you cuddling up with your quaint little Amish girlfriend. Now my apartment is packed up and loaded into a storage unit and I'm deployed again and stuck with a self-righteous, arrogant, little jerk who can't see past himself far enough to know his actions have consequences for everyone around him."

Raines turned and abruptly marched over to her seat. Camp wasn't accustomed to letting people inside his closed off world. But he didn't think Raines would have it any other way.

BATON ROUGE, LOUISIANA

A ventilated box truck passed through security and backed up into the loading dock at the Gulf Shores Research Center. The driver buzzed the back door and was finally met by a graduate student.

"Got a delivery here for a Dr. Stern."

Keith looked out at the truck and then down at the paperwork the driver handed him.

"I don't think we were expecting any deliveries. What do you have?"

"Not sure exactly, but they're alive. I think the guys at the airport were saying they're monkeys. Anyway, you got thirty-nine of them."

Keith shook his head. "Listen, I've got to call Dr. Stern and clear this."

"Call whoever you want but in ten minutes you're gonna have thirty-nine monkeys running around on your loading dock."

Keith walked outside by the truck and called Stern from his cell phone. Stern was already in his car driving to the university.

"You're kidding me. We cancelled that order after the whole Animal Humane Fund thing. In fact, I'm meeting with the chancellor next week, and it looks like we'll be shutting down all of our animal research indefinitely. Tell him we reject the shipment."

Keith walked over to the driver to explain.

"Dr. Stern cancelled that order more than three weeks ago. He told me to reject the shipment."

"Guess you didn't read the contract. These are live primates ordered from the Philippines. You had cancellation privileges for seventy-two hours after the order was placed. Now these are American monkeys. Actually, they're Gulf Shores's monkeys now."

Keith punched in his security code and opened the back door.

"I don't care what your contract says. We reject the shipment."

The driver went to the back of the truck and unlatched the door. "It makes no difference to me. Hopefully, these guys will still be on your loading ramp when the TV cameras come. If you make me leave them here I'm calling Channel 2 News before I reach the street."

"Okay, okay, we'll sort it out later. Bring them in. I'll call for some help."

DIEGO GARCIA

The plane taxied to a stop on the tarmac. As the engines started to cool, the hydraulics on the craft squealed to life, and the back door began to rise. The view outside was completely obstructed by three pallets of equipment, an M1 Abrams tank and personal luggage stowed between the passengers and the back door. Three forklifts quickly pulled up. and within minutes crew and passengers deplaned. Two plain-clothed men in t-shirts and tactical cargo pants walked up toward Raines and Camp.

"Commander Campbell, Colonel Raines, welcome to Diego Garcia."

Camp was bewildered. He didn't expect to see these two.

"Special Agent Daniels, Special Agent Jackson. You boys are quite a fair distance away from Langley. What brings you out here?"

"Special Ops assignment, Commander, welcome to the team."

Camp smiled and heaved his rucksack over his head and dropped his Oakleys down over his eyes and started walking.

"Sorry boys, but my Special Ops kinetic days are long gone. I'm on a special research project now."

Jackson and Daniels followed as Raines stayed quiet.

"That so? Guess General Ferguson didn't get that memo. Might want to read your orders, Commander," said Daniels as he slapped some papers into the open pocket on Camp's pack.

"Feel free to shower and hit the DFAC for some midnight rats starting at 2030 hours. First team meeting is at 0700 in the XO's TOC."

Daniels and Jackson split off, and Camp came to a complete stop as Raines walked up beside him and dropped her pack.

"Thanks for the heads-up, Raines."

"You slept the whole way here. Frankly, you now know as much as I do. Hell, you know more than I do. So how come you know who these two spooks are?"

Camp ignored the question and scanned the buildings.

"Come on, let's find billeting and get some hooches. I'll tell you all about the Black Death plague after I get a shower," Camp said.

"Black Death plague?"

PART
TWO

13

DIEGO GARCIA

The rain fell hard but peacefully. It was not so much a storm as it was a predictable daily watering. The steam rose above the cement runway as temperatures headed towards the standard eighty-three degrees.

Diego Garcia is about 400 miles south of the equator and isolated in the middle of the Indian Ocean. It's a living coral atoll. The coral reefs and island are comprised of a seemingly infinite supply of living organisms. Once an active volcano, all that is left now from the remnants is the atoll surrounding a central lagoon. Thanks to its tropical location and heavy rainfall, the island is heavily vegetated with coconut palm and ironwood trees.

Diego Garcia was discovered by Portuguese explorers in the early 1500s and is the largest of fifty-two islands from which the Chagos archipelago form. The name of the island is believed to have come from either the ship's captain or the navigator. Once discovered, the island just as quickly disappeared from maps of the Indian Ocean for many years until it was relocated and claimed by the French in the early 1700s. Diego Garcia remained under French control until after the Napoleonic Wars—about 1814—when possession was ceded to the British.

In 1965, with the formation of the British Indian Ocean Territory, Diego Garcia was under administrative control of the British government of the Seychelles. With the formation of the BIOT, a formal agreement was signed between the governments of the United Kingdom and the United States in 1966, making the island available to satisfy defense needs for both governments. In 1976, the Seychelles gained independence from England, and the BIOT became a self-administering territory under the East African desk of the British Foreign Office & Commonwealth.

Following the overthrow of the Shah of Iran in 1979, Diego Garcia saw the most dramatic build-up of any location since the Vietnam War era. And in 1986, Diego Garcia became fully operational with the completion of a $500 million construction program.

Its strategic location and full range of facilities make the island the last link in the long logistics chain that supports a strategic U.S. and British naval presence in the Indian Ocean and North Arabian Sea.

Diego Garcia is a full 3,000 miles away from the nearest hospital that can treat serious injuries or illnesses. The island served as a strategic staging point for Operation Enduring Freedom in Afghanistan and was only a six-hour flight to Operation Iraqi Freedom in Baghdad, two facts that were all too familiar to Commander Seabury Campbell, Jr.

Seated around the conference room table in the commanding officer's wing of the Tactical Operations Center, or TOC, was an assortment of Special Ops and INTEL players. Titles, ranks, home agencies and formal names were checked at the front door. No one was on the team or at the meeting by accident and that's all anyone really needed to know. Special Agent Daniels was clearly the team leader and the briefing was his.

"We have been watching this AQ training camp in Algiers for a few years now, but our HUMINT on the ground reported substantial activity about six weeks ago. Before we could even assess what was going on forty of the faithful were dead with not so much as a bullet or rubber-band being fired. HUMINT ascertained that chemical weapons were the cause and, frankly, we did, too. Fortunately our newest teammate, Camp, gave us an eyeball and told us that the chemical weapons dog didn't hunt. He postulated a more diabolical bioterror scenario, a biological disaster of medieval proportions in the form of Black Death. Forensics confirmed Camp's hunch."

"It wasn't a hunch." Raines shifted awkwardly as all eyes flashed on *her* since she was sitting next to *him*.

"Regardless, the jihadists were experimenting with Black Death. But since it killed just about all of them, we're not totally sure what their end game was."

The team seemed smaller than what Camp had remembered from his days in Afghanistan, but he knew that the technology would have evolved beyond his recognition, which reduces the need for extra footprints. Team members sitting around the XO's teak conference table seemed young, calm and confident. Seven members of the U.S. Navy's Naval Special Warfare Development Group, or DEVGRU, sat on one side of the table. Formerly recognized as SEAL Team Six, they had arrived on a transport only hours before Camp and Raines.

The XO's door opened and a stocky sailor with graying, short-cropped hair and a half-cocked, ear-to-ear grin walked in.

"Gentlemen. Ma'am."

Camp looked up when he heard the familiar voice.

"That's right, Camp, a voice you'll never forget," the man said before Camp could speak.

"Kentucky. How the hell are you?"

"I never thought I'd ever see your white ass on a Special Ops mission again. How've you been, Camp?"

"Keeping my head down."

"I lost track of you after Iraq. You must have set endurance records there."

"It was intense, but nothing like the caves of Tora Bora, Kentucky."

The grin left his face for a brief moment. "No, there was nothing like Tora Bora, to be sure."

Daniels took his meeting back. "Gentlemen, you can reminisce on the flight tonight. For those of you not in the fraternity of friends, Kent Jefferson here is the DEVGRU team leader.

"Call me Kentucky, please."

Jackson and Daniels were joined by two SAS officers from CIA. Special Activities Staff is one of the least known of the covert units working on behalf of the U.S. Government. SAS teams were seldom any larger than twelve and could be as few as one. They were particularly skilled in counterterrorist and hostage rescue situations.

"Okay, we're wheels up at 1750 today so don't get too comfortable. Our team is fourteen deep thanks to the addition of Camp and Raines. Kentucky and the rest of DEVGRU will get us on the ground and deliver us to haji and his buddies. Jackson, me and our SAS take care of the threat with backup from DEVGRU. Raines and Campbell are mission specialists for all things bio and infectious. Camp is a former Special Ops veteran and a medical doc with three years in the OIF theater and brings substantial trauma experience. So if you get a boo-boo, Camp gives you the Band–Aid."

"What if Camp is compromised?" asked one of the SEALs.

"Pack an extra Band–Aid," Camp responded without looking up.

"We're tracking for a wet drop at 0400 in the Mediterranean where the USS *Bataan* is waiting for us. The *Bataan* is an amphibious assault ship. She's fast, flexible and doesn't draw much attention beyond routine patrols in international waters. Kentucky will take it from here."

"As soon as we touch, the Bataan will send over our two LCACs. The Landing Craft Air Cushions are part plane, part boat. We literally fly—or hover—over the water. These ladies cost $22 million each so treat 'em well. Tracker and Ezra are craft masters. Shane and Worm are your engineers. Raines, Camp and Daniels fly with Tracker. Jackson and the SAS boys fly with Ezra. We already know our assignments."

"A wet landing anywhere in particular, Kentucky, or are we just bobbing up and down in the Mediterranean?" Raines asked.

"If all goes according to plan, it'll take us seventeen minutes by LCAC to the coastal caves in the islets around Algiers where friendlies will provide cover and ground transport. We'll be four-wheeling in soft-shell Citroens. Algiers is the capital and located in the north-central part of Algeria. We hope there'll be about 3 million folks sleeping during our forty-five minute visit."

Kentucky powered up his laptop and entered a password to log in to his secured account. Tracker got up, turned the projector on and pulled the screen down as Daniels hit the lights. An aerial shot of the crescent bay city filled the screen.

"Martyr's Memorial will dominate the landscape as we enter the city. It stands ninety-two meters high and you can see it from just about anywhere in the city. If we get lost or separated—and we won't—Martyr's Memorial will be your bearing."

"Can we hit some of the stalls on Rampe de la Pêcherie? Dar Lahlou has the best couscous anywhere in the Mediterranean."

"That's a negative, Worm."

A detailed street map of Algiers was the next slide.

"The city is divided into three parts. The lower section is the French area and is where they put up their administrative buildings back in the day. We're talking office buildings and government centers. We'll be driving through wide boulevards past theaters, cathedrals and museums. You'll be tempted to think Algiers is nice, until we move into the second district. The upper part, or the old section of Algiers, is where we're going. The area is called the 'kasbah' and over the last twenty years it has evolved into a slum and breeding ground for radicals and fundamentalists. These are some of the worst living conditions in North Africa. The kasbah was built in the 1500s as an Ottoman fort but looks more like Sadr City in Baghdad on steroids."

"Marvelous," grunted Camp with obvious disdain.

"Our target is a machine shop located behind the Ketcha-oua Mosque. We go in locked and loaded with small arms and a few other goodies. No sound. HUMINT says we may find a bio lab in the garage. We know they started playing with Black Death in Tizi Ouzou Province, but they accidentally killed forty of their playmates with it. We suspect that this may be part of Abdelmalek Droudkal's Al Qaeda in the Islamic Maghreb, or AQLIM. Nothing to suggest we'll be coming across our dear friend Abdel or any of his seventy-two virgin-makers. We're just looking for a simple bio lab."

"And when we find it?"

"When we get the green from Camp and Raines, we wrap up all their goodies and take 'em home."

"Resistance?"

"We're expecting low-level technicians and maybe some scientists. We would, however, like to bring some visitors back to the Bataan with us if possible."

"What about this Black Death shit?"

"Good question, Tracker. We're assuming it is everyday garden-variety plague. All of you will process through medical after this briefing to make sure your vaccinations are current and appropriate. Camp and Raines will be loaded with antibiotics if necessary. Anything else? Good. We stage at 1650. There won't be a meal service on this flight so stow your tray tables and load up with rats before we fly."

14

The two LCACs and all of the parachute gear were stowed in the caves by American Special Ops team members from the Bataan as the DEVGRU fourteen split up into four Citroëns. Each car's GPS had been pre-programmed for a different route to the machine shop behind Ketchaoua Mosque. The last thing the team needed was to have a convoy of four Citroëns stopped by the DRS. Raines and Camp rode with Special Agent Daniels and their driver, Samir, a long-trusted human intelligence officer.

Their Citroën climbed a small hill and then followed a wide boulevard past Martyr's Memorial. The street was nearly deserted as a subtle breeze moved through the date palms and other trees that lined the avenue.

"Actually a beautiful city," Raines said as she looked back over the Mediterranean Sea reflecting an early morning glow of twinkling stars. Camp put his head back and closed his eyes.

"You may be inclined to clarify your opinion in about four kilometers," Daniels added from the front seat. "The kasbah is a slum of staggering proportions. It's a perfect breeding and recruiting ground for Al-Qaeda in the Islamic Maghreb as DRS hardly ever goes in for any reason. They have some random checkpoints set up just to make sure kasbah dwellers don't go out unless they have good reason."

"Was this a French colony?"

"You could say that, I suppose. The French were sick and tired of the Algerians attacking and pirating their trade ships so in 1832 they attacked Algiers, and for the next 130 or so years, they controlled the place. In 1942, this was the headquarters of the Allied Forces in North Africa. Algiers became the center of the Algerian War of Independence and finally the capital of free Algeria in 1962 when the remaining French packed it up and went home to drown their sorrows in red wine."

The four-lane boulevard abruptly condensed into two lanes as their car passed beneath an arched iron gateway. The sides of the road were filled with cars, and old Datsun pickup trucks were parked in a myriad of random directions. Houses were more like shanties and perpetually interconnected. Where one house ended and another began was anyone's guess.

Trash and all forms of waste covered the ground, which featured patches of old concrete and centuries' old stones, rocks and dirt.

Homemade electrical lines patched homes into power lines wherever someone could get high enough to splice in. The locals tried to tap into the power grid during outages. But every week or two, somebody's grid timing was off by just a few seconds, and they'd be electrocuted, to the horror of their families and the delight of neighbors looking for some good public square entertainment.

The GPS indicated the Ketchaoua Mosque was less than a kilometer away.

"Camp?"

"I'm awake."

"Just to review, anything goes wrong and we're separated, use your tourist papers and get to the port at Crescent Bay. The ferry connection will have you in Marseille and sipping a fine French bordeaux by dinner time."

"Why don't we just do that instead?" Camp asked.

Raines smiled at his sarcasm.

"After what Kentucky told me, I guess that doesn't surprise me," said Agent Daniels.

"Excuse me?"

An awkward second or two passed.

"Nothing. Just a bit unusual that a SEAL would be combat-averse."

"I'm a medical doctor, Daniels, a researcher. I don't fight anymore."

"Did you ever?"

"What exactly *did* Kentucky say?"

Raines was silent.

"I thought he got over all that," Camp said under his breath.

The car lights were turned off as it pulled up to its assigned coordinates. The satellite-regulated countdown watch Daniels was wearing indicated they had fewer than three minutes before all four teams would converge on simultaneous green.

The plan was simple enough. The DEVGRU Special Ops guys would enter and secure. Daniels, Jackson and their two

SAS officers from Langley would handle interrogation and investigation. Raines and Camp would assess the bio threat, if any, and Camp had medical responsibilities if anyone went down.

Worm was the first at the door as Tracker and two more SEALs took to the roof and closed off all other points of ingress, or in this case, potentially hot and rapid egress.

Worm pointed to Kentucky and gave him a hand signal that the door was unlocked, open and slightly ajar. Worm and his teammate Ajax entered the room. Their night vision goggles made the room light as day, albeit in varying shades of green. The room was empty with no traces of a heat source other than smoldering embers in the center of the shop from a recent fire.

The machine shop appeared to be legitimate. There were several parts from cars, appliances, scooters and bicycles strewn all around. A rudimentary set of tools was visible, as well as a small blowtorch and welding supplies.

Jackson and Daniels started to explore the back room, which was filled mostly with trash and a few opened boxes.

"Check this out."

Jackson was holding a handful of electric garage door openers.

"Anybody see a garage door on the way in?"

The guys, including Kentucky, had a quick laugh.

"Care to enlighten the rest of us?" said Raines, showing her displeasure of not being in the inner circle of the boys' club.

"They use these for remote detonation of IEDs. Cell phones are easier to use but easier for us to jam. Choose the vehicle you want to attack and—presto—open the garage door from hell." Kentucky had seen far too many of these things.

Camp was away from everyone else looking at a car on jacks in the back of the main shop. Other than a missing front right wheel, the old, red Datsun seemed to be in good shape. Pointing his flashlight into the cab of the truck, he saw a half-full pack of Marlboro's and a box of purple latex gloves.

"Raines."

Raines walked over to Camp and followed his flashlight beam into the truck.

"Looks like we might be in the right place," she said.

Camp walked around to the back of the truck. A canvas tarp was heaped up over the bed. He handed the flashlight to Raines. Camp pulled out a pair of sterile latex gloves, then pulled the canvas back.

"Holy shit."

There were more than two dozen Tecniplast rodent cages piled under the tarp. None of the cages had any bedding or water. They were all empty but clearly had been recently used.

"Maybe they were planning to open a Pet Smart out here," Raines joked, as Camp started pulling the cages out one by one. "Think we can get any swabs for analysis?"

"Better than that."

Camp reached and pulled out the very last cage. An oversized rat, quite dead at this point, was on his back. The cage was stuffed with newspaper.

"We've got something," Raines said in a low voice as Jackson and the two SAS officers came over.

Jackson saw the rat and quickly covered his face. "Get it bagged and sealed. We're out in two minutes."

Daniels and Kentucky were squatting in the center of the room around the embers that were still warm to the touch.

Most shops and houses used fires in the center of the room for cooking. But, based on the ember debris, this was not a cooking fire.

Daniels carefully sorted through the ashes. The edge of an ivory piece of paper caught his eye. It was a business card. Half of the card was burned beyond use, but the first half was readable. The top line read "Hassina," then "Economic," and finally, "U.S. Embassy Ra—"

Each tactical watch began to vibrate at the same precise moment. Camp and Raines took their bagged and sealed rat out of the building, followed by the SAS team and Kentucky. Worm and Ajax backed out of the machine shop as Tracker and his unit followed behind. The entire DEVGRU team was back at the islet cave in less than fourteen minutes and on the LCACs and out to sea. The entire mission lasted forty-five minutes, just like it was planned.

The team convened in a meeting room adjacent to the Bataan XO's wardroom. Daniels sent an image of the card back to Langley for analysis. Camp and Raines had the rat down in the medical lab where it was going through toxicology and microbiology studies.

The flat-screen panels in the meeting room were instantly connected back to Langley. The business card mystery took the CIA less than three minutes to solve. Hassina al Batir was a Moroccan national who worked for the State Department at Embassy Rabat. She worked in the ECON section tasked with helping Moroccan's start and launch new businesses. She had no clearances and no prior personnel issues. Basically, she had had a clean folio for almost seven years.

"Camp, what do we know about the rat?" asked Daniels.

"Black plague, Black Death, bubonic plague—call it what you want but it's all basically the same thing. This little guy is loaded with the plague but he died from a lack of food and water. This is a bacterial disease. It enters through the skin and travels through the lymphatic system. Left untreated, you'll die a horribly painful death in two to six days."

"So you shouldn't be in the same room with these things, breathing the same air?"

"Not quite, Kentucky. That would be a viral disease, a virus that could infect you through inhalation. Plague is usually transmitted by flea bites. So, while Agent Jackson was quick to cover his face when we found this guy, he should have been more worried about the fleas that were landing on his shoes and crawling up his pant legs."

The DEVGRU team had a great laugh as they started to shift in their chairs. As though on command, everyone started to move and scratch areas of their bodies that seemingly had no itch triggers. Camp couldn't resist.

"Looks like you have a flea in your hair, Jackson."

Jackson jumped out of his chair and brushed his hair frantically over the table. The SEAL team went hysterical as Jackson stormed out of the room saying something about a shower.

"The bacterium is called *Yersinia pestis* and it can be grown and cultivated in a petri dish just like any other bacteria. Bubonic plague is not usually spread directly from person to person. Small rodents, such as rats, mice and squirrels, carry the infection. Fleas that live on these animals act as the vectors that carry the infection from rats to humans. People may get exposed to the bacteria from flea bites or from direct contact with an infected animal. But during the Black Death outbreak hundreds of years ago, many people became sick with pneumonia from *Yersinia pestis,* which morphed the disease into pneumonic plague thereby allowing sick people to spread the disease to each other through coughing and sneezing. It killed 75 million folks back in the day."

"What about today?"

"Antibiotics and vaccines do the trick. If you're traveling to areas in the Middle East or Africa where Black Death is typically found, then get a vaccine. If you contract the disease, then we give you antibiotics like streptomycin or tetracycline and that usually does the trick."

"Usually?"

The meeting room door opened, and a lab technician walked over and handed Camp the initial lab report.

Daniels rubbed his hands through his thinning hair again. "So I don't get it. Al Qaeda wants to unleash Black Death on the population using a bioweapon that we can easily cure?"

"It's all about the fear and terror," Kentucky said. "Look how this room full of adults has been shifting and scratching just thinking that this shit could get in us."

The room grew silent as Camp put the lab report down.

"What's up?" Raines finally asked. Camp handed her the report since she was the infectious disease expert.

"Okay. This is not good."

Camp stood up and left the room quickly as all eyes followed him, then snapped back to Raines.

"This rat is a hybrid. Not the rat itself, but rather the infection is mixed."

"What do you mean?"

"The *Yersinia pestis* bacteria have been modified, altered. Actually, enhanced is a better word. The animal has incredibly high traces of what we call viral hemorrhagic fever. The hemorrhagic fever viruses, or HFVs, are a diverse group of organisms that are all capable of causing clinical disease associated with fever and bleeding disorders. These organisms can be divided into four distinct families of viruses."

Kentucky couldn't handle anymore.

"Okay lady, enough of this scientific mumbo-jumbo crap. What's in the damn rat?"

"It's a Category A bioweapon disease. We'll need further testing, but it looks like Ebola, maybe even Rift Valley fever."

"No big deal right? Antibiotics and vaccines?" asked Worm optimistically.

"Unfortunately, there are no antiviral medications that are effective on HFVs. The only vaccine we've ever developed has limited impact on yellow fever."

"So how do you treat people who get it?"

"The approved method, Agent Daniels, is called supportive. Simply provide care and comfort. Unfortunately, 90 percent of people infected with Ebola die. The only effective treatment is to quarantine the area and prevent the further spread of the disease."

Tracker was pulling up information on Ebola off the CDC web site as Raines spoke.

"It says here that Ebola is transmitted to humans from primates. Now, I ain't no zoologist or anything, but that four-legged rat did not look like a monkey with a spindly little tail to me."

"You're sort of right. The initial transmission of Ebola is usually caused by a human coming into direct contact with an infected primate. But humans can spread it to each other through direct contact, too. Clothing, bed sheets, and touching are common transmission methods."

"So how did Ebola get into this rat?"

"That's the hybrid part. I'm not sure how, but I'm fairly certain it wasn't by accident."

The door flew open and an agitated Captain John Swelling entered the room. The DEVGRU team immediately stood, though Daniels and his two SAS officers remained seated.

"Just great. You cowboys bring Ebola on my ship in the middle of the damn sea? Medical is now quarantined to prevent infection and acceleration. Just what in the hell am I supposed to do for my crew now?"

"Sir, we'd request that your LCACs take us over to Marseille and drop us off so we can continue the mission."

"The hell you will. You can stay confined to this ship just like the rest of us."

"Sir, with all due respect, we can play this through the director's office and the White House if you prefer."

"Fine. Have the White House call me because you're not going anywhere."

Camp was already on a secure line to Washington in his personal quarters when he finally got through to General Ferguson, who was sound asleep in his Virginia home.

"This better be good, Commander."

"Sir, we've isolated what we think is the bioterror threat. Al Qaeda in the Islamic Maghreb was playing with the Black Death plague up in the hills of Tizi Ouzou Province. It looks like they may have gotten some help as they appear to have been able to weaponize the plague by introducing an HFV into their rats."

"Are you suggesting Ebola? In rats?"

"Affirmative, that's what it's looking like, sir."

"How the hell could they do that in some cave?"

"I'm guessing they've had some assistance."

"Any idea what they're up to, how far along they are?"

"Not yet, sir, but we've got some leads."

Captain Swelling left the meeting room as fast as he had entered. Daniels went to his quarters to make his call to Langley as Camp came back in and took a seat next to Raines.

The silence in the room was deafening.

"Ma'am, how bad is Ebola?" asked Ajax.

Raines paused for what seemed like an eternity.

"The incubation period for Ebola ranges from two to twenty-one days. The illness is abrupt, comes quickly and without warning. It starts with a fever and headache, then joint and muscle aches, sore throat, and weakness, followed by diarrhea, vomiting, and stomach pain. A rash, red eyes, hiccups, internal and then external bleeding rages before you die. Some live, but most die."

Daniels came back into the room and whispered something into Kentucky's ear.

"Okay, folks, grab your gear and head to the LCACs. We're going to France."

MARSEILLE, FRANCE

The team checked into the Sofitel Marseille Vieux Port, a five-star luxury hotel overlooking the water.

"Damn, I love traveling with spooks. You guys always get the finest establishments," said Kentucky, as they walked into the expansive hotel lobby dressed in civilian clothes. "One hundred and eighty Euros per night? That's we get paid in a week."

"Les Trois Forts restaurant is on the top floor," explained Special Agent Daniels. "Chef Dominique Frerard will take care of us in a private room overlooking the harbor tonight.

Wine at seven followed by dinner. And please, dress it up a few notches. This is haute-couture Mediterranean gastronomy at its finest."

"What the hell did he say?" asked Worm.

"The food is good," Tracker translated.

LES TROIS FORTS RESTAURANT

Four bottles of Chateau Guiraud Sauternes were spread among the DEVGRU fourteen with a bottle of an Italian pinot gris thrown in for good measure next to Raines.

"Not in the mood for a manly red?" chided Camp.

"It's a waste of money. You dirtbags wouldn't know the difference between Boone's Farm or bordeaux. As for me, I prefer a reasonably priced Turonia Rias Baixas Albarino."

"Sounds more like a bacterial strain."

"Before our meals arrive, let's get through the briefing. Each one of you has a packet with your specific roles and responsibilities. We'll have weapons and we'll be covert but this is not a hot mission. Everybody tracking?"

Daniels continued.

"Kentucky's group will provide tactical support and eyes on the ground. Jackson and my group will work the INTEL angle through Embassy Rabat and try to determine why Ms. Al Batir's business card was smoldering in an Algerian fire pit some 600 miles away. Any questions?"

"Camp and myself are doing what exactly?"

"Raines, you and your *husband* will be checking into the Royal Hotel Rabat on Allal Ben Abdellah Avenue as Mr. and Mrs. Roger Whitcomb of Toronto, Canada. You have Canadian passports and the obligatory wedding rings in your packets."

"Sounds enchanting," Raines muttered sarcastically.

"Which part? The hotel or being married to him?" said Kentucky.

Raines shot him a glance.

"Pick your poison."

"The Royal Hotel Rabat has sixty-seven rooms of ample luxury. You have requested twin beds since Mr. Whitcomb is a notorious snorer. The hotel does not have Internet, but Kentucky and his team will set up robust Wi-Fi with secure channels for you before you check in. You are small animal veterinarians on a sightseeing holiday and you'll make sure that everyone you come in contact with knows that you are vets. The agency suggests that the Rabat Zoo be your first stop. The zoo is large and expansive, but a lack of funding has left the exhibits a bit sparse. Make sure the zoo authorities know your background and ask for special views. Our INTEL suggests that zoo ownership is a bit tawdry and perhaps nefarious."

The door to the private dining room opened, and fourteen waiters entered simultaneously and placed each bowl of soup with the precision of a synchronized swim team.

"Morocco is no piece of cake, folks. Even though Morocco has a relatively liberal brand of Islam, state law is still influenced by, though not rooted in, Sharia Law. So no public displays of affection from the Whitcomb family please."

"That goes for you too, Worm," Kentucky added with a huge laugh.

"Don't ask, don't tell, sir."

"Not anymore."

"Since the 2004 terror bombings in Casablanca, there has been a definite spike in Islamic extremism and recruiting. The Moroccan Islamic Combat Group is closely tied to our boys from Al-Qaeda in the Islamic Maghreb, as well as the Tunisia-Islamic Fighting Group. So, we'll be on the ground in Rabat until we know more. That's all for now. Let's enjoy a marvelous evening. Doctors Whitcomb and my team will be on a Ryan Air flight tomorrow afternoon at 1300 hours. Kentucky's team will be on Royal Air Morocco into Marrakech Menara and then a convoy to Rabat at 0800."

"Great. That's code for we get an overcrowded bus and a Motel 6," said Tracker as he lifted his wine glass. "Here's a toast to our last supper."

The view out Camp's hotel window was nothing short of spectacular. The harbor was filled with tall mast sailboats and power yachts so expensive that he could never pay for one even with a lifetime's worth of Navy O-5 paychecks.

He figured it might be his last chance to make a few phone calls back to the States so he took advantage of the opportunity. He dialed the number that had never changed since he was born.

"Hey, mom."

"Seabury, is that you? Sea Bee, get on the other extension. It's Seabury calling."

Camp could hear the click on the phone.

"Where are you, son?"

"I'm overseas. Just had a minute or two and thought I'd check in. How are the girls?"

"Your sisters are doing just fine," his mother said. "We have the grandchildren over all this week, at least each afternoon when they get out of school. They like to help with evening milking. They're pretty excited about Christmas break coming soon."

"Seabury, you remember Chip Smith from your high school football team?"

"I think so, dad. Harvey's kid?"

"Yep, that's the one. Well, old Chip is a multimillionaire these days."

"Say what?"

"Harvey converted his chicken business into a poultry farm for vaccine research. Then he sold it to some New York company for $12 million. He gave Chip and his older brother $3 million each, and old Harvey and Mildred Smith cashed in and moved to South America, or some darn place."

"Isn't that just the darndest, Seabury?"

"Sure is, mom."

"Your father wants to sell the dairy farm now. Says he'll take only half that much."

"I bet you would, dad."

"You gonna be home in time for spring planting, Seabury?"

"I hope so. We'll see what Uncle Sam wants. Well, I better get going. I love you."

"We love you too, son."

Camp closed up his phone and looked out over the harbor. He wondered if he could be looking at Harvey Smith's new yacht out there.

Opening his phone again, he pressed the speed dial on key #2.

"Lightner Farms."

"Hello, Eileen."

15

Dr. Whitcomb put the metal key into the lock and opened the door to their second floor room as Mrs. Dr. Whitcomb watched.

"I thought he said we had twin beds."

Camp put his luggage against the wall and walked around the sparsely decorated, little room that measured twelve feet by fifteen feet. The white tiled floor was clean but stark. A checkered bedspread covered the double cherrywood bed and two very old and very flat pillows adorned the top of the bedspread. A radiator was on one wall and a petite make-up table with mirror and chair were against the other. A small, round bistro table sat in the center of the room beneath a red tablecloth. Two chairs faced the table, which had a small vase and some artificial flowers in it. The tiny bathroom was just large enough for a toilet, bathtub, and a sink but no counter space. The only window in the room faced out over

Allal Ben Abdellah Avenue but the view was mostly blocked by the crackling neon sign that flashed "Hotel."

"I'm not anymore thrilled than you are. You can have the dresser."

They unpacked for a few minutes in awkward silence.

"You hungry?" Raines asked.

"I could eat."

They walked for several blocks along the Rue des Consuls. Embassies from various countries filled the streets on both sides, interspersed by an assortment of restaurants and office buildings. The air was warm, and the sunshine was penetrating. People of all nationalities filled up the sidewalks along with them. Rabat was certainly an international town.

The enticing music coming out of the Le Ziryab restaurant was more than they could ignore.

The Ziryab was in the heart of the medina dining district. The sitar music sounded like a beautiful blend of both Persian and Moroccan influence. It was as romantic as it was mysterious.

A turban-clad host wearing the traditional Islamic robe led them down a marble-tiled walkway with high arched ceilings. He carried a burning oil lamp to light the way as fire torch sconces lit the arches. Disappearing around a corner, he took them to an eating area that was set off with an archway and drapes on each side of the table. Red upholstered chairs surrounded an elegant table with embroidered fringe.

"Mr. Whitcomb, you devil, you. Taking your bride to the fanciest joint in town on our first date?" said Raines.

The waiter spoke broken English but well enough for a couple of Canadians to understand him.

"Chicken is our specialty. It is served with beldi and

bread. The bread is made with anise, olives, whole wheat flour and other bread festivals. It is homemade and cooked in our oven the traditional way. Couscous is traditional as well. It's white, complete, bendeq, barley and is rolled by women. The lemon confit, olives and many other preparations are also made in the ancient cuisine tradition of Ziryab."

Camp gave Raines an amused look. "Perfect. We'll take two."

"I can't wait to taste the barley that is actually rolled by real women," Raines said as the waiter walked away.

Another server brought a kettle of hot tea and poured it for them.

"Listen, I want to apologize. I was kind of an ass to you on the flight into Diego Garcia, and I'm sorry," said Raines.

Camp looked into her eyes. She was sincere and gentle which forced him to look away.

"Well? Apology accepted?"

"Actually, I guess it was my stupidity that got us both sent to Diego Garcia in the first place," Camp said.

"Is that an apology, too?"

Camp looked back at her, and they both smiled.

"Yes, Les, that's an apology, too."

"You called me, Les. This must be love…Seabury."

"It's Roger. Roger Whitcomb."

"Right. Sorry, again. Can I ask you something?"

"I don't think my saying no is going to have any impact so go for it."

"Kentucky has issues with you, doesn't he? But I know you guys were teammates, fought in Tora Bora together. Hell, you even earned the Navy Cross for heroism in that fight. What does he mean by you being combat-averse?"

"It's a long story, Raines."

"We're married, Dr. Whitcomb. We've got a long time ahead of us so try me."

"It was December 12, 2001, just seventy-two days after 9/11. The invasion of Afghanistan was approaching the end of the first phase. Al-Qaeda fighters had taken refuge in the Tora Bora region. We were working with anti-Taliban tribal militia as we continued a tough advance through rugged terrain. Air strikes by the U.S. and British cleared our path. Besides the militia, there were maybe a dozen British SBS commandos, a signal specialist, a couple of dozen SAS, and our SEAL team with yours truly and Kentucky. We got into a major fire fight. The AQ boys had the higher terrain position advantage on us as we went through a deep crevasse. Northern Alliance fighters were getting mowed down like carnival fodder. All of us were taking casualties. Our medic was one of the first killed. The fight seemed out of control. The wounded were piling up. I thought if we could get enough suppression fire up on the cliffs, then maybe I could get some people to cover."

"So what happened?"

"I put my weapon down and started dragging people to cover, one after another, after another. There was no way I could get to everyone, but I tried. Once we got them to cover there wasn't much we could do for them. It wasn't like we were equipped with triage or anything."

"How many did you pull out?"

"The citation says forty-seven men. Most of them were Northern Alliance militia."

"And for that Kentucky holds a grudge?"

"Kentucky is a warrior's warrior. He defines what a Special Ops warrior is. He was pissed that I put my weapon down. SEALs fight first and then rescue their own."

"Is that why you left the SEALs?"

"I was in the first major battle after 9/11, and I never even fired my weapon. And who gets the Navy Cross for heroism? Me. Right, that went down well with the rest of the team. So I applied and the Navy sent me to med school. I fast-tracked and basically did my residency in Balad for three years. I learned how to be a surgeon on the job, eighteen hours a day. Some days were even longer than that. I just couldn't leave. I guess it was as much Tora Bora guilt as it was that I found my calling."

"What happened to Osama bin Laden?"

"We think he was there. Hell, we know he was there, or they wouldn't have ambushed us. We thought Pakistan was shutting down the border and we also thought our boys in the sky would be dropping Gator mines to block his egress. NATO nixed the Gators. The Pakis were nowhere to be found, and the Afghan fighters quit the battlefield at night for prayers, which AQ took full advantage of. Nothing like checking your watches and calling off combat because you gotta pray."

"You were wounded."

"No biggie. The first was just a little bullet to the thigh, clean through and through, no bone."

"I read the citation as well. Says you were wounded early but kept rescuing others."

"Whatever. I have no idea how many survived or even *if* they survived."

"Because of the grenade, right?"

"Yeah, that one sort of ate my lunch. I never felt a thing, but shrapnel went right through my neck, as well as an assortment of other places. Lost a lot of blood and—as you so eloquently pointed out—spent ten days in a coma and woke up in Diego Garcia. Not real pleasant."

The chicken, bread and couscous were served. The aroma was beyond comprehension and the flavor was to die for.

"Bon appetit, Dr. Whitcomb."

"And to you as well, Mrs. Dr. Whitcomb. Now, may I ask you a question since we're doing all of this bloodletting bonding and introspection?"

"Fire away."

"Why did you trail me all the way to Gettysburg?"

"Easy. I wanted to see if your ass was worth saving and then to save your ass."

Camp smiled and took a huge bite of the bread.

"Oh my God, this *is* delicious," he said.

"So who is this mystery woman you were with at Lightner Farms? I want to know who my competition is."

16

NEW YORK

The central newsroom at the national headquarters of CBS News was in chaos as breaking reports came in from all over the country. The cable news channels had broken to live coverage but the executive producers at CBS wanted to gather as much information as possible in order to reduce wild speculation that might incite widespread fear and panic.

Local affiliates were reporting tainted beef supplies from supermarkets in Florida, Minnesota, Iowa, Washington, Oregon and Kansas. Local hospitals had already confirmed seven fatalities, and more than 200 were sickened, some in critical condition.

What wasn't clear was if the beef was contaminated accidentally or poisoned intentionally.

A seasoned producer in her fifties ran through the newsroom yelling and holding up a piece of paper.

"We just received this communiqué from the Animal Liberation Front. It reads:

Negotiation is now over. Animals will be treated with dignity and respect from this point forward. We have poisoned the entire beef supply from Seattle to Miami, from Boston to San Diego and all points in between. A legion of liberators has each pierced the cellophane packaging of at least one package of beef in every city with needles of ricin. We are animal rights activists calling on America to adopt a strict vegan lifestyle. We are your grocery store checkers, supermarket managers, stockers, waiters and busboys. We will not rest until animal agriculture ceases, biomedical research facilities are closed, and pet stores are put out of business. Non-human animals are morally equal to human animals.

Another producer hung up the phone after an urgent call. "My guy at the FBI says we've also got an *e. coli* confirmation from some beef that traces back to a processing plant in Warrenton, Minnesota."

Images on the screens from the various affiliate stations showed widespread panic as people emptied out their refrigerators and freezers and started throwing out all beef and meat products.

The anchor got behind the news desk and took a final powder as the set manager did the ten second countdown.

"Stand by. We're breaking live in ten, nine, eight—"

"This is like the Tylenol scare on steroids," he said.

"Three, two and…"

"Good evening. We're breaking in live with devastating news. An animal rights extremist group is claiming responsibility for poisoning America's beef supply with ricin. We have also confirmed an *e. coli* contamination in meat products across various parts of America."

General Ferguson turned the TV off with disgust and rubbed his balding head. The telephone started ringing immediately.

"Yes, sir…I just saw it…right now it appears to be a criminal issue. The FBI seems to have a handle on it…yes, sir… I'll keep you informed…Sir? Gulf Shores Research Center? Monkeys?...Yes, sir…I'll run that by our field agents."

17

Hassina al Batir sat nervously in a small office. She had no idea who the men were who were meeting with her supervisor, but she knew she'd find out soon enough.

Her boss came in followed by Daniels and Jackson.

"Hassina, these gentlemen are U.S. government employees and they'd like to ask you some questions. Don't worry, you're not in trouble. They just have a few questions for you."

"Hassina, describe for us what you do here at the Embassy."

"Well, I work in the ECON section. I work with the local Moroccan population and help them with micro-finance loans to start businesses and then learn the basics about marketing."

"How do you identify potential businesses or people that you might work with?"

"Typically, we work with the GOM, or government of

Morocco, to identify those that we might be able to support."

"Do you give them money?"

"Not usually, but sometimes we'll make small grants. Maybe $500 or even $1,000 on occasion."

"That's not a lot of money."

"It is if you're Moroccan. One thousand U.S. dollars is almost 8,500 MAD or Morocco dirham."

"Do your clients ever want anything besides money?"

"Distribution. If they make blankets, or hats, or pottery, they often want to know how they can sell it to the West. But that's usually about it."

"What about networking? Do they ever want help finding strategic partners, tapping into trade groups, that sort of thing?"

"No, not that I can think of. Oh, wait. There were a couple of brothers I met several weeks ago at a trade fair. It was held in Tangier. King Mohammed the Sixth sponsored an international 'Invest in Morocco' conference in the Tangier City Center. It's a very modern city and the conference was held at the Mazagan Beach Resort. It's a luxurious five-star hotel and resort."

"That's where you met these brothers?"

"Yes, they came up to my table. They appeared to be very wealthy, well-dressed, and very polite."

"What did they want?"

"They were starting a pharmaceutical company. They said it would be the largest in North Africa. They were looking for trading partners into Russia and China."

"So why were they talking to the American embassy?"

"I guess because I am Moroccan. They thought I could help them find the right people."

"And did you?"

"Our counterparts at the Russian embassy are hardly helpful. But I knew there was a small company, a Russian company, in Rabat that was financing oil deals. I told them to start there."

"Did you give them a business card?"

"I don't know. But I had my cards there on the table along with hundreds of brochures."

Jackson and Daniels looked at each other briefly.

"Is there anything else?"

"Yes, one more question, Hassina. What kind of pharmaceuticals did the brothers say they manufacture?"

"I don't know. I didn't even think to ask."

"What is the name of the Russian company you sent them to in Rabat?"

"They are called Gospodstvo Ventures. They have an office in Moscow, too."

RABAT ZOO

The veterinarians on holiday from Canada paid their admission tickets and entered the Rabat Zoo. The exhibits were stark, unkempt and seemed almost cruel for the animals inside. The Whitcombs asked the information desk if they could meet the head zookeeper or any of the veterinarians on staff. They were told that there were no veterinarians, but the zookeeper would be delighted to meet them.

Abdul Hakim was in his mid-thirties and as a child was raised as a goat tender. He had no formal training with animals which was quite apparent from the condition of both the exhibits as well as the animals. He spoke only a few words of English but his assistant, A'zam, was educated in

London and had traveled extensively throughout Europe, the Middle East and even Southeast Asia.

"Welcome to our facility. Mr. Hakim seldom meets professional veterinarians."

"The pleasure is all ours. We're looking forward to seeing your exhibits. As you might imagine, we don't often get to see African mammals up close in our practice in Canada," replied Camp.

Mr. Hakim laughed after hearing the interpretation from A'zam.

"May we offer you a personal tour of the exhibits?"

"That would be wonderful," Raines said.

The four of them began the tour at the large animal exhibit. There were three elephants and a rhinoceros in the exhibit.

"What age do you expect the rhino and the elephants to live to here in captivity?" asked Raines.

"The elephants can live up to seventy years but that's not common in a zoo. Some rhinos can live fifty years, but again that's uncommon," said Mr. Hakim through A'zam's translation.

"They are beautiful African bush elephants."

Mr. Hakim leaned over and asked A'zam a question.

"Yes, Mr. Hakim would like you to examine one of the elephants and see if you know what could be wrong with his health."

"Well, we certainly don't mind, but I must tell you that we typically work with small animals, such as canines, felines, rats, mice and rodents," said Raines.

"We understand. Please follow."

Mr. Hakim led them through the back door of the enclosure and grabbed some treats for the elephant. While the mammal nibbled on the treats, Camp and Raines walked around the pachyderm and gave it a quick examination.

"Well, it's a male in fairly good health. His feet look fine, but he has some skin issues. Do you have a consistent mud hole wet enough for him to wallow around in?" asked Raines.

"He has plenty of drinking water, but unless we get rain he doesn't have much mud to play in."

"Mud on his skin protects him from the sun so you might want to dig out a mud hole for him and let him stay covered. He may not look as nice for your visitors, but his skin will get browner and he'll be healthier."

"How long have you had this elephant?" asked Camp.

"Mr. Hakim received him less than one year ago. Why?"

"Well, judging by his teeth, I'd say the real problem is that he's rather old. Elephants cycle through several sets of teeth in their lives. Once they are ground down into stubs like these, it usually means they are very old and there's not much time left," said Camp.

Mr. Hakim grew visibly irritated when he received the translation from A'zam.

"Mr. Hakim says that he was told the elephant was only eighteen years old when he bought him."

"Well, I'm sorry about that, but this fella has been around a long time. He's healthy enough but just old."

The tour lasted for another hour until A'zam finally walked the Whitcombs back to the entrance.

"Dr. Whitcomb, you mentioned that you have expertise with small animals, even rats, mice and rodents. Do you only focus on domestic animals?"

"Actually, we are hired quite often by research universities. For example, researchers are always looking for better ways to study human cancer and other diseases inside rodents. It's a great way to test the power of new drugs and therapies. If you can treat and cure a disease in a mouse, then you have a fighting chance of treating a human with that same disease, too."

"Fascinating. How long will you both be on holiday here in Morocco?"

"We plan to stay in Rabat for another three days then we want to see Casablanca and Tangier. Our hotel is in a perfect location to see the area," said Raines.

"Oh, you must be staying at the Golden Tulip Farah near Hassan Tower?"

"No, we are just poor veterinarians so we're staying at the Royal Hotel Rabat."

A'zam laughed at the suggestion they were poor.

"I see, well the Royal Hotel is a very fine place as well. Well, enjoy your holiday. Perhaps you will meet other opportunities in Morocco that will make you wealthy."

"We can only hope," Raines said. Camp shook hands with A'zam as Raines lowered her eyes and smiled politely.

Camp and Raines walked out of the zoo and towards the street to flag down a taxi.

"So where'd you come up with the whole dry skin thing and mud holes?" Camp asked under his breath.

"Me? Talk to me about nubby teeth."

"Late night television on *Animal Planet*," quipped Camp.

"Me, too."

GOSPODSTVO VENTURES, RABAT

Special Agent Daniels sent his two SAS officers over to Gospodstvo Ventures. Borysko and Fedir were Ukrainians who had worked for the agency for seventeen years and were some of the first Langley recruits after the fall of the Soviet empire.

Following the collapse, the former republics were left on their own to develop counterterrorist capabilities. Counterterrorism needs became more urgent in recent years as the rising problem of organized crime taxed internal security resources that would normally be sufficient to deal with domestic terrorism. Ukraine responded by creating the Berkut detachments, or Golden Eagles, that were under the authority of the Ministry of Internal Affairs. These units originally formed in 1992 and were based heavily on Special Purpose Militsiia Detachments, known as OMON, that dealt successfully with many of the same problems still facing Ukraine. The headquarters of the 5,000-man Berkut regiment was located in Kiev, with battalion- and company-sized detachments based in larger Ukrainian cities.

Borysko and Fedir were highly trained Golden Eagles, and they had used their skills to monitor Algerian warlord Abdelmalek Droudkal at the Al-Qaeda training camp in the cave hideouts of Tizi Ouzou Province in Algeria for more than three years.

"Доброе утро. У нас нет назначения, но мы хотели бы говорить со старшим менеджером сделки," said Borysko as they entered the front lobby.

"You speak Russian. Is that a Ukrainian accent?" asked the middle aged woman at the reception desk.

"Yes, we are from Kiev," said Fedir.

"I'm not sure who could see you today. As you said, you don't have an appointment. Are you looking for funding for a business?"

"Actually, we wish to explore a joint venture. We have

290 million rubles to invest and we need a partner for the remaining shares."

"I see. Perhaps Arkady Iksanov could meet with you briefly. He is our general manager."

The two SAS agents were led into Iksanov's office, where the room was filled with smoke from a recent chain of unfiltered cigarettes.

"Miss Shvydkoy informs me that you're looking for a strategic partner and that you have $10 million to work with. What sort of venture are you exploring?"

"We have purchased drilling rights to an oil field in Tindouf and we need a partner, preferably Russian, to help us explore."

"Tindouf, not far from here, but why don't you speak to someone in Algiers?"

"There are no Russian venture capitalists in Algeria. You were the closest and the largest one we could find," said Fedir.

"Well, I'm not sure we're entertaining any more energy projects. As you know, Russia has much oil and natural gas production. Are you experts in petroleum?"

Borysko and Fedir exchanged glances and started to laugh. "No, actually we are scientists with medical backgrounds. We did research on drugs for medicines," said Borysko.

"I see. So how did you arrange to have so much money to invest?"

"We were very successful at what we did. Now it is time to do something else," said Fedir.

"You might even say we were a bit bored. It is time to make lots of money," added Borysko. "Sick people may feel better, but we can't make lots of money just by discovering new drugs."

They all shared a good laugh.

"Well, I don't know if our central office in Moscow would be interested or not. But if you like, you can make a good faith deposit and I will ask our president's council to review your business plan. If he likes the plan, he would invest, and you would receive credit for your deposit. If not, then your deposit is the fee he charges to review your plan."

"How much is the deposit?"

"Fifteen million rubles, $500,000 in cash."

Borysko and Fedir looked at each other, and the two thought through the offer. Iskanov scribbled some numbers on a piece a paper and handed it to Fedir.

"Well, think it over. If you decide to proceed, then here are wiring instructions for our account at the Bank of Moscow."

The two agents stood up and shook hands and gave Iskanov their business cards.

"You can reach us on either cell number."

ROYAL HOTEL RABAT

Camp's secure cell phone lit up as Raines sat on the bed reading a magazine while he was peering out the window past the buzzing neon sign.

"Yes."

"Please stand by for General Ferguson."

"Camp? We've got a huge problem back here."

"Sir?"

"An unexpected shipment of monkeys arrived at the Gulf Shores Research facility in Louisiana a few days ago."

"Sir, I swear I didn't steal them."

"Cute."

"I thought the president's Executive Order put an end

to the use of non-human primates, at least for the one-year moratorium?"

"It did. The university cancelled the order from the breeder in the Philippines, but the shipment came regardless."

"So send them back."

"That's not the problem. They're all dead."

"Dead? How?"

"Every one of them infected with Ebola."

"What about the staff and the researchers?"

"Well, they were exposed. Some of them are sick, but we've not seen any fatalities. The problem is the press. It was leaked to the press immediately, and the whole damn country is going ape shit now."

"How can I help, sir?"

"This Ebola…are we at risk of an outbreak here? What do we tell the people? I can't get a damn straight answer from the CDC."

"Sir, let me put Colonel Raines on the line. She can probably give you a better answer than I can."

"Raines is with you?"

"Yes, sir. In fact we're sharing a hotel room together, but that's a long story."

"I bet it is."

"General Ferguson, this is Colonel Raines. I understand you have an Ebola situation."

"Is this going to be an outbreak, Colonel? Should the public be concerned?"

"Well sir, it is unusual—but not unheard of—to have Ebola infected primates sent to a research lab. In 1989, Hazleton Labs in Reston, Virginia, received a shipment of crab-eating macaques and they had Ebola. It was non-pathogenic to humans, but all the monkeys did, in fact, die. They were euthanized. The media outlets went crazy and set off widespread fear and panic. But you say that some of the researchers and staff are ill as well?"

"No blood hemorrhaging or classic wild-ass Ebola images, but some pretty hefty fevers. We don't know the pathogenicity of this particular Ebola yet."

"Well, let's hope its REBOV, the Reston Ebola virus."

"Agreed. I'll be in touch."

18

Raines nursed a cup of Turkish coffee and nibbled at the last remains of her khobz, the Moroccan round flat bread used to scoop and eat food, instead of using a fork.

Camp was buried behind his newspaper and his dark Oakleys. "You're not supposed to eat your utensils."

"I can't help it. This bread is delicious."

Raines enjoyed watching all of the people passing by along their sidewalk bistro. A familiar looking man in a wild and bright African shirt sat down at the table next to them.

It was Daniels.

"Americans?"

"No, we're Canadians."

"Great. What do you recommend from the menu?" asked Daniels.

"The bread is good," said Raines, as Camp shot her a glance. "Well, it is."

"You're going to get a visit from your friend A'zam. If he

makes you an offer, take it and go. We're tracking and eyes are all around you."

"The coffee is incredible. They also serve a pastry, similar to baklava that I'd recommend," Camp said. He folded up his newspaper and left 165 dirhams to cover their breakfast. "Well, enjoy your day."

"Can I get a doggie bag?" Raines pleaded, as she finally got up and followed Camp.

The Whitcombs took a leisurely stroll back to the Royal Hotel Rabat. They noticed a very nice, very new, black Mercedes-Benz 360 parked out in front of their hotel.

As they walked inside the lobby, they were greeted by A'zam.

"Drs. Whitcomb, how wonderful to see you again."

"A'zam, what a delightful surprise. How are your elephants doing?"

"I'm pleased to tell you that Mr. Hakim has dug out a large ditch and filled it with water. The elephants are in there almost all day long. They seem very happy. And the children love to watch them play in the mud."

"That's wonderful news, A'zam. Thank you for letting us know," said Raines.

"The other day you said you had plans to visit Casablanca and Tangier. Is that still your plan?"

"Yes, nothing definite. We have never been to this part of the world before so we thought we'd explore Rabat first," said Camp.

"Well, I was wondering if you might like to visit Yemen."

"Yemen?"

"Yes, it is a beautiful country in the Middle East. A very short plane ride from here, actually. In fact, we have a private jet."

"We? You and Mr. Hakim?"

A'zam laughed. "No, Mr. Hakim is my cousin. I work with my brothers. We are launching a pharmaceutical company. We want to bring more industry and economic growth to our country."

"So you're from Yemen?" asked Raines.

"Yes, but my family has homes in many countries. My brothers are everywhere."

"Well, it sounds like an interesting trip. Perhaps we could consider it on our next holiday."

"That would be wonderful. But I was hoping I could entice you to visit our facilities for a few days now. You see, we are setting up a vivarium so that we can continue our applied research. We need to make sure that our drugs are being developed safely and efficaciously. We know the basic science, but now we must develop the applied science. Getting the drug to the exact spot of the disease is very important, as I'm sure you know."

"Well, it is A'zam, but we're not researchers, just simple veterinarians. Both of us did a lot of research in veterinary school, but that was a long time ago."

"But that's perfect. We are only seeking your guidance, like consultants, to show us how to set up our labs. I consider our meeting to be Allah's providence. We were exploring how to hire consultants when all of a sudden—inshallah—God brought you to us."

"Well, I'm not sure what to say. What do you think, Peggy?" Camp asked.

"It might be fun, Roger. Something different," said Raines.

"We would, of course, compensate you for your time. Perhaps, 50,000 Canadian dollars?"

Raines and Camp exchanged high fives as Camp reached out his hand to A'zam. "A'zam, you have a deal."

"Outstanding. My driver will pick you up at 3:00 p.m. today and take us over to the Rabat-Salé Airport. I will, of course, be traveling with you. Does that give you enough time to pack?"

"Yes, I can be ready by then," said Raines.

A'zam reached into his bag and pulled out an envelope. "As promised, please accept the $50,000 in Canadian as a token of our appreciation. You can use it to come back to Casablanca someday."

Camp and Raines walked upstairs and put the metal key into the lock. Camp opened the door slowly, only an inch or so. The small piece of fabric he had placed above the door jamb was already on the floor.

"Something wrong?" asked Raines.

"Someone's been in our room."

Camp picked up the fabric and showed Raines. They searched through their belongings enough to know that nothing was missing. By design, there was nothing to be found by intruders that would suggest anything other than two veterinarians from Canada enjoying a holiday in Morocco.

US EMBASSY RABAT

Agents Daniels, Jackson, Borysko and Fedir were in their quad office in the INTEL section of the embassy when Fedir's cell phone rang.

"Hello?"

"Здравствуйте, а как ты сегодня?"

"Mr. Iksanov, how nice of you to call. Did you receive our deposit?"

"Aa, and Mr. Pahvchik might be interested to discuss

more with you. He has asked if perhaps the three of us could meet again here in Rabat to discuss the details of your proposal. I was hoping you could join me for dinner tonight."

"We would very much like to do that, but me and Borysko are leaving on a business trip for about one week. Perhaps we could meet then?"

"Certainly. Call me when you return and we'll discuss more. Where is your trip taking you?"

"We're considering an investment in a pharmaceutical company so we are flying to Sana'a."

"In Yemen? Perhaps we are closer partners than we think. Mr. Pahvchik has investments in Yemen as well."

"Well, don't let him get to our deal faster than we can," Fedir laughed.

"I will let him know. Please call me when you return, Fedir. Give my greetings to Borysko. Good-bye."

19

The multimillion-dollar yacht slowed its engines and pulled into the dock on a remote island in the chain of islets around Incheon International Airport. Large cargo vessels were easily seen passing by near the shore out in the Yellow Sea. Dokwang had a poultry facility for vaccine research down in Ulsan along the Sea of Japan, but this lab was easier to get to by both sea and air.

The deck mates tied off both bow and aft as Tae Sook Yoo stepped off port side followed by their guest and Mr. Lee. Mr. Lee walked several steps behind them.

Yoo and his guest were joined by translators.

"When did the samples arrive?"

"We received them only twenty-one days ago. That is not much time. I hope you understand," said Mr. Yoo.

"But you had the benefit of understanding the bacteria long before that. You know how the samples were made. I suspect that makes your job much easier?"

"There is nothing easy about this job."

The three men passed through what looked like a boarded-up tin door to an old warehouse and then into a modern atrium that fed into a series of three vapor-locked doors. They entered a curved observation deck with thick glass, halogen lights and leather chairs. It almost felt like they were looking down on a surgical suite from luxury sky boxes at an NFL game.

"Mr. Lee will update you on our progress."

"As we suspected, the DNA is very complex, but we believe we are close to developing a working antibiotic. As you know, finding an antibiotic for such a bacterium is perhaps impossible."

"That's what I am investing in, Mr. Lee, the impossible. There will be many patients. I need a cure and a prevention."

"We understand," said Tae Sook Yoo. "What is your time frame, Mr. Pahvchik?"

"If I like what I see here today, I am prepared to buy 49 percent of your company for both common and preferred shares. I'd like to see our products ready by January."

"As in the January that begins next week?" asked Mr. Lee.

"Shall I look elsewhere? Is there a problem?"

"Not at all. We will have a workable vaccine and antibiotic. I guarantee it. Mr. Lee, let's show our guest the research we're doing with chickens, rats and some of the non-human primates."

"Chickens? You're using chickens for research?"

"Yes, as a matter of fact we recently acquired 60,000 from an infectious disease research facility in America just before they shut down all animal research during the one-year moratorium. I can show you some of them now if you like. The rest are in Ulsan."

SEATTLE, WASHINGTON

He parked his 1994 Toyota Corolla in the lot next to the Seattle Ferry Terminal and walked the three blocks up to 816 3rd Avenue. The FedEx Kinko's was empty. He knew he would stand out but this might be the last posting he ever made.

He went to the front counter and asked for a computer to rent. He gave the clerk ten dollars and said he didn't have a credit card. He was given an hour of time.

He inserted his flash drive into the USB port, then decided to read the communiqué one last time before he logged onto Google mail.

> *Negotiation is over. Animal agriculture is over. The atrocities of animal research are over. America's beef supply has been poisoned and now the freaking president of the United States has even issued a decree, an Executive Order, to stop all animal research. But our animal brothers and sisters are still being held captive in laboratories and farms all over the world. We know that researchers and farmers have only one choice left and that is to kill their prisoners. Liberators unite. Make this a Christmas that our animal friends will never forget. Join 2 million animal liberators worldwide as we break into every university, every research facility and every farm and let the animals go. Liberate them and let them return to their natural habitats. Some die through liberation struggles, but all animal brothers will be murdered through captivity if we don't act.*

He logged on to his Google email account and pressed "send" knowing full well that he had less than six minutes to get back to his car.

He stood up and walked quickly to the door.

"Need some change?"

"No, I'm good," he said, as he reached for the handle. The glass door opened before he could reach it. Two men stepped in as he dropped his eyes.

"Rick Prescott?"

"Nope, wrong guy."

"Mr. Prescott, Agents Dandridge and Yetter with the FBI. We'd like to ask you a few questions."

Dandridge and Yetter took Prescott out of the store as Yetter turned back and gave the FedEx clerk a big thumbs-up.

20

A'zam nodded, then dismissed the two room-service waiters. A feast of couscous, bastillia, sfiha and a full platter of mezze spread out before him like a banquet lunch fit for a prince.

He picked up his cell phone and made the call.

After fifteen years of Somali warlords ruling Mogadishu, Islamists, along with legitimate businessmen took over and formed the Islamic Courts Union, or ICU. Within a year, the Ethiopian military ousted the ICU and tried to restore the legitimate government that had long remained in exile in Kenya.

Several Somali insurgency groups continued to rule the streets, but no group was more powerful—or ruthless— than al-Shabaab. Al-Shabaab, though radicalized, served more as nefarious criminal masterminds. They considered themselves Al-Qaeda by proxy and were waging jihad to bring Islamic sharia law to Somalia. But more than anything else they were motivated by money.

Al-Shabaab had been training and arming the Mudug pirates of southern Somalia in exchange for a share of the spoils. The network of pirates made ocean transit through the Horn of Africa a crapshoot at best.

At any given time, the Mudug pirate-infested waters and the long arm of al-Shabaab had twelve ships held hostage while negotiating $25 million in ransom for each.

Shabaab means youth, and young Moktar Ali Zubeyr, who had already fought in the Afghan jihad, now controlled almost half of Mogadishu and all of the Mudug pirates.

"Assalam allikum, Moktar, kaifa halluk?"

"I am well, A'zam. Kaif yamkanee masadatika?"

"The event is ready to begin. I know you have received the money transfer and our products. Are your Mudugs ready? Are the cages ready?"

"Na'am. Have I ever disappointed you yet, brother?"

"Of course not, Moktar. You are the most faithful. My business friend in Russia will post the coordinates, plans and names of the vessels. Make sure that there is no harm. The operations must be quick. Simple theft first, and while they are detained then release the fahr faras. Make sure they are uncaged near the food and grains. We want them to live long and enjoy the voyage."

"You say they are the Malak a-Maut?"

"Na'am. No brothers. Only Mudugs."

"Ashtoufik badain. May Allah be with you."

HORN OF AFRICA

Seven speedboats towing skiffs without motors left a dimly lit pier. A band of thirty-five Mudugs hoped to intercept their targets under the cover of darkness. The pirates were all fishermen, and they knew the waters both personally and professionally.

It was perhaps the oddest mission they had ever received from al-Shabaab. But the money was good. Each fisherman was paid $10,000 in cash at the pier that they handed over to their families. Unlike other missions, they did not need to control the ship and wait months for a ransom to be paid. This would be quick. They were to board the ships, round up the crew, steal watches and wallets, deliver the products and leave within ten minutes.

Several hundred yards out into the sea, the speedboats started to split up and head toward their seven targets.

Each skiff would have to travel 80 to 120 nautical miles before they could reach the right locations at the right times in the shipping lanes. The cruising lights of the *Samho Dream* were spotted first.

The *Samho* was flagged from Singapore and was carrying millions of barrels of crude oil from Iraq to the United States. With hardly any effort, noise or commotion, the skiff sped up, crossed the wake of the mammoth vessel and tethered itself on the rear port side. Four gunmen scurried up the side of the ship and disappeared into the galleys, berth deck and finally the bridge deck. Within minutes, the ship's twenty-four crew members were sitting on the floor on the bridge deck with three AK-47s pointed at them. One of the gunmen passed a bag, and each crew member deposited rings, wallets, iPods, and anything else of value.

Just as al-Shabaab promised, this would be the bonus bounty for the bandits to split among themselves for such an unusual job done so well.

A rope was lowered over the rear port to the speedboat

and trailer skiff tethered below. The fisherman pulled the tarp back, and fifty cages teeming with rats came to life with new activity. One by one, each cage was tied to the rope, then pulled to the main deck above.

A second Mudug untied the cage and threw the rope back over the side. The third pirate waited until he had a cage for each hand and then sprinted off to the food galley.

The food prep area was typical for a large ship. The pantry held supplies that would be needed for a long voyage. The young man opened the first cage and set twenty rats free into the pantry hold that was filled with boxes of grain, cornmeal, oats and rice. Uncaged, the ravenous rats were finally free from their cramped quarters and food was plentiful and to be found everywhere.

The dining room was quaint and less than clean to begin with. Crew members would pass through a small serving line, then sit at a seat in one of two long rows. Half-eaten plates of food were still on the tables, serving evidence of where hungry sailors had first encountered Somali Mudugs just minutes before.

The young man put the second cage on the table and opened the gate. Twenty more rats emptied out and began to feast on the plates before them.

As quickly as he left, he ran back to the aft port side where six more cages were already staged and waiting for him. With a mighty heave, he tossed the empty cages out into the ocean where they sank to the bottom, as instructed.

Fourteen minutes after it began, the speed boat and empty trailer skiff was untethered and the pirates started the long ride home to the pier just north of Mogadishu.

There would be plenty of time to divide up the bonus

bounty but not enough time for Combined Task Force 150 and the U.S. Navy to interfere with their work.

That was part of the plan as well.

Four days later, after a relaxing stay at the Sheraton, a caravan of four SUVs streamed through the desert as A'zam entertained the Whitcombs.

"I hope you found your accommodations in Aden to be acceptable. Most say that the Sheraton Gold Mohur Resort is one of our finest in Yemen."

"Watching the sunset over the Gulf of Aden was spectacular. I thought we were coming here to work and yet you treated us to a spectacular holiday," said Raines.

"We felt bad that we were infringing on your holiday asking you to do some work. It was the least we could do. I must say that the Sheraton was perhaps a step up from the Royal Hotel Rabat."

"Ah, how about a million steps up," said Camp.

"How far is your factory from here?"

"It's a bit quaint right now, but we certainly hope it will rise to the level of becoming a factory within a year. Money is not the problem. We must make sure the technology is correct. Ta'izz is only 175 kilometers from Aden. We'll be there shortly."

Camp kept looking out the tinted windows hoping that he would see some signs of DEVGRU nearby. If ever he needed Uncle Sam's Naval Special Warfare Development Group, now was that time.

Instead, he saw miles and miles of sand.

A single white building started to emerge on the distant

horizon as they descended out of the Yemeni Highlands. It stood isolated. Not a tree or hill or other building was visible for miles.

The SUVs rumbled into the checkpoint, where armed guards raised the barrier and let them pass. The vehicles kicked up a cloud of dust as they pulled into the circle drive in front of the building. An engraved sign next to the front door featured the word "ASP" in large letters with the logo image of Cleopatra's venomous snake next to it. Beneath the letters and image were the words "Aden Sea Pharmaceuticals" in both English and Arabic. Camp noticed several guards on the roof, satellite dishes and a barbed wire perimeter.

"This is definitely *the* place," Camp said to Raines with double entendre intended. Raines reached over and squeezed his hand. She'd never been in any situation like this before.

"Ready to work, Dr. Whitcomb?" Camp asked.

"I am, indeed, Dr. Whitcomb. Let's have a look at these critters," said Raines courageously.

Outside the vehicles they could hear the distinct humming sound of generators. There were no power lines in sight. A'zam led them into the building.

A greeter met them at the door with a tray full of tiny glass cups decorated in gold lace and filled with hot chai tea.

"Please, let us sit and enjoy some tea before we work. I'll have the drivers put your luggage in your quarters. Let me be the first one to welcome you to Aden Sea Pharmaceuticals."

They sat in large, overstuffed sofas that lined the outer walls of the room. Vertical LG air conditioners kept the room temperature comfortable. A staff member walked over to A'zam and handed him a printout from the computer.

"Did you hear what happened in America today?"

"No."

"The news says '*a mass liberation and coordinated effort to break in to research laboratories was conducted by thousands of animal rights activists this morning. Millions of mice and rats have been freed at universities everywhere.*' Maybe this will be good for our business," A'zam said laughing at his own irony.

"Does it mention if anything has happened in Canada?" Raines asked.

"Yes, several universities in Canada and London were also attacked. Perhaps you will have a pest problem when you get home."

A'zam finished his chai as Camp and Raines followed his lead. He was now ready for work.

"Now then, shall we go to our lab?"

A'zam led them out of the greeting room and down a set of stairs. The air was already damp and cool. The familiar smell of animals filled each breath.

"I was under the impression that you wanted our guidance on how to set up a vivarium. But judging from the smell of it I guess you already have animals," Camp said.

"Yes, we have crafted our own version of an animal laboratory, but we need the next version to meet safety standards around the world. No point of discovering a breakthrough drug if the protocols are wrong or incomplete."

The animal lab was crude at best, but the equipment was top tier.

"This is our pride and joy. The small animal imaging suite allows us to make great strides. Are you familiar with Positron Emission Tomography?"

"Well, I heard about PET imaging in vet school, but I've never seen one like this in person," said Camp.

"What does it do?" asked Raines.

"Well, in most labs, test animals must be removed from their vivarium to be scanned in order to see whether or not the drug being tested is having any impact on the disease the rat has been given. In applied science we want to know if the basic science we learned at the academic level can be used to precisely target the disease or affliction we're studying in the rat. Many of the rats we are studying have compromised immune systems so we want to keep the imaging suite right here in the vivarium. Keeping the equipment inside the barrier makes it easier to conduct experiments without disrupting the rats, but it limits our accessibility and requires that we wear gloves, masks and gowns."

The lab was active behind two barriers of glass walls. Two technicians were actively at work. As many as 2,000 Tecniplast cages were in sight.

"Geez, looks like you have a few thousand rats already," observed Raines.

"Actually, Dr. Whitcomb, we have ten more labs just like this. We house 20,000 rats in research at any given time. If you can help us develop a vivarium that houses all of them in one room, then we can be much more efficient."

"What kind of research are you conducting? Is that a flow cytometer over there?" asked Raines. Camp shot her a quick glance. Her eyes quickly recognized the mistake. "I saw one in one of our veterinary magazines, Roger. They can use it to see if dogs and cats have an infectious disease."

"Precisely correct, Dr. Whitcomb. We are studying infectious diseases. Our dream is that Yemen becomes the world headquarters for immunology and vaccine development. We've also got two high-performance liquid chromatography systems. The equipment will be used for biological sample separation and testing, nucleic acid analysis, pipet-ting robotics and high precision cell characterization."

"I'm afraid those words are a bit above me. You must have an incredible education A'zam," said Camp.

"My parents sent me to Oxford in England when I was only sixteen years old. I earned my PhD in biomedical engi-neering last summer."

"Very impressive."

"We want to focus on understanding the immunology of infectious diseases, both existing and emerging, and devel-oping vaccines to prevent them, especially diseases caused by bacterial pathogens. The rest of the equipment is fairly routine: microscopes, centrifuges, pipettors, electronic scales and power supplies. Well, shall we gear up and go inside?"

YEMENI HIGHLANDS NEAR JABAL SABER

The DEVGRU team had set up their observation camp in the cliffs on the distant mountains in the Yemeni highlands. They still had sight RECON on the building, but they were three clicks away. If things went wrong it would take almost ten minutes to get to Camp and Raines.

That could be the difference between life and death.

Satellite coordinates had already been fed to NSA, and more than one drone was locked in. Thermal indicators sug-gested that the compound had no more than forty people, including the Whitcombs.

Borysko and Fedir had already taken a flight to Moscow to see if they could sniff out Pahvchik. The Langley file iden-tified Pavel Pahvchik as being Bratva, a brother of the Russ-kaya Mafiya, part of the organized Russian mob syndicate. Pahvchik did not appear to be connected with any Islamic extremism or terrorism, but he had a long track record of financing shady business deals and nefarious ventures of all varieties.

Daniels and Jackson were left with eight SEALs on the cliffs of Jabal Saber somewhere below 9,800-feet above the desert floor.

"I don't like the distance. We're too exposed if we go any farther in, but we're too far out to help if this thing goes to hell in a hand basket," said Daniels.

"Sir, I can have my team 100 feet outside the wire in three hours. No vehicles, no noise. It's a bit of a belly crawl, but we can do it. We can pop up from the sand at the first sign of trouble. We can stay hidden beneath the sand for up to three days. After that we're snake food so don't forget to come get us," said Kentucky.

Daniels thought it over.

"Can you and Jackson take care of yourselves up here if we leave you?" Kentucky chided.

"Go. Get into position."

A'zam gave the Whitcombs a tour of the small, Aden Sea Pharmaceuticals facility. He explained the research and the hopes of the company.

"Do you think it's possible to build one facility, one vivarium, where we can conduct all of our animal research and testing?"

"Not in this structure and certainly not with 20,000 animals. Can we see where the other animals are housed?" asked Camp.

"Actually, the other rats are no longer part of this study. We continue to examine these 2,000 rats until our breeder sends us a new supply of African rats."

"Were the others part of a terminal study?" asked Raines.

"Yes, you could say that."

"Well, depending on what infectious diseases you're studying the risk of cross-contamination might be too great in just one facility. You might be better off having a separate facility for each disease. That's going to cost you more in equipment, but the study results will be much more accurate and safer in the long run," said Camp.

"Fortunately we are focused on one disease, well, one condition for now. With success will come more products. Inshallah."

"And what's that?"

"The Middle East and Africa have bacteria and viruses that you won't see in Canada but, unfortunately, are all too common for us. Neither the Americans nor the Europeans spend any of their time or money trying to solve our diseases. So we must. Let me show you."

A'zam led them over to a series of microscopes. Images from previous tissue scans were printed in color the size of posters and mounted on the wall above the microscopes.

"Black Death is a bacterial infection called *Yersinia pestis*. There have been three main forms of Black Death. Bubonic plague was most common. The mortality rate was between 35 and 75 percent. Pneumonic plague was more lethal. It killed 90 to 95 percent of those it infected. If it happened today less than 10 percent would die from it thanks to modern antibiotics. But septicemic plague was the most deadly. The mortality rate was near 100 percent. Even today there is no cure. Symptoms are high fever and skin turning deep shades of purple due to DIC, or disseminated intravascular coagulation. In its most deadly form, DIC causes a victim's skin to turn dark purple. The Black Death got its name from the deep purple, almost black discoloration. Victims usually died the same day symptoms appeared. In some Middle Ages cities, as many as 800 people died every day."

"How does one contract septicemic plague?" asked Raines.

"Septicemic and bubonic plague were transmitted from direct contact with a flea, while the Pneumonic plague was transmitted through airborne droplets of saliva coughed up by bubonic or septicemic plague victims, which then infected other humans. Fleas, humans and rats served as hosts for the disease. The bacterium, *Yersinia pestis*, multiplies inside the flea, blocking the flea's stomach and causing it to become very hungry. The flea then starts voraciously biting the host. Since the feeding tube to the flea's stomach is blocked, the flea is unable to satisfy its hunger. As a result, it continues into a feeding frenzy. During the feeding process, infected blood from the flea, carrying the plague bacteria, flows into the human wound. The plague bacterium now has a new host, a human host, as the flea starves to death."

"Lovely. Anyone care for a bowl of crawling rice?" said Camp.

"But, A'zam, we know that if we can get the infected patient into isolation we can usually knock down the bacteria with streptomycin or gentamicin in about ten days," added Raines.

"You have learned many things in your veterinary magazines, Dr. Whitcomb. All of these rats in our facility are infected with septicemic plague. But that's not the problem."

"Seems plenty big to me," said Camp.

"Africa, especially the Congo, has had many outbreaks of Ebola since the mid-1970s. There are no treatments for Ebola, as you know. So we have created a new rat model and cross-contaminated it with septicemic plague as well as Ebola."

"Good God almighty," Raines said quietly.

"But why?" asked Camp. "How can you possibly combine bacteria like the plague with a virus like Ebola? Besides, the Ebola virus in animals is non-pathogenic to humans, at least from rats. It won't spread to people from rats, will it?"

"That's what we thought, too. Ebola is transmitted among humans through bodily fluids. Up until recently, the wild reservoir for the virus was simply unknown. The best that scientists could ever come up with was the hypothesis that fruit bats carried the virus. Then we began to study the flea, the smallest insect of all."

Camp was visibly disturbed as Raines began to breathe faster.

"The flea is the vector, the common denominator. It feeds off the rat. The *Yersinia pestis* bacterium in a rat with plague causes the feeding tube to the flea's stomach to close up. The flea bites more and more, and bites anything around it because it is literally starving to death. The ravenous flea is the vector that carries the plague—and, more importantly, whatever other infection that is being carried in the rat, such as Ebola—is then transferred to each human wound it creates with the very next bite. During the feeding process, infected blood flows into the human's wound. The plague bacterium now has a new host, and the Ebola virus is transferred from human to human through bodily fluids; in this case, from flea bite to flea bite."

A'zam finished his oration as though he was proud of a major discovery. His energy and passion conveyed nothing less than the high ideals of a medical scientist.

"So, has this been a problem in Africa or the Middle East,

this Black Death rat laced with Ebola? Is that common?" asked Camp.

"Not at all. In fact, unheard of until now. But we think it may come very quickly. These rats, are in fact, carrying dual infections. They carry plague bacteria and Ebola virus. I have called this new disease, Malak al-Maut. Literally translated, it means angel of death."

"Are you telling me that all of these rats in here are infected with Ebola?" asked Raines.

"Yes, this strain is Ebola-Zaire. Scientists have been focusing on gorilla-to-gorilla transmission. But it was never the gorilla. It was the flea. Same as in Black Death."

"But there is currently no licensed Ebola vaccine for humans and no Ebola treatment that will cure the infection once it begins. So, why are we still standing in this lab?" asked Camp.

"Simple. We have the technology in place to eliminate fleas in this facility. Unless you were foolish enough to be bitten by one of the rats, it cannot go anywhere. There is no vector. But you raise an important question, Dr. Whitcomb. We must develop a vaccine to prevent Malak al-Maut as well as an antibiotic to cure people who may get it. That is my other reason for inviting you here to our facility."

"You want to develop vaccines and antibiotics for a disease combination that does not exist outside this lab?" asked Raines.

"Correct. We must know if it is remotely possible or if we are dealing with a dual infection that is beyond man's ability to solve."

"What do you want us to do?" she continued.

"Review our research reports. Review our immunology and microbiology work. Tell us if there is anything we've overlooked."

"Okay. Then what?" asked Camp.

"A few hours of analysis then we will have dinner tonight. I'd like you to meet my brothers and share your findings. Then tomorrow, if you're all done, we'll drive you back to the airport. Fair enough?"

"A'zam, you understand that we're not epidemiologists?" asked Raines.

"One last question, A'zam. How sure are you?"

"We believe this dual infection could be lethal in pandemic global terms."

"No, I meant that your facility is flea-proof," said Camp.

"Inshallah."

A'zam left them alone with the two technicians working on the other side of the lab.

"This place is dirty beyond words," Raines whispered under der breath.

"Ground zero for worldwide bioterrorism," said Camp.

"And it's filthy. How could you ever get a good outcome in squalor like this?" protested Raines. "What do we do?"

"Give him the analysis he wants, get the hell back to the airport, and then call in some Predator drones."

The sand opened ever so slowly, just enough to allow Worm to get a clean look through his night vision goggles. He heard three cricket clicks in his headset as three armed guards walked past his end of the perimeter. It was now clear.

The DEVGRU eight had belly-crawled three miles and then buried themselves in the sand surrounding the compound, one on each corner and one in each middle section.

Worm edged his way to the barbed-wire fence, crawling beneath a sand rug. He gently passed a volt meter beneath the wire. It was not electrified, and there was no sign of laser security or motion detectors. The lab's isolation and heavily armed fortification probably reduced the need for additional high tech security and gadgetry. He cut the bottom wire and tied it off just high enough to allow sufficient room to move beneath it. Once inside the perimeter he placed an audio detection device no larger than the circumference of a quarter, on the bottom right corner of the window glass to the dining room. He put a suction cup camera next to the audio chip and made sure they were both activated.

Immediately inside his night vision goggles a new picture popped up on the screen. He could see servants placing fruit bowls and food on the table. The table was wide and long. There were five seats on each side, one seat at each head.

Worm heard two long clicks in his headset. He turned his head slightly and saw two vehicles with headlights speeding toward the compound. They had been traveling through the desert with lights off but were now tipping their arrival.

He moved quickly over the sand to get back to the wire, then underneath. He settled under his sand rug as the two vehicles passed within inches of his buried body.

He had earned his nickname once again. No one could move through the earth undetected like Worm. DEVGRU now sat by patiently with eyes and ears turned on.

After quick showers and a change of clothes, Camp and Raines were escorted into the dining room. The bowls were overflowing with fruit, breads and dates.

A'zam walked into the room immediately after them and on cue followed by two well-dressed men, wearing traditional white galabiyya robes and white cotton kufi skull caps.

"May I introduce my brothers. Umer is the president and Omar is our international director of marketing. May I present Dr. Whitcomb."

"Welcome to ASP. A'zam has told us much about you.

I trust your accommodations have been acceptable," said Umer.

"Indeed, and it's our pleasure to meet you as well."

"We are not often joined by women for dinner but this is a special occasion. It is Christmas, as you say. Mrs. Whitcomb I am a man of great modesty, and I would only ask that we be allowed to hide some of your immeasurable beauty."

Two servants walked up behind Raines and covered her hair with a paisley leaf square hijab.

"To honor our guests, we ask that you please sit at the heads of our table as we partake in all that Allah has blessed us with."

Raines and Camp were seated at opposite ends of the table. Camp's back was against the window, just a few feet from Worm's camera and audio detection device. Raines was closest to the hallway.

After an early course of fruits and breads, several enormous platters of goat were placed on both sections of the table. Umer reached to his belt line and removed a jambiya from the sheath and cut a large piece of goat meat away from bone.

"Have you ever seen one of these, Dr. Whitcomb?" asked Umer.

"Very impressive dagger. Is that gold?" asked Camp.

Umer, Omar, A'zam and their six body guards laughed wildly. "Yes, of course. The scabbard is called Omani, and the hilt is cut from rhino horn and mounted with silver panel on its front. All jambiya fittings are chased silver, covered with a thin gold foil. This one is probably Jordanian. Perhaps eighteenth century," said Umer.

"What does jambiya mean?" asked Raines.

"It's the Arabic word for a dagger, as mounted on one's

hip," A'zam said to Raines as an aside, quietly hoping to convey that she ought not to speak.

When the goat pull was complete, small plates of date palm sweets were placed in front of each person. More chai tea was served.

"I can't begin to thank you enough for such a wonderful feast. This has been a delightful experience," said Camp.

"All praise be to Allah," Umer said.

"My brothers would like to know your findings. Is it possible to develop both a vaccine and an antibiotic for this Malak al-Maut?" A'zam asked.

Camp and Raines exchanged quick glances. They had already discussed a response.

"First, I must extend congratulations. I believe you have bioengineered a rat model that simply defies modern explanation. Your scientific genius is worthy of the most intellectual journals and magazines throughout the world. I look forward to the day when your research is published. If, and when, the people of the Middle East or Africa are confronted with this Malak al-Maut, I am certain that you and you alone will have the necessary science to prevent their illness or treat their symptoms. But my wife and I have concluded that developing a vaccine or antibiotics will be very difficult."

Umer stood from his chair quickly and began to pace in the back of the dining room.

"Are you implying, Dr. Whitcomb, that you don't think we *can* engineer such vaccines or antibiotics or that you think we *won't*?" Umer demanded.

"No, sir, I'm just saying it will be very difficult at best. The DNA is so complicated. The wild reservoir for the Ebola portion of the dual infection is still unknown," said Camp.

"I need more than that, Dr. Whitcomb," said Umer, who was clearly growing more agitated. His eyes were lit with fire. "If Malak al-Maut were unleashed on the planet, could other researchers beat us to the discovery of a vaccine and antibiotics?"

Camp felt the perspiration on the back of his neck. "I'm not sure I understand. What do you mean unleashed?"

Umer stood directly behind Raines. "How long would it take for others to discover treatments?"

"I don't know. Maybe years. Maybe never. Our best hope is to make sure Malak al-Maut is never, as you say, unleashed."

Umer reached to his hip and withdrew the jambiya and raised it above his head. "Dr. Whitcomb, it has already been unleashed." His hand swung down with lightning speed and immeasurable force as the dagger penetrated through the right side of Raines' chest and exited her back and went into the chair. The room was filled with the sound of ribs breaking like small sticks. Umer withdrew the dagger as Raines gasped for air in excruciating pain.

The bodyguards had already withdrawn their knives. But before they could turn towards Camp a red spot appeared on Umer's forehead as blood splatter hit the back wall. He was dead before he hit the floor.

The sand outside the compound erupted like hellfire. Eight more shots fired almost simultaneously as four guards fell from the roof, two more dropped at the checkpoint and two crumbled to their knees outside the front door.

Kentucky blew through the front door before the bodyguards had made it to their feet in the dining room.

Omar was in the hallway and was just pulling his AK-47 out of his galabiyya when Kentucky unloaded a three-round burst into his chest.

Before Camp could get to his feet, the guard next to him slashed wildly opening a cut across his cheek. Camp gave him a quick stiff arm to the neck before the blade sank deep into Camp's upper left arm. The glass window behind Camp exploded with the full force of Tracker's body lunging over Camp and onto the guard. Tracker snapped the man's neck then plunged a knife deep into the throat of the guard next to him before he could stand.

Camp was in a daze. All he could see was Raines in the seat across from him. Blood poured out of her wound. Her breathing was labored, almost impossible.

When he got to her side, her eyes were wide and pupils fixed with terror. After three years of trauma work in Iraq at the Balad Air Base, he knew instantly that Raines had, at best, a chest flail. He feared it could be much worse. Half of her chest was moving in as one half moved out with each breath.

Camp pulled her to the floor and rolled her onto her right side, the same side where Umer's dagger had entered. The wound was down. He pulled two pillows from the chairs and elevated her feet, hoping to keep shock from taking hold. He pulled the hijab off her head, rolled it into a ball and placed it gently under her injured ribs.

Her body started to shiver, but her breathing improved slightly.

"Raines! Leslie!! Come on, woman. Stay with me here. Stay with me! We still haven't seen Casablanca yet."

Camp quickly unbuttoned her blouse and reached his hand into her shirt and applied pressure over the wounded area trying to keep the chest wall from moving.

Raines tried to speak.

"Don't get fresh with me, sailor," she whispered, as she started to flutter in and out of consciousness.

Kentucky ran into the dining room followed by Ajax and Tracker.

"I need two bags filled with sand and some tape, STAT," Camp yelled as Ajax and Tracker left as fast as they had arrived.

"You've got a pretty serious bleed out, Camp," said Kentucky as he wrapped a tourniquet around Camp's upper arm.

"That's because I don't do combat, remember?" Camp muttered in anger.

"The hell you don't. You're on my team any day."

Tracker and Ajax brought in two burlap bags full of sand. Camp reached them under Raines as gently as possible.

"Cut off his man-dress. I need to get some clean gauze around these bags."

Tracker cut through A'zam's galabiyya and handed the white fabric to Camp. A'zam was still alive but gurgling up blood.

Ajax handed Camp the tape. He secured the injured side of her chest, the right side, across the front of her body to her left chest, careful not to tape around her back. The pressure and the tape allowed her chest to rise and fall normally on both sides.

Kentucky handed him small gauze strips and tape so Camp could apply pressure and stop the entry and exit wounds from bleeding. If the flail didn't kill her, the bleed-out certainly would.

Special Agents Daniels and Jackson were watching and listening from afar as Aden Sea Pharmaceuticals was transformed into a killing field in fewer than twenty-three seconds. Daniels knew from the video feed that Raines was hurt badly. He wasn't the least bit worried about the DEVGRU team.

Langley patched him into the USS *San Antonio* in the Gulf of Aden. They quickly dispatched two, big, heavy and loud CH-46 Sea Knights that would cut through the Yemeni highlands with anything but stealth silence. Two Predator drones were already circling above and waiting for instructions.

A Predator team from Creech Air Force Base in Nevada came over the COMM, telling Daniels that two more vehicles were speeding through the desert towards ASP with lights off.

Daniels gave the word and two hellfire missiles took out both vehicles, lighting up the desert sky as Daniels and Jackson got into their SUV and raced toward the compound.

DEVGRU was locked down as the remaining fifteen armed ASP guards had taken positions of cover while sending sporadic rounds of AK-47 fire.

Tracker put a bullet in A'zam's neck, finished off the other dinner guests, then went room to room looking for the rest of Umer's "brothers."

Daniels and Jackson ran into the compound.

"One wounded, Colonel Raines. Compound is all clear," yelled Worm.

The sound of incoming CH-46 Sea Knights could be heard in the distance.

"How do we move her Camp? We've got birds landing and drones waiting to blow this shit up," said Daniels.

"We need a solid litter. Get her on a board, rip a door off the wall if you have to, but don't change her from this position. Daniels, you can't blow this thing up yet. We've got to get some of the rats from downstairs out of their vivarium," said Camp, frantically as the DEVGRU team started to move Raines onto a newly dislodged door. "We've got

2,000 dirty rats down there, infected with Black Plague and Ebola."

"Then blowing this shithole up is *exactly* what we need to do. We aren't taking bio-hazards on the birds, Camp," said Daniels.

"Listen to me. They had 20,000 at one time. They've already unleashed these things. The only chance we have at identifying a vaccine or antibiotics is getting these things to a lab at Diego Garcia."

Daniels struggled for an answer.

"Are we at risk?"

"Hell, yes, we're at risk. So is the rest of the planet."

Kentucky helped Camp to his feet as Raines was carried outside. "How many do you need, Camp? I'll go get 'em."

"Kentucky, you've got to gear up. Mask, smock and gloves. Get as many as you can into canvas or burlap bags and seal them up good in a plastic bag with tape."

"Roger."

Kentucky turned and started to run out of the room.

"Kentucky…you're a good man."

Kentucky smiled and ran down to the vivarium. He knew there was no time to gear up. Two technicians were huddled on the floor in fear. They had no weapons.

Kentucky grabbed a large canvas bag and went to the Tecniplast cages. One by one he opened them up and grabbed a rat by the tail from each. The bag was full with eight so he double-bagged it in plastic, then sealed it with tape for extra security. He suspected the rats would suffocate but hopefully whatever Camp needed from them he could just as easily get from dead rats as well.

The doors to the big Sea Knights closed, and the birds lifted off. The DEVGRU team had a bird's eye view as two drones lit up the ASP compound like it was a Fourth of July exhibition.

The Sea Knights flew fast and low over the Gulf of Aden until the USS *San Antonio* came into sight. She was the flagship of Combined Task Force 151 and part of the anti-piracy naval force off the coast of Somalia.

Raines was lucky. The *San Antonio* was the nearest American ship and it had a Fleet Surgical Team 8 with level-two surgical capability to deal with trauma, surgical care, critical care and medical evacuation needs.

As the birds touched down on the sturdy decks of the *San Antonio* a trauma team was standing by. Raines was put on a gurney and started with an IV before Camp ever made it to her side.

She regained consciousness momentarily. Camp grabbed her hand as they rushed her inside the ship.

"Where am I?" she whispered.

"The *San Antonio*," Camp said tenderly.

"Home?"

They rushed her into surgery. Camp was treated for the laceration on his face and the wound to his arm. Kentucky took the bag of rats to the HazMat officer who was less than excited to see his new passengers. The bag was put into deep isolation.

THREE

21

Raines was stable thirty-six hours after emergency surgery but was being kept in an induced coma. She had lost a significant amount of blood.

The *San Antonio*'s XO gave Camp an extra day to recuperate from his stab wounds before the debriefing.

Captain Jacob Delaney's wardroom was filled with some of his staff as well as Special Agent Daniels and Kentucky.

"So when Umer raised the hypothetical 'what if,' was it your assumption then that they had already 'unleashed' 20,000 of these Malak al-Maut rats?" asked Delaney.

"I can't speak for Raines, but that seemed to be the implication to me, sir."

"So what was your role? Why'd they take the risk of letting you see the facility?"

"Pure speculation here, sir, but I think they were getting a bit cocky, a bit arrogant. They stumbled across two independent variables, two professionals, who could independently assure them that no possible vaccine or antibiotic could be manufactured quick enough to solve what they had created."

"Clearly, this was a one-way ticket," said Daniels. "There was no leaving."

"We figured that out within the first ten minutes. We were expecting execution after our last supper. But I never saw Umer's theatrics coming. I figured we'd get dessert at least. Raines wanted some Baklava. I guess he thought if Raines' life was in danger I might confess that a cure existed. I don't know. But I was very relieved to see his brain splatter on the back wall."

Kentucky grinned from ear to ear.

"What about this Malak al-Maut?" asked the ship's chief surgeon. "Are you suggesting that a Septicemic-Ebola dual infection is even scientifically possible in a rat?"

"We had less than two hours to look at everything they had. The research reports that I saw were all written in Arabic. I have no idea what Raines found. But the screenshots they printed from microscope samples seemed to support their theory. Of course, they could have doctored the images."

"So you're not sure."

"No, I'm not. I have my doubts about the Ebola. But septicemic plague alone is enough to kill a lot of people. A combination of the two could wipe out two-thirds of the planet."

"What's next, Commander Campbell?" asked Delaney.

"Sir, I need transport to Diego Garcia. It's the only functional animal research center the U.S. has anywhere left on the planet. I need to get a clean chain of tissue samples on the rats that Kentucky got. That's the only way we'll really know what's going on."

"How soon can you be ready?"

"Today. But I need to bring Raines along. She's an infectious disease expert."

"That won't be possible. We're keeping her heavily sedated until she's stabilized. She was within an hour of death," the physician said.

"I understand. We transported severely injured warriors in induced coma states from Balad to Landstuhl, Germany, every day. I'll attend to her the entire way. I am a trauma doc."

"Captain Delaney, I won't sign off on this. She's lucky to be alive."

""With all due respect, sir, I can clear this with the Pentagon or the White House if necessary."

The wardroom was quiet.

"Very well. The birds can take you to Qatar and we'll arrange for a C-17 medical evac from there," said Delaney. "Agent Daniels, how long will you be staying with us?"

"Jackson and I will join the trip as far as Qatar and head back to Washington from there."

"One last thing, Commander..."

"Yes, Captain."

"Did you find any evidence to suggest they ever had 20,000 rats in the first place?"

"No, sir. Two technicians in the vivarium kept providing us with photos and reports. We saw cages for 2,000 rats. There could have been other rooms, but we didn't see anything to support their claim."

Captain Delaney and his staff stood and gathered their papers.

"Sir, if you'll excuse me, I'd like to check in on Colonel Raines."

Delaney nodded and Camp left the wardroom followed closely by Daniels.

"Camp, do we have a bioterror event here or not?" Daniels asked in the hallway.

"I don't know."

Kentucky and the DEVGRU team had been on Delaney's ship a few months earlier during an infamous hostage situation. Somali pirates had captured the crew of a VLCC or very large crude carrier.

"Kentucky, I'd like you and your DEVGRU boys to stay with us for a week or so. I've put a special request in to CENTCOM and AFRICOM."

"More pirates?" asked Kentucky.

"Yes, and they've been acting odd. A few days ago they seized seven ships, both cargo and crude. They isolated the crew on one end of the ship and then taunted them with weapons and threats, while the rest of their gang went through the ship's compartments stealing cash and jewelry."

"No ransom demands?"

"That's the thing. Before any of the Navy vessels got to them, they left the ships and high-tailed it back to the Somali coast."

"All that risk for a couple hundred dollars and a few cheap watches? It does seem odd," said Kentucky. "Maybe they're finally getting the message."

"Maybe. Or maybe they're up to something else. Either way, I'd like to have your team along for the ride."

22

After Camp received the call he sprinted down the sidewalk past a Main Street of barracks until he came to the medical unit. He suited up quickly and put on his mask.

Raines was moving in her bed. Her doctors had started to withdraw the medicines that induced her coma.

Camp reached for her hand.

"Les? Les, can you hear me?"

Her eyes fluttered, and she finally opened them. The tube down her throat prevented her from speaking, but her eyes spoke volumes.

"Hey, girl, welcome back."

Camp's eyes filled with tears, an image Raines would never forget no matter how many drugs were poured through her system.

A nurse tapped on the glass to the ICU and held up a sheet of paper. URGENT CALL FROM USS SAN ANTONIO.

Camp squeezed her hand.

"You're going to be alright, Les. You're back now."

Camp walked out to the hallway, threw the mask into the trash can and pushed the blinking light on the desk phone.

"Commander Campbell."

"Commander, this is Captain Delaney on the *San Antonio*."

"Yes, Captain. What can I do for you?"

"It's Kentucky. We had to put him in isolation last night. The man's a terrible sort of sick right now."

"From the rats?"

"We don't know for sure, but that's what everyone's guessing. Stand by. I'm going to put you on speaker. Commander Sharon Plotkin is handling his case."

"Dr. Plotkin, what are Kentucky's symptoms right now?"

"When I left him in isolation maybe fifteen minutes ago, his fever had risen to 104.2 with no end in sight. He has chills, severe abdominal pains and a very rapid heartbeat. He's vomiting blood, and he's damn near delirious. He's got several black patchy rashes on his skin and hundreds of bumps on his skin, almost looks like insect bites."

"So much for a clean lab without fleas," said Camp. "Sounds like bacterial endotoxins are causing disseminated intravascular coagulation and probably ischemic necrosis from the clots. Have you started him on any antibiotics?"

"We started streptomycin intravenously about 0400 hours this morning, but—Commander, please hold a second... I'm so sorry, but Chief Petty Officer Kent Jefferson just died."

Camp's face went numb. A million thoughts poured through his mind simultaneously.

"Geez. Doctor, how long was it from onset of symptoms to death?"

"Maybe seven hours...tops."

"So what the hell does this mean for the rest of my ship, Commander?"

"Captain Delaney, you'll need to do an entire inventory of who came in contact with Kentucky in the last seventy-two hours and get them into isolation and treatment."

"Brilliant. We're talking about 360 sailors and another 700 Marines. The whole damn ship is an isolation ward now. What the hell did he have, Campbell?"

"Sir, I'm doing molecular studies on tissue samples right now. These rats appear to have all the markers of a hybrid. I think we're dealing with two infections."

"Two? That Malak al-Maut shit?"

"Yes, sir. It appears to be Black Death, sir, and some form of Ebola."

Camp hung up the phone. There was no time to mourn Kentucky. The rats were clearly lethal.

23

General Ferguson and his staff sat glued to the bank of TV sets in the Pentagon's ready room. INTEL was coming in faster through the 24/7 cable channels than it was from his own intelligence agents.

Field producers were streaming video into CNN's international news headquarters in Atlanta at an alarming pace. No one really knew what was unfolding, but everyone suspected the worst.

The CNN anchor read the report: "The South Korean-operated and Singapore-owned *Samho Dream*, which was carrying more than 2 million barrels of crude oil from Iraq to the United States, arrived at the port of Mobile, Alabama last night. While it's not uncommon to have a crew member die during transatlantic voyages, it is uncommon to see three deaths. The tanker's crew of five South Koreans and nineteen Filipinos sought immediate medical attention when they made port. Since then, forty-seven dockworkers have fallen ill with a mysterious ailment and have been hospitalized in critical condition, and four of them have already died."

Reports were coming in from a total of five U.S. ports including the ports of Miami, Savannah, and Charleston. But nowhere was the news more dreadful than the port of Wilmington in Delaware. The news bulletin from the Associated Press sent shockwaves throughout the CNN central newsroom: TRIAGE AND ISOLATION UNITS BEING SET UP IN A WAREHOUSE AT PORT OF WILMINGTON. MORE THAN 7,000 PEOPLE STRUCK WITH MYSTERIOUS ILLNESS. HEALTH OFFICIALS REPORT 103 CONFIRMED DEATHS WITH NUMBERS EXPECTED TO GROW SUBSTANTIALLY BY THE HOUR.

PORT OF WILMINGTON

Timothy Anderson was like any other twelve-year-old boy who grows frantic when his labrador retriever goes missing. He was worried and desperate to find Molly.

Timothy often went to the shipyards with his dad, a port supervisor. The Christmas break meant he and Molly could spend entire days playing around huge ships and longshoremen.

Molly saw something more enticing than the green tennis ball Timothy was throwing to her in the morning, and she took off. By the time Timothy found her around noon, she was muddy and in trouble. By the way she was scratching herself he suspected that she was covered with fleas. He knew his dad would be mad and his mother would make Molly sleep outside.

But by mid-afternoon Timothy was starting to feel miserable, too.

By dinner time, Timothy's dad was in a panic himself. The port of Wilmington was in the middle of a disease outbreak, and neither Timothy nor Molly were anywhere to be found.

Timothy and Molly had curled up between some large ocean storage containers. He had hoped to get out of the sun, even though it was only forty-four degrees outside. He was burning up and chilled at the same time. Weakness and lethargy had set in, and his stomach was in unbearable pain.

The sun had already set, but the port lights illuminated the dark spots on his arms and hands. The reflection of emergency lights flickered on the sides of ships and containers. He was too weak to cry out for help.

A sudden surge of pressure from his stomach burst through his chest and out his mouth as he vomited all over himself. He was too sick to even roll up on his side.

He recognized the peculiar taste of blood in his mouth. His heartbeat was rapid, so advanced that he was almost out of breath from breathing so hard.

Finally, thankfully, he thought his breathing was about to stop, and he could go to sleep just like Molly.

PENTAGON

One of the coffee-pouring majors handed General Ferguson the telephone.

"Yes, sir, the CDC is in contact with port authorities in Mobile, Miami, Savannah, Charleston and Wilmington. No one knows for sure what the common denominators are since each port received cargo and petrochemicals from various parts of the world."

The *Samho Dream* offered the best hope of determining

what was making people sick and where it came from.

CNN was preparing to give its on-camera anchors an update on the breaking story when the newsroom feed from Al-Jazeera Television ran a special report. A soft-spoken Arabic woman read the press release as the graphics operator tried in real-time to type the story on screen. The news was fresh and breaking quickly.

"A few moments ago Al-Jazeera received this release from Al-Qaeda in the Islamic Maghreb and has confirmed the document's authenticity. It reads: ALL PRAISE BE TO ALLAH AND ALL BROTHERS WHO WAGE JIHAD IN THE NAME OF OUR ONE TRUE GOD. AL-QAEDA IN THE ISLAMIC MAGHREB HAS UNLEASHED PLAGUE ON THE GREAT SATAN OF THE WEST, FOR THEY DID NOT TURN FROM THEIR EVIL. WE HAVE SENT THOUSANDS OF WARRIORS TO AMERICA AND THEY NOW CARRY MILLIONS MORE WHO WILL WAGE JIHAD IN THE NAME OF ALLAH. MILLIONS OF AMERICANS WILL DIE, CURSED WITH THE BLACK DEATH OF MALAK AL-MAUT THAT KNOWS NO MERCY. ALLAH THE MERCIFUL ASKED US TO SEND A WARNING FIRST SO WE SENT MONKEYS TO LOUISIANA. THEY WERE YOUR DISEASE SENTINELS. ALLAH SENT YOU AN EARLY WARNING SO THAT YOU COULD PROTECT THE LIVES OF THE INNOCENT, TURN FROM EVIL, AND SERVE THE ONE TRUE GOD. BUT YOU IGNORED THE SENTINELS. GOD'S NAME BE PRAISED."

General Ferguson's phone at the Pentagon lit up. The CDC, NSA, CIA and 1600 Pennsylvania were all urgently looking for answers. No one had ever heard of Malak al-Maut, but now it was the IED du jour in the War on Terror.

The President called an emergency meeting of his top medical and military advisors, and General Ferguson was whisked away in a Marine helicopter across the Potomac and was now sitting in a room at the White House less than fifteen minutes after the Al-Jazeera news story broke.

"What are we dealing with here, folks? And what's the reference to Louisiana?" asked the president.

CDC Director Janis Vitter was on the speaker phone. "Mr. President, a research facility in Louisiana received an unexpected shipment of thirty-nine rhesus macaques—non-human primates—and shortly after the shipment arrived, every one of the monkeys died. It's rare but not uncommon. Same thing happened in Virginia a few years back."

"Sir, we confirmed that these monkeys at Gulf Shores did, in fact, have Ebola. Some of the staff became ill, but no one has died," said General Ferguson.

"Well, we've got more than 100 dead Americans today and it's not even seven o'clock yet. Are these reports suggesting that Ebola has been weaponized through monkeys? I haven't heard any reports of wild monkeys running through the streets of Savannah or Wilmington."

"Ebola in research animals is typically non-pathogenic to humans. I think that's what we saw in the Gulf Shores case a few weeks ago," Vitter added.

"So how the hell do we stop this thing? What's being done right now?" the president asked.

The room full of top ranking military officers, Presidential advisors and infectious disease experts grew deafeningly silent.

"In a word…nothing," said Director Vitter.

"We're in the middle of a bioterror attack and our best and brilliant minds are doing nothing?"

"Sir, we have shipped some vaccines and antibiotics to the port authorities from some of our previous work, but we don't have the capacity to research any new vaccines or treatments here in the U.S. right now. Perhaps if we can determine exactly what the disease is and how it is being passed, then we could infect other living systems in order to test the efficacy of any vaccine or antibiotic we can create."

"Then do it."

"Sir, we'll need your help with foreign governments, perhaps the Chinese and Singapore," said Vitter.

"For what?"

"We don't have any viable, or at least operational, animal research facilities in the U.S. after the one-year moratorium was imposed. I'm afraid we have no other choices but to work with the offshore facilities of other countries."

24

DIEGO GARCIA

Camp's cell phone started to vibrate annoyingly on his night stand. He cracked his left eye open just wide enough to recognize the number of an incoming call from the Pentagon.

"Camp, have you been tracking the news?" asked General Ferguson.

"No, sir, I've been in the rack for three hours."

"We've got a hundred Americans dead and thousands more in critical condition in four port cities on the Atlantic and another one in the Gulf. Al-Qaeda in the Islamic Maghreb is claiming to have unleashed some shit called Malak al-Maut on the evil empire."

Camp was silent. He couldn't determine if he was having a nightmare or being awakened into one.

"Copy that again, sir. Did you say Malak al-Maut?"

"Affirmative. You know what it is?"

"Raines and I started to get a look at it, General, but we were not able to do any molecular work or even review the bacteriology reports. We saw what seemed to be some real looking tissue samples, but they were only photographs. I've got some forensic samples I'm working on right now here in Diego."

"You've already got it? How close do you think you are to a vaccine or antibiotic?"

Camp jumped out of bed and turned the light on. "Whoa, sir. We don't have a clue what 'it' is let alone if it really is a pathogen capable of being transmitted among humans."

"Campbell, are you deaf? One hundred Americans are dead just today alone. Is that enough pathogenicity for you?" shouted Ferguson. "So this really is Ebola? How the hell could they have weaponized this?"

"Sir, that seems unlikely to me."

"Tell that to the thirty-nine monkeys who died from Ebola last month in Louisiana. The AQ brothers say that was our warning. Is that what they mean by 'Malak al-Maut'? They were just playing with us…toying with us…playing with Ebola?"

"I don't think so, sir. But I am fairly certain they had successfully raised a colony of dirty rats. Rats that were either bred to have, or susceptible to getting, the Black Plague. Malak al-Maut is their hybrid disease, dual infections of plague and Ebola. It means…angel of death."

Now Ferguson was silent.

"Sir, how many ports did you say have been infected?"

"Five."

"So that could mean literally, as few as five ships, could be the culprits."

"I'm not following you Campbell."

"Sir, every oceangoing vessel—from the earliest mariners to present day super tankers—have been besieged with rats and rodents. They live on the docks, get into the ships, scurry through the grains and cargos and emerge from ships thousands of miles from home and where they started. Rats from ships are vectors for all sorts of diseases, and these animals are well established in port areas. They have spread epidemics of plague, murine typhus, salmonellosis, trichinosis, leptospirosis and rat bite fever to many seaport cities. It's not the monkeys, sir, it's the rats."

"So five random ships just happen to be carrying Malak al-Maut-laced rats?"

"Sir, you need to contact the USS *San Antonio* immediately. When I was briefed by Captain Delaney he mentioned some odd behavior by Somali pirates recently."

"Go on."

"They seized several US-bound freighters in the Gulf of Aden. After rounding up the crew and holding them hostage, they ransacked the ship's living quarters and stole whatever cash and jewelry they could find. But before any muscle showed up, they let the crew go. No hostages, no ransom demands."

"Routine, Campbell. That's why they call them pirates."

"Sir, this happened with exactly seven ships. Maybe those seven ships are now anchored at our five ports. The crew members only reported what was stolen. They never mentioned if anything might have been *added* to the cargo."

"Roger that. Delaney can probably get us the names of each ship, which gives us a ground zero in each port. Then we send out Orkin Pest Control and have them catch and kill a bunch of African biting rats."

The phone line went silent.

"Sir, you have a much bigger problem than that."

"I'm not sure this can get any bigger, Camp."

"The rats won't bother humans unless they touch dead carcasses. It's the fleas, the fleas on the rats. The fleas are ravenous by now. You could lose entire cities in less than a week."

"Good God Bless America…we're afraid of nukes getting in the hands of terrorists, a suitcase nuke that could take out an entire port city. And now you're telling me that Al Qaeda sent fleas?"

"Sir, I'm heading over to the lab now. I'll call you when I know something."

25

A thick mixture of rain and snow had begun to fall. A grey sky covered the horizon with no hopes of a sun break visible as temperatures hovered near freezing.

The Pushkin was a place where one felt like an aristocrat of early nineteenth century Russia. It was a literary café and restaurant with an interesting collection of items—an antique library with 15,000 old books, maps, globes and telescopes, all of them original articles from Pushkin's time.

The place held a special place among the city's restaurants, and Moscow mayor Vleshkov brought his guests there often. It was carefully styled after the luxurious yet cozy Moscow mansions of Pushkin's era. All parts of the cafe—the drawing room, the antique pharmacy, the stairs, and even the elevator—had artificially aged floors and tiles. Every item in the interior was absolutely genuine.

The waiters were dressed in old, grey Russian servant frock coats, and even spoke the Russian language of historic Pushkin. The menu offered traditional Russian dishes prepared according to old recipes with a touch of French cuisine flare, typical of the early nineteenth century.

Pavel Pahvchik sat at the small, round table as two members of the Bratva stood near the serving counter and two more stood outside the Pushkin. He and his guest were mired in a quiet conversation.

"Are you sure you're ready?"

"Indeed. We have a 90 percent success rate on all of our tests. We are ready to announce," said Mr. Lee as he sipped his cappuccino.

"Good. Make sure you get on Bloomberg Television. I love Bloomberg."

"Consider it done, Mr. Pahvchik."

"Will you stay in Moscow for a few days? Enjoy our weather?" Pahvchik laughed at his own joke.

"No, my apologies, but I'll be flying to New York immediately to join Mr. Tae Sook Yoo at the press conference tomorrow."

"Very well. Perhaps next time then." Pahvchik stood up and placed 1,500 rubles on the table, more than enough to buy two nice bottles of wine, let alone two cappuccinos. He walked a few paces, then turned back. "Remember: Bloomberg."

Mr. Lee nodded his head in understanding, finished his coffee and grabbed his travel bag.

Special Agents Borysko and Fedir kept eating their eggs and sausage at the window table as they watched Mr. Lee hail down a taxi.

DIEGO GARCIA

Raines was sitting up in bed with all tubes disconnected other than an IV. She was weak but quite alert. She had been moved out of ICU and into the staging area next to the critical ward. A smile fell across her parched lips as Camp entered and sat on the bed next to her.

"Look whose back among the living."

"Thanks to you," she said softly, her voice still not strong enough to fully fill a secret being whispered. "You saved my life, Camp."

"It was nothing. Besides, I had wanted to get into your shirt for a long time, and finally—boom—there was my chance."

Raines started to laugh, but the laughing caused her broken but healing ribs to hurt. She winced in pain.

"Okay, sorry, no jokes yet."

"Any news about our friends in Yemen?" she asked.

"Nothing other than they had a barbeque as soon as we left."

"What about the rats?"

"Bad news there, Raines. They got some of them onto ships sailing into American ports. One hundred dead just yesterday alone. Worldwide television news centers are covering it wall to wall."

"Al-Qaeda?"

"Our boys in Algeria are taking credit. Raines, we managed to get eight of the rats out of the ASP facility. They're obviously dead, but we're running all sorts of molecular and bacterial tests. Hopefully. We'll know something in a few hours. A'zam told us about the septicemic plague and I think that's accurate. I just can't get my head around the Ebola. How on God's green earth could they get a pathogenic virus like Ebola and a bacteria like plague into the same rat and make it contagious? I just don't get it."

Raines motioned for the glass of water on her stand. Camp bent the straw and put it into her lips. She swallowed hard.

"What about the Russians?"

Camp smiled and brushed the hair off her forehead.

"Russians? They're giving you some pretty hefty drugs, Colonel. Enjoy them while they're free and legal."

Raines shook her head.

"No. When I looked through all of the research reports, they were all in Arabic. Then I found it: hundreds of pages in Russian."

26

The emerging situation called for a dramatic shift in meeting rooms. The first meeting had taken place in a small conference room outside the Oval Office. But now Al-Qaeda had launched a bioterror attack, and all hands were in the Situation Room.

The White House Situation Room is a 5,000 square-foot conference room and intelligence management center located in the basement of the West Wing of the White House. It is run by the National Security Council staff for the use of the president and his or her advisers to monitor and deal with crises both home and abroad.

Once labeled the low-tech dungeon of the free world, the Situation Room was now bursting with every high-tech gadget imaginable.

The current watch team included three duty officers, an intelligence analyst and a communications specialist.

Seated around the large mahogany table were the heads

of CIA, Homeland Security, the director of National Intelligence, the director of the Center for Disease Control, the surgeon general, the heads of the Joint Chiefs and General Ferguson.

"Mr. President, we're thirty-eight hours into this thing. The five port authorities are now reporting 1,136 fatalities and more than 14,000 people severely ill and in isolation," the Secretary of Homeland Security said. "With the help of the USS *San Antonio,* we've identified the seven ships that are the source of the outbreaks. We have National Guard members on site in full HazMat gear trying to eliminate the rats, but it's a very slow process."

"Madame Secretary. Have there been any reported cases of this Malak al-Maut farther inland away from the ports?"

"So far the farthest inland report is fewer than three miles."

"General Ferguson?"

"It's worse than that, Mr. President," said General Ferguson. "Think of the millions of rats that will scamper from trash can to bushes in the street light shadows of every large American city tonight. Each one of them carries a legion of fleas. Which ones are infected? Which ones aren't dirty? They are creating unprecedented sheer terror. That's what we have to be afraid of."

The President was silent.

The cue light on the satellite video link from Diego Garcia flashed green.

"Yes, Commander Campbell."

"Madame Secretary, the National Guard is wasting their time trying to kill the rats. General Ferguson is correct. The rats aren't biting people. The issue is simply this: the bacteria in the plague shuts down the feeding tubes in fleas. They sense they can't get any more food from the rats, so they jump to people looking for food. The fleas are transmitting the infections from human to human, not the rats. Aerial spraying may be your best, and only, bet for containment."

"That may be fine for the plague, Commander, but what about the Ebola?" asked the president.

"I don't know, sir. I doubt there's an Ebola component to this but I'm not sure."

Dr. Janis Vitter, director of the CDC, spoke up.

"Mr. President, we have definitively confirmed the presence of the Ebola virus in the thirty-nine research monkeys at the Gulf Shores Research Center. Al-Qaeda took credit for that attack and warned us that we ignored their sentinels. I'm afraid we must assume that there is, in fact, a Black Death-Ebola mix in play here."

"Commander, you have use of the only up and running animal research facility we own right now at Diego. My briefings suggest you have more than sufficient staff and resources. How long do you project before you have a working vaccine and viable antibiotics?" the president asked.

"With all due respect, sir, research doesn't work that way. Yes, I have sufficient staff. Yes, I have all the equipment imaginable. And yes, I have thousands of animals to test on from numerous species. But I have no body of work to refer to. I have no publication trail from basic science that tells me what works and what does not work for this bacteria or virus. We're trying to bypass basic scientific research and discovery and jump right in to applied testing and research. Sir, this is why our universities come up with hypotheticals, write their grants, and then conduct basic research."

"I don't need a lecture from you, Commander. I need a vaccine."

"Yes, Mr. President, it is in fact too late for a lecture. We're working on the vaccine and antibiotics 24/7. But I suggest you'll have a better shot at containment then you will with treatment."

The video feed from Diego Garcia went black as Camp abruptly shut down and disconnected. The chairman of the Joint Chiefs shot a stern look over in the direction of General Ferguson. Camp was Ferguson's man and everyone knew it. Camp's tone with the president was out of line and the chairman would get his pound of flesh.

The watch team's duty officer walked over to the president's chief of staff and whispered in his ear.

"Ladies and gentlemen, we should probably take a look at a television news conference coming out of Manhattan near Wall Street," said the chief of staff.

"Good God, has this thing reached New York City?" asked the president soberly.

"On the contrary, sir, a foreign company is claiming to have both a vaccine and a working antibiotic."

"That's impossible," demanded General Ferguson.

Four flat-panel TV screens tuned simultaneously to the financial channel as the press conference began.

"Good morning, my name is Tae Sook Yoo. I am president and chief executive officer of Dokwang Pharmaceuticals, Ltd in Seoul, South Korea. After 9/11 our company began to role play various bioterror scenarios. If we could think it up, we knew that terrorists could, too. A few years ago we started to develop prototype vaccines and antibiotics for both Black Death and different strains of Ebola viruses. When terrorists created Malak al-Maut from plague bacteria and Ebola virus, we immediately tested our development drugs to see if they were both safe and efficacious. I am joined today by the chief medical examiner for the State of Delaware, Dr. Anastasia Merrill."

"Good morning. The Port of Wilmington has already seen almost 600 fatalities. Our triage and isolation centers are located in warehouses right at the port. We have more than 4,400 confirmed patients. Yesterday afternoon we tested Dokwang's experimental antibiotic on 50 patients and a placebo on another 50 patients. In those given Dokwang's Roderemycin, we saw fifty fevers break and remarkable improvements within eight hours. Alternatively, we saw the conditions of the fifty patients given placebos continue to deteriorate."

"Thank you, Dr. Merrill. Several months ago our labs conducted what we called bio-war games in order to develop a bio-terror vaccine through friendly competition between our own research scientists. One team injected research mice with the Ebola virus subcutaneously, just under the skin. The mice did not get sick, but they did develop an immune response to the Ebola virus. Another research team injected lab mice intraperitonealy or directly into the abdomen. These mice got sick with the Ebola virus and died within eight days.

"Then we had an idea. It was an accidental discovery, serendipity, if you will. What if we collected serum from the mice which had been injected with Ebola in the skin and tested that serum's ability to prevent the deaths of mice injected with Ebola in the abdomen? You see, serum is the liquid that's left over when you remove all the red blood cells and all of the white blood cells from blood."

"The serum protected all mice that were injected. We then realized that if we could get serum from people who survive or have an early stage Ebola virus infection, then we could successfully treat humans who are lethally infected. Dr. Merrill?"

Tae Sook Yoo yielded the podium back to Merrill.

"We have also administered Dokwang's Malak al-Maut serum to seriously infected people, as well as a vaccine to first responders and other members of the incident command team who are at risk. Symptoms from our most severely ill have improved, and all vaccinated personnel are still symptom-free after eight hours."

"With that, I'll take some questions," said Mr. Yoo.

The stock ticker crawl on the Bloomberg Television screen focused on DKWL, Dokwang's American business publicly traded on NASDAQ. The stock had closed the previous day at $1.80 per share but was poised to explode after the 9:30 a.m. opening bell on Wall Street. Stock futures on DKWL were skyrocketing.

General Ferguson shook his head and rose to his feet. "Mr. President, this is just not feasible. There's no way this company could possibly know the pathogenicity of this virus this soon. I really think we need to get Commander Campbell on this."

"I think Campbell has already run his course on this one and came up predictably empty," the chairman said.

The head of the Food and Drug Administration spoke up.

"Mr. President, this could be a marvelous breakthrough, but we know little, actually nothing about this company or their products. We could certainly fast-track our review process." "Review process? We've got 1,400 dead and 14,000 more dying in isolation. We've got millions of fleas going ape shit in a feeding frenzy, and you want to talk to me about a review process? How about a blue-ribbon panel and town hall meetings, too! Dr. Vitter, get up to Wilmington immediately and verify the data. If this is the real deal, I'll issue an Executive Order. Let's make sure Dokwang can manufacture the quantities we need."

The President stood up and the room rose to their feet as one. "Chairman, I'd like to see you and General Ferguson for a brief moment in my office."

MOSCOW

Pavel Pahvchik motioned to his Bratva to turn the television off. He poured a glass of premium vodka in celebration.

"Did you see that?" he said to no one in particular. "It was on Bloomberg. That's something, isn't it? Come, it's just about time to sell some of our stock on Wall Street."

27

The animal research facility at Diego Garcia was buzzing with activity. The researchers had positively identified the bacteria as Black Death. A'zam was correct. It was septicemic plague.

The virologists were still struggling to identify anything tangible and definitive as being Ebola from the Malak al-Maut rat tissue samples. They still needed more time.

Camp's cell phone started to vibrate. He recognized the incoming notation and figured this was the ass-chewing call he'd been expecting.

"Campbell."

"Commander, you do understand decorum, do you not?"

"Yes, sir."

"You do understand chain of command and the president—whether you like him or not—is, in fact, your commander-in-chief?"

"Yes, sir."

"Well, apparently you'll have an opportunity to reflect on all of that during a long flight back to Washington. You embarrassed the chairman and pissed off the president."

"General Ferguson, we have a bioterror attack and you want to pull me out of the lab so I can get a face-to-face dress-down? Consider it done, sir. I get it. I apologize, and it won't happen again. Now, if you're through, I really need to get back to work."

"You're through alright, Commander. Your research is over. Shut the project down."

"Sir?"

"The South Koreans have just announced both a vaccine and antibiotic for Malak al-Maut. The chief medical examiner from Delaware verified its effectiveness, and the CDC warranted both drugs. The FDA still wants a review process, but the president has signed an Executive Order and help is on the way."

Camp dropped back into his Vietnam-era, Army-issued green vinyl and steel swivel chair. He couldn't believe, let alone, fathom, what he was hearing.

"That's impossible. It simply can't be done that quickly."

"My thought as well. But, apparently it can and obviously it was. You're a trauma guy, Campbell. It was just too much to ask of you to accomplish without the help of Raines."

"General, we've only just barely identified the bacteria. I don't see how they could have released a vaccine or an—."

"Doesn't matter. They did. As soon as Raines is fit to fly, you're to return to Washington immediately where I'll help you reassess your career and determine what's best for both you and the military."

Camp heard the general's phone click as he sat motionless staring into Diego Garcia's busy research lab.

28

The Defender 90 pulled off I-270 north from Virginia and crossed into Pennsylvania on US-15 North. Camp and Raines rode together in silence after a long flight into Andrews Air Force Base.

Raines was recovering nicely. She still felt some pain when she walked but other than being weaker than normal she was feeling like her old self again, nothing that a few more weeks of recovery and fresh air couldn't fix.

"Did you tell her I was coming along?"

Camp was focused on the road while his head was in a lab 8,000 miles away.

"Camp?"

"What?"

"Did you tell her I was with you?"

"Eileen? Yeah, I called her from Andrews. She knows."

Raines looked out across the snow-covered hills.

"She's okay with it?"

"Raines, everything will be fine. You've got two weeks of medical leave, and I'm taking twenty-one days of personal leave. Cell phones off, great food, a hot fire and we can clear our minds."

"That's not what I meant. I mean, I did sort of spy on the two of you, you know?"

The Defender pulled into the parking lot at Lightner Farms. Before Camp could even get the key out of the ignition, the front door opened, and Eileen came out wearing her North Face fleece and a cute hat.

A welcoming smile beamed across her face as she met Camp at his door.

"Welcome home, sailor," Eileen said as she gave him a tender hug. Eileen reached through the truck and grabbed Raines' hand. "Welcome, Leslie. I am so glad Camp talked you into coming."

Raines smiled. "I'm not sure I had much choice, really. I hope I won't be an imposition."

"Not at all. I'll walk you in while the sailor grabs the bags."

With a wink from Eileen, Camp opened the rear compartment as he watched Eileen and Raines walk into the lodge. He knew this would be uncomfortable at best.

Eileen walked Raines over to one of the oversized leather chairs in front of the fireplace. A warm and crackling fire was already ablaze. Raines sat down and Eileen covered her legs with a red blanket she had purchased years earlier in Muskogee, Oklahoma, at a Cherokee Indian retail store. The sound of a tea kettle hissed from the stove top in the kitchen as Brazilian flutes and acoustic guitar melodies filled the room from a nearby CD player.

"What do you like in your tea, Leslie?"

"A splash of milk and a dash of sugar if you have it."

"Got it."

The wooden lodge door opened, and Camp came in carrying their bags.

"Let's put Leslie in six. And I know where you're going," Eileen said with a wry smile.

Camp marched upstairs as Eileen served the tea. He stayed upstairs for what seemed like an eternity to Raines. She felt very awkward.

"Have you lived in Gettysburg your entire life?"

"Heavens, no, I bought this bed and breakfast about five years ago now. I'm a Texas girl, born and raised."

"I live in Texas, as well. I've got an apartment in San Antonio. Well, I did. At least my furniture lives in a storage unit there."

"I'm from Muleshoe, about halfway between Amarillo and Lubbock. It's a one-stoplight-don't-blink sort of town."

"Sometimes they're the best. How did you settle on Gettysburg?"

"I went through a divorce and needed a change so I took a road trip. I wanted to see New England's fall foliage. The plan was to do B&Bs all the way to Maine. But I never made it any farther north than Gettysburg. Shortly after I bought the place, I met Camp."

"How long have you two been together?" Raines asked hesitantly as shock lit across Eileen's face. "I'm sorry. Am I being too nosey?"

The upstairs door opened and closed, and Camp started down the stairs.

"Are you two causing trouble yet?" he asked, coming down the steps.

"Almost. Are you ready for your surprise?" Eileen asked him.

"Surprise? Do I detect some apple cobbler in my future?"

"That can be arranged as well. But first you need to take a tour of the garage."

"The garage? Eileen, you shouldn't have. Did you buy me a Harley?"

"In your dreams, sailor. Go take a look and tell me what you think."

Camp shrugged his shoulders and went outside. Eileen turned back to Raines.

"Leslie, what has Camp told you about *us*?"

"Nothing, I swear, not even a word. I was out of line."

Eileen took a deep breath and went into the kitchen and returned with the tea pot along with some more milk and sugar.

"Can I warm you up?"

"Please."

"Leslie, I'm sure he doesn't know what to say so maybe it's best if I tell you. When Camp was in Iraq at the Balad trauma center, he was putting in fourteen- and sixteen-hour days. Every time choppers would bring in wounded soldiers, he and a team of nurses would meet the helos outside and quickly try to stabilize the wounded as they wheeled them in. He was always somewhere between surgery, the helo pad, and his bed, seldom anywhere else."

"I know he spent three years there."

"They couldn't get him to leave. Worse than that, they couldn't afford to lose him. He saved more lives than you could possibly imagine."

"He's never talked about all of that."

"He doesn't talk about it with anyone. Well, there was an Army helicopter pilot who flew more medevac missions into Balad than practically anyone else. She was a captain and for several months she'd fly them in, drop them off, and go get more. She worked more hours than Camp did. They became friends through the glass of her chopper and his gurney on the tarmac."

"Was that you?"

"No. She was based at Balad, too, so they stole moments for quick meals and occasional conversation in the trauma center. Quickly, they fell in love. Camp asked her to marry him. She agreed, and they set a date."

"It sounds very romantic, at least in a war sort of way."

"It was. A dust storm moved in like they often do in Iraq as Jane's chopper and another bird were picking up wounded outside of Ba'qubah. The trip back to Balad was less than thirty minutes. They thought they could make it in time. Jane lost her bearings in the sandstorm, the rotors malfunctioned from the grit of the sand and they crashed in the desert outside of Balad. The nurses told Camp that Jane's chopper went down, and he left surgery and joined the medics in Humvees as they rushed to the accident site. Camp went to Jane immediately. She had obvious and massive head injuries. The medics basically ignored her and went to the others, the ones who were still moving and appeared to have a chance. Somehow, some way, Camp brought her back. They got her back into the trauma center. And six hours after surgery she was on a C-17 to Landstuhl in Germany. But she was on all forms of life support."

"Camp did the surgery?"

"As much as he could. He doesn't remember any of it."

"Did she survive?"

"Not really. Jane suffered severe brain damage. After four more surgeries, she finally emerged from coma but she never became aware. She opened her eyelids and went through various sleep-wake cycles, but there was no cognitive function. No awareness, no cognitive function, and total life support. Doctors determined she was in a persistent vegetative state."

"And Camp couldn't pull life support from her, could he?"

"Not exactly. Since they were only engaged he had no legal standing. It was up to her next of kin."

"And her family?"

Eileen looked away as a tear streamed down her cheek.

"He really hasn't told you anything, has he? One of the daughters went into nursing and the other went into the Army. Jane is my sister, the Army pilot. I worked as an ICU nurse out in Lubbock until my divorce. When I bought this place, I planned to give up nursing. Then this accident."

"Oh, Eileen, I had no idea."

"I take care of Jane every day. She's upstairs in Room #3. Camp comes to see her faithfully and sleeps on the floor next to her bed. If it were up to me, I'd let her go peacefully. But he still loves her. He won't let go. He can't let go. He moved over to research hoping against all odds that he could find something that would one day bring her back. How do you close the door on hope when that kind of love stands in the way?"

Eileen broke down into tears as Raines got up and held her. They were both sobbing when Camp came in from the garage.

"So...you kept all the rats I brought out here. Raines, you've really got to see what Eileen did out here. She built a freaking lab around these little guys, probably equivalent to a Class 100 clean room. And they've multiplied."

Eileen dabbed her eyes with tissue.

"I wasn't an ICU nurse for nothing."

Camp walked over to the fireplace and threw another log on.

"Camp, you should've told me about Jane."

He stood silent, staring into the flames as they licked and roared around the new log.

"Is that why you brought the lab rats out here? For Jane?"

Eileen looked over and nodded.

RURAL PENNSYLVANIA

They had been driving on old Highway 30 for almost an hour. Raines loved the drive, especially through the old and quaint downtowns. She finally broke the silence.

"I love these old towns. So much character. Is this Lancaster?"

"Stonybrook. Lancaster is a metropolis compared to this. And even this town makes Bird-In-Hand look tiny."

"Have your parents always lived out here?"

"Mom and dad took over my grandparents' farm when dad got back from Korea. Dairy farmers don't get vacations so they've been there ever since."

"So, why did we have to bring Eileen's shotgun along?"

"Just in case."

"Just in case of what? Al-Qaeda?"

"Crows."

The rolling hills passed them by in silence. The snow was all but gone, yet there would always be more to fall.

"She's beautiful, Camp."

He said nothing.

They passed Smoketown Airport and slowed down for an Amish buggy. Raines waved to the children sitting next to their father.

The letters on the mailbox read SEABURY CAMPBELL, SR., which certainly meant to Raines that it must be a big deal for "Junior" to come home.

Three cars were parked along the road at the top of the driveway. Protest posters were still out and leaning against the cars as a few people stood chatting. Camp pulled up and got out.

"Folks, we're here from Washington, D.C. This is Lieutenant Colonel Leslie Raines, and she's an infectious disease expert for the Army. I suppose you're all wondering about the outbreak on this farm?"

The protesters looked puzzled. "What outbreak?" asked one middle-aged woman.

"These cows have developed a flesh-eating bacteria and, frankly, you're standing much too close. It's a slow horrific process as a patient's flesh starts peeling away from the bone. You may already be infected."

"What the hell?" said one young man has he gathered up his poster and opened his car door.

"If you get over to the county health department they may have some antibiotics left but I can't guarantee anything."

The protesters all started moving quickly.

"Oh wait a minute. You're all animal rights activists, correct?"

"Yes."

"Well, then I'm not sure you can take those antibiotics anyway. They've all been tested on animals. You probably can't take the medicine on 'moral' grounds. Oh geez, you could be in some real trouble."

Tires spun and the three cars left in a hurry. Camp quickly reached into the Defender and pulled out Eileen's shotgun. He fired twice into the open field across the street and started to get back into the Defender.

Camp's mother's face could be seen in the kitchen window, probably washing the breakfast dishes by hand as she had done for fifty years.

"Did you hear that? Sounded like a shotgun," the elder Seabury said as he got up from the table. They both looked out the window in time to see the tail lights from three cars as Camp put the shotgun back into his car.

"Seabury? Seabury!! He's here. Our son is here," his mother yelled, as she dried her hands on a dish towel.

Seabury adjusted his glasses as a smile covered his face. "I'll be damned. Will you look at those people go. He just shot some crows. Now that's my boy!!! He just shot the crows."

"Sweet Mother of Jesus, he brought a girl with him, too. Oh, Lord, I need to freshen up. Go out there and stall them."

Raines looked at Camp in complete astonishment as they drove up the long driveway.

"Flesh-eating cows? What the—Camp, do you mind telling me what that was all about?"

Camp smiled. "Just telling my daddy that I love him."

Seabury walked out the farmhouse door as Mrs. Campbell scurried up the stairs to brush her hair, powder and change out of her house dress.

Camp got out of the Defender and hurried over to his dad. The hug was genuine and sincere.

"Dad, I want you to meet Colonel Raines. She's Army."

Raines came around to the front of the vehicle and extended her hand. "Please call me Leslie, sir."

"Only if you don't call me 'sir.'"

"Deal. You have a beautiful farm here, Mr. Campbell. Camp has told me so much about it."

"Who? Oh, Seabury. Well, he used to love this place. Now I can't even get him to come back and visit anymore."

"Where's mom?"

"She had a wardrobe malfunction as soon as she saw Leslie in the car. She'll be right down."

Mrs. Campbell burst out of the door wearing one of her nicer dresses. Her hair was combed and fresh patches of rouge decorated her cheeks. She immediately went to Raines.

"Welcome. I'm Seabury's mother, Ruth. I'm so glad you came to visit."

Camp went up to his mother and picked her up and twirled her around.

"Hey, good looking. Did you miss me?"

"You look tired, son. Are you eating well?"

"Like a cow."

The elder Seabury cleared his throat. "Speaking of which, I have some bad news. Mira died last week."

Camp dropped his head a bit and smiled.

"Well, she certainly lived a long life. The old girl must've been twenty-five years old."

Raines seemed concerned. "Was Mira a member of your family?"

"Practically ran the barn, she did. Mira was the Holstein that Seabury rescued when he was only a boy."

"My first surgery."

"Well, let's get inside. Ruth just bought a new can of Folgers."

The four sat in the simple living room and sipped coffee. An old wooden Zenith TV console was in the center of the back wall surrounded by floorboard heaters. The vinyl covering was still on the two lampshades Ruth had purchased at K-Mart two years prior.

"Well, Leslie met Jane this week."

"How's she doing, son? Any changes?"

"No. I'm afraid not, mom."

"Well, we still pray for her every Sunday in the adult Sunday school class."

"Thanks."

"Eileen is quite a trooper, isn't she Leslie? That's what I call sisterly love."

"Eileen is wonderful. She's an incredible woman," said Raines.

"Seabury, after you called to say you were coming, I called Chip Smith. Hope you don't mind. He wanted to stop by and say hello."

"Fine. Did he ever hear from his dad or mom yet?"

"Not a peep from them. That's just not like old Harvey Smith either. Hell, he never even said good-bye to me either," said Sea Bee.

"It's only been a few months. Maybe they're too busy spending their millions in Costa Rica."

"Maybe."

The sound of an approaching truck cutting over the gravel driveway made them all get up and look out the living room window together. A visitor was a big deal in Bird-In-Hand, Pennsylvania.

It was Chip Smith in his brand new F-350 bought and paid for from his chicken inheritance.

"That's Chip? He's added a few pounds since high school, like maybe two hundred."

Chip opened the back kitchen door without knocking

and lumbered into the house. No need to knock when you're farm neighbors. Camp and Chip worked to catch up for the almost seventeen years since high school graduation.

"So, Chip, have you heard from Harvey yet?" Camp asked.

"Nope. Darndest thing, too. The new owners removed all of the chickens, just about 60,000 of them. They left about 200 or so behind and not a soul to tend to them. I go over and feed 'em every day, make sure they're cared for. But the property is vacant."

"How do you move 60,000 chickens?"

"Smoketown got a 747 awhile back in the middle of the night. Maybe they got first class tickets? You remember where our farm is, don't ya, Camp?"

"Miller Lane."

"It's only a mile or two from here. Mind taking a look?"

"You boys head on over while Leslie and I get some lunch going," said Ruth, already up and on her way to the kitchen.

"Don't make her butcher anything on the kitchen table, mom. She's recovering from some pretty serious injuries."

"Mind your own business, son, we'll get along just fine."

The adhesive letters on the mailbox still read HARVEY SMITH. Chip and Camp pulled up to the farmhouse in Chip's new Ford. There were no other cars. The place looked abandoned. The biometric key reader was hanging in shambles, probably from Chip's sledgehammer.

"You gotta see what they did in here first."

Chip led him into the house.

"Yikes, they gutted everything. No walls and steel I-bars holding up the second floor? Guess they didn't buy the place to live in it."

"Or to raise chickens. Let me show you the barns."

The barns were eerily empty, quiet and desolate. There was enough food left in the feed silos to feed those 60,000 chickens for another two months.

"I've got the leftover chickens back here in the old coop. Can't eat 'em. Don't know what the hell to do with 'em but can't just let 'em die either."

"You said your parents sent you a letter?"

"It was from Mildred. Mom sent one to me and one to my older brother. They wired us each $3 million and said they were off to Costa Rica."

"Had they ever talked about selling the farm to you before?"

"Sort of I guess. Dad said that if neither of us boys wanted the farm he was going to sell it. This whole region was turning into a vaccine research corridor. It was like another gold rush. Folks were selling, and corporations were buying left and right. Guess they stumbled across a quick deal or one stumbled across them."

"Any idea who bought it?"

"Well, I checked that out with the county office. Some company called DKW Limited with a post office box in New York City. That's all I know. So can you help me?"

"Find your parents?"

"No, with these chickens. Can you take a few of them off my hands? Maybe take some back to your parents' farm?"

The sun was just starting to set as Camp and Raines passed back through Stonybrook again, on their way back home to Lightner. The smell of chicken poop from ten little chattering chickens in the back of the Defender was more than either could handle. The windows were down, and the heater fan was on high.

"It smells like hot chicken shit in here. Can we turn the thermal oven down at least?" Raines asked, trying to control her laughter.

"It is not my fault."

"Eileen will be thrilled," Raines howled with laughter.

"What was I supposed to do when my dad refused to take them?"

"You're a good son…Junior."

29

A new car was in the parking lot as Camp and Raines pulled into Lightner.

"Guess she has some paying customers now," Camp said. "Would you mind holding some doors open while I move these chickens out back to the coop?"

"Sure you don't want them to just bunk up with your rats?"

When they entered the lodge a gentleman was sitting in one of the leather chairs in front of the fireplace, sipping tea and chatting with Eileen. He stood as they entered.

Camp and Raines were surprised.

"Special Agent Daniels, are you just randomly vacationing here in Gettysburg?"

"Good evening, Commander. Colonel, it's nice to see you back on your feet again."

"To what do we owe this friendly visit?" asked Camp, washing his hands at the kitchen sink.

"Actually, I'm here to see Colonel Raines. Something she wrote in her After Action Report."

"Was something wrong with my AAR?"

"Leslie, you sit. I need to go and feed the rats," Eileen said as she left.

Daniels was more than perplexed.

"Might as well feed the chickens while you're out there, too," Camp said as he winked at Eileen.

"Okay…"

She had no idea what he was talking about.

"You indicated in your AAR that you found documents in the ASP lab that appeared to be written in Russian."

"They were definitely written in Russian, but I have no idea if they came from Russia or one of the former Soviet bloc countries."

"Do you remember the business card we found in Algiers?"

"Hassina something if I recall."

"Exactly. Hassina al Batir works in the ECON section of U.S. Embassy Rabat. We caught up with her, and she told us about some brothers who wanted assistance funding a pharmaceutical company. She put them in touch with a company called Gospodstvo Ventures in Rabat."

"Russian?"

"Yes. Gospodstov sells itself as a venture capital funding group. Most of their work is legitimate, though shady, and typically focused on all things petroleum. The mastermind behind the company is a charming fellow by the name of Pavel Pahvchik. He is a Bratva, a brother of the *Russkaya Mafiya*."

"Do you think he funded ASP?" asked Camp.

"Don't know. And of course all the evidence was torched

along with a couple thousand dirty rats after we left and the drones moved in. Borysko and Fedir are still in Moscow. They're keeping a constant eye on Pahvchik but so far nothing."

"Got anything yet you can share?"

"Files? Not really. But they snapped a few photos of him at a bistro meeting back in January."

Daniels handed them a few photos.

"Who's the Asian guy with him?"

"Goes by Mr. Lee and works for some trading outfit in New York called DKW."

Camp looked closely at the photo again.

"I may know something about your Mr. Lee. Can I keep this?"

"What do you know?"

"There's an old high school friend of mine out in the Lancaster, Pennsylvania, area. His parents sold their chicken farm to a vaccine research firm out of New York. They go by the name of DKW Limited."

"Now that *is* interesting."

"That's not the half of it. They bought the family farm for $12 million. Parents wired each of the kids their 25percent, then they literally flew the chicken coop to Costa Rica."

"They've got good tastes."

"Except that they haven't been heard from since the sale went through. The new owners cleared out almost all of the 60,000 chickens and left town."

"Took them back to New York?"

"No idea. But now the farm is empty. The parents are AWOL, and the two sons have an extra $3 million each on their ATM cards."

"You said a vaccine research firm. Is that like a pharmaceutical company?"

Raines and Camp caught quick glances.

"Exactly like a pharmaceutical company," said Raines.

"Guess we need to look into DKW Limited in New York. Why do you want the photo, Camp?"

"I'd like to show it to my friend, snoop around a bit, and see if anybody remembers seeing this Mr. Lee fellow."

Daniels reached out and took the photo out of Camp's hand.

"Thanks for your time. We'll take it from here."

Daniels grabbed his bag and went to the door.

"Well that's a relief. I'm glad the Agency is on top of it. Guess you probably already know where their farm is and what my friend's name is. Tell him 'hey' for me."

Daniels stopped and paused. A sheepish smile broke across his face. He walked back and gave Camp the photo.

"Enlighten me, Commander."

"Harvey and Mildred Smith's place is on Miller Lane, Bird-In-Hand, Pennsylvania. Their son is Chip Smith. Petite fellow, drives a Hyundai and talks with a lisp."

Daniels nodded his head.

"Hope your recovery goes well, Colonel. Good night."

PENTAGON

The chairman of the Joint Chiefs asked Ferguson to take the call. He was tired of dealing with her.

"General Ferguson."

"General, Janis Vitter, at the CDC."

"Good morning, Dr. Vitter. How may I help you?"

"General, we have an emerging threat coming out of

Eastern China, specifically the Fujian Province in the south-eastern sector along the coast of the East China Sea."

"I presume a disease threat that CDC is tracking."

"Yes, but the implications for America are critical. After the Malak al-Maut outbreak everyone's on high alert. Sensitivities are heightened, and it wouldn't take much to trigger an all-out panic, both in terms of public health and agriculture."

"What's the problem?"

"Two thousand birds were culled from a farm in Fujian a few days ago. Birds on adjacent farms are also sick or dead. The Chinese Ministry of Health and the China CDC believe we have a new strain of HPAI H5N1."

"Forgive me, doctor, but I'll need a translation in peasant English, please."

"Avian influenza. Bird flu. Bird-to-human transmissions leading to clinically severe and potentially fatal human infections."

"I'm sorry to hear that. But after the recent H1N1 swine flu hysteria, I'm not sure anyone will take your sky-is-falling concerns very seriously. How can the military help you?"

"Well, we've isolated the virus and we need to get some strains to your research labs in Diego Garcia. We're concerned that with every generation of this virus the disease will continue to mutate. The vaccines we developed for the 2006 strain of avian influenza aren't touching it. As soon as the media catches wind, we'll have a pandemic of fear long before the highly pathogenic influenza A subtype H5N1 virus delivers a pandemic threat to our shores. We think millions of birds are about to die in the region. And speaking of wind and the migratory habits of these birds, we might see H5N1 in our jet streams within a month."

"Dr. Vitter, the president shut down the facility at Diego Garcia after the South Koreans delivered the vaccines and antibiotics. There are no more animal research facilities under American control. I suggest you contact Dokwang in Seoul."

"I'll do that. In the meantime, we have already arranged for the immediate transport of some of the infected birds. They are in quarantined containers but must be handled carefully and properly."

"Well, I wish you great luck with them."

"General, they are packed on one of your planes. CDC China made arrangements with the commanding general of the 8th United States Army in South Korea. Since this is a threat to national security, they sent the birds to Andrews Air Force Base and then on to Fort Detrick in Maryland."

Ferguson pounded his desk, a thump not lost on Vitter.

"Detrick no longer has an infectious disease research center, Dr. Vitter. As I said, all animal-based research in America and under American control is shut down for one year under the president's moratorium."

There was a long pause on the other end.

"Then I suggest you incinerate those birds immediately. May we send more to your commanding general in Seoul so that he can get them over to Dokwang?"

"I will contact them. Keep me posted if this thing gets out of control."

"Sir, that's why I'm calling you now. We know enough to know that 'this thing' is already out of control."

"I presume you briefed the White House?"

"Yes, and the chairman sent me to you."

"Wonderful."

30

The Dokwang research facility had taken delivery of their third set of infected birds from the Fujian Province. Command Sergeant Major Cummings from the 8th US Army was in no mood for another round of excuses.

"The CDC and the Pentagon need some guidance. Are you close to developing a vaccine? What are we dealing with here, folks?"

Mr. Lee was cautious.

"We've run all of this strain's genomic sequence data through the NIAID Microbial Sequencing Center at the Institute for Genomic Research in Rockville, Maryland. Unfortunately, there are no GenBank matches. This is something the world has never seen before."

Cummings was a typical CSM. "I don't care about that muckity-muck bullshit. When will you have a vaccine?"

"This is beyond our current capacity. We will continue to work on it but there can be no guarantees."

"Wait a minute. You solve a freaking Ebola outbreak in seventy-two hours, but you can't cure some sick geese, chickens and a few turkeys?"

"We're working on it, Sergeant Major."

GETTYSBURG

Camp was sound asleep on the floor at the foot of Jane's bed when his cell phone started to vibrate.

"What?"

"So that's how you greet your commanding officer now?

"I'm on leave, sir."

"Actually, your leave ended at 2400 hours last night. Now you're back on my clock. As promised, I'm calling to help you reassess your career."

"Let me save you some time, General Ferguson. I plan to drop my papers today. I'm resigning my commission."

"You're five years from your twenty, Captain. Are you sure you want to do that?"

"Sir, I'm—did you say Captain?"

"I'm pushing those papers across my desk, now pending, of course, the outcome of our conversation."

"Do I detect a quid pro quo in here, sir?"

"Camp, we've got an emerging situation with an H5N1 outbreak. On 1 March, China CDC culled 2,000 infected birds. That number has now reached 250,000 birds, and seven humans have died in rural provincial clinics. We've got reports of sick birds and sick people in Laos, Vietnam, and Thailand. CNN has the story in the cue now, and they've called for comment."

"And?"

"Well, we've assured them that American military epidemiologists and infectious disease experts are working on the virus at an undisclosed biomedical research facility."

"That was stupid. We're shut down."

"That's why I'm calling, Camp."

"Wait a minute. You want to throw H5N1 at me after you, the chairman and the president threw me and my team under the bus? You've got to be kidding."

"I wish I was."

"Hell, General, I wouldn't know where to start. I'm not in any mood to fly to East-freaking-China to scoop up dead birds. I just acquired ten chickens the other day, and they're already more than I can handle."

"There's no need for a China flight, Camp. We've got infected carcasses in isolation at Detrick and another flock of the walking-wounded en route from Andrews this morning. As you know, that's only thirty-six miles from Gettysburg."

Camp was silent.

"How is Jane anyways? Any changes?"

"No. Still the same."

"I'm sorry, Camp."

"Raines met her."

"Raines? She's with you?"

"She took her medical leave here in Gettysburg. Eileen has two patients now."

"Raines is an infectious disease expert."

"And she had a massive chest flail and nearly died. She's recuperating, sir."

Raines opened the door to number three and entered the bedroom as Camp lay talking to Ferguson on the floor beneath Jane's bed.

"I'm recuperated. What does he need?"

Ferguson heard her voice.

"Captain Campbell?"

"Yes, sir," Camp responded, with complete exasperation in his voice.

"Fort Detrick is all yours. Run the research any way you want to. The call is yours. No one from the Pentagon or Pennsylvania Avenue will interfere."

"You're desperate."

"You have no idea."

"You're working other options, I presume?"

"We've got Dokwang, our Malak al-Maut golden boys, working on it, but so far DKW has run into a dead end."

Camp jumped to his feet.

"Dokwang is DKW? Why the hell is it so hard for everybody in Washington to just talk to each other and connect the dots! All these damn little fiefdoms drive me nuts."

"Captain?"

"Raines and I are wheels up to Detrick. I'll keep you in the loop. Expect a call from Special Agent Daniels from the CIA."

The Lightner Farms animal research lab in Eileen's garage was active and running at full capacity. They estimated an ever-expanding colony of rats to be more than 400 and counting; ten chickens from Harvey Smith's farm were in the coop; the carcasses of four geese from Fujian Province, China were in Eileen's deep freezer; and three sick turkeys from Laos were lying down behind the shed.

"Move over, Captain Campbell. Now you're in my kitchen," said Raines, feeling feisty and ready to work.

"Actually, it's my garage but no point being picky now," said Eileen, as she watched the two get ready to work.

"Okay, first thing we've got to do is isolate the virus. Get one of the turkeys and let's do a blood draw. We're going to start growing this stuff up in a cell culture. Then we'll need to inject the cultured virus into a living system."

"Because?" asked Eileen.

"Because viral populations do not grow through cell division since they are a-cellular. So they use the vehicle and metabolism fuel of a living host to produce multiple copies of themselves and then they assemble in the cells of the living system. That, my dear friend, is just one of the reasons why we do animal research."

"I thought some research was done in test tubes?" asked Eileen.

"*In vitro* and *in vivo*."

"I love it when you speak Latin to me, Colonel," teased Camp.

"In what? You lost me, Leslie."

"*In vitro* literally means inside glass, like a test tube. *In vivo* is Latin for inside a living organism. We're going to grow the culture inside glass but then we must get it to grow inside an organism so that we can figure out how to treat it. Pathogenicity will require whole animals in order to see where the virus grows, how it grows in birds, and what organs it attaches to."

"What difference does it make?"

"Metabolism, blood flow, the energy of just water pushing through cells—it all has an impact on how a disease, bacteria, or in this case a virus, moves through a living organism. None of that occurs inside glass. Besides, if we cure cancer inside a test tube, does it really matter if it doesn't translate to a living system? Then, if we cure cancer in a mouse, does it really matter until it translates to people? It's all part of the research process. So, what are we going to use for the living host, Camp?"

"I believe we have ten chickens who have volunteered for duty. How long do you think it'll take to grow the culture?"

"You're talking about our Phase One trials. Well, we'll have a culture in two to ten days. But it takes six months from growing cultures in chicken eggs until a vaccine is potentially on the market."

"We've got the eggs from these few chickens but we don't have six months. If this avian strain has combined with an H3N2 human influenza strain co-infected and mutated to something we've never seen before, it'll kill millions."

"I'm working as fast as I can, Captain Campbell," Raines said, with a smile in her voice.

"How do you keep this sense of humor?" Eileen asked.

"I focus on what's possible, Eileen, and ignore everything that seems impossible. But we can't put this stuff in chicken eggs, at least, not yet, anyway. It'll simply kill the eggs. Know any good genetics guys, Captain?"

"I used to link up with some folks from Chiron and Aventis."

"Chiron's part of Novartis now, right?"

"I don't know. I think so."

"Well our only shot at this may be to develop a DNA-based vaccine. It's going to be much faster to produce than typical protein vaccines."

"What's the plan?"

"Once we have the virus isolated and grown, then we put it through a process known as reverse genetics technology. We need to engineer a modified strain of the virus that both grows in eggs and protects against the natural bird virus."

"Can you do that?"

"Some of it. But we'll need some help from your Chiron friends."

"Ferguson will get us whatever we need."

"DNA vaccines are still somewhat experimental. There are technical hurdles," said Raines. "That's why I think we need to do our research on parallel paths, both in glass and in organisms. There's no way that we can solve this influenza. But maybe we can hand off the baton in the first leg of the relay."

"I'm listening."

"We've got to find efficient ways of getting the DNA into human cells. Then we have to make sure the gene is expressed once it's inside the human cell. The DNA can't integrate into the genome or disrupt the other genes in the human clinical trial."

"Raines, we can't do this. We don't have the time. It's utterly im—"

"Don't say it. Focus only on the possible. If we can contribute 10 percent skill and find 90 percent luck, we'll have a vaccine in two months. We're only handing off a baton."

"That's what they were doing with vaccines for HIV, herpes and hepatitis, right?"

"And influenza. So call your Chiron, Novartis and Aventis guys. We're on the clock."

31

The President arrived in the Situational Room as Special Agents Daniels and Jackson put various photos up on the screen. The Joint Chiefs were assembled as well as General Ferguson, the head of Central Intelligence, the FDA administrator and Director Vitter from the CDC.

"Okay, Special Agent Daniels, what do you have for us?"

"Mr. President, we've uncovered what appears to be an extended circle of collaboration. There are three major players: Al-Qaeda in the Islamic Maghreb based in Algeria, a Russian mafia organization in Moscow, and a start-up pharmaceutical company in South Korea."

"Dokwang?"

"Yes, Mr. President. On 19 January 2009, forty Al-Qaeda operatives were killed by an outbreak of Black Plague in their hideout in the mountains of Tizi Ouzou Province. We believe they had finally learned how to weaponize the Black

Death bacteria at that point but were ill-equipped to protect themselves from it."

"They were capable of doing this research themselves?"

"No, Mr. President, we believe they turned to a venture capital funding shell the Russians had set up in Rabat, Morocco, called Gospodstov Ventures. This organization was pure Russkaya Mafiya. We don't believe this operation had state sanction or that the Russian government knew anything about it."

"Pure criminal intent to kill Americans?"

"Al-Qaeda wanted to kill Americans, Mr. President. Their only interest in the Russian mob was for funding and scientific help. Pavel Pahvchik is the head of the Bratva, the brotherhood in this organized crime syndicate. He provided the funding and probably the scientific expertise. I don't think he cared if he killed a few Americans, but his endgame was clearly pure financial profit."

"Though I'm sure he's heartbroken that innocent Americans were killed. Dokwang?"

"Yes, sir, Pahvchik's organization invested $75 million and bought a 49 percent share of Dokwang or DKW Limited. We believe that once they weaponized the Black Death that Pahvchik delivered the plague strands to Dokwang to develop both a vaccine and an antibiotic."

"So how did this Russian mobster get the rats to our shores?"

"Mr. President, we believe that Al-Qaeda activated its cells in Somalia and paid them to stop seven oceangoing vessels headed for America. Under the guise of being Somali pirates they ransacked the cabin crews, stole money and jewelry, and then let the crews go without hijacking the ships or demanding ransoms. We believe they dumped hundreds of infected rats on each ship, maybe thousands. The fleas did the rest of the work when the flea-infested ships got to port."

"And what about the Ebola?"

"Sir, we believe the Ebola was just a ruse designed to stir panic and terror. Although possible, we believe it was highly unlikely that they could mix an Ebola virus with a plague bacterium in the same rat and have it be a pathogen to humans. The rats were dirty, just not that dirty."

"Are you positive?"

"No, Mr. President."

"But we had thirty-nine monkeys die with Ebola at Gulf Shores. Al-Qaeda said they were their sentinels and our warning system."

"True. Ebola-Reston, such as we saw in a Virginia research lab several years ago, is uncommon but not unheard of. That strain of Ebola, however, was non-pathogenic to humans. The lab workers at Gulf Shores fell sick with fear, probably nothing more."

"So they sold us a crock of shit about Ebola and the entire country went hysterical."

"People were dying from the plague. We'd just been through the beef poisoning attack throughout the country. Lab animals had been, as they say, liberated and fear was at an all-time high. It all happened so quickly, and it uncaged a perfect bioterror storm."

"What about Dokwang?"

"We're not convinced they knew Al Qaeda was involved on the front end. They knew that they were dealing with the Russian mob, but we think the outbreak escalated from fear to deaths faster than they could have ever imagined. But they had been working on a vaccine and antibiotic for several months before the outbreak hit our shores. Sir, they essentially were part of a larger plot to send in the fire department long before the arson was even ignited."

"And the Russian?"

"He cashed in brilliantly when Dokwang's stock shot through the roof. There were no other options in the American research community, thanks to the moratorium on animal research. They were the only game in town, or at least the only ones who came to town with a viable answer within thirty-six hours."

"Arrests?"

"We have no jurisdiction, Mr. President. No Americans were involved in this to the best of our knowledge."

"Anything else?"

"No, Mr. President. We have one more loop to close with Captain Campbell, but other than that, our investigation is closed."

"Special Agents Daniels and Jackson, thank you for your fine work. If you'll excuse me I need to meet with the Secretary of State. I think it's time we speak to our South Korean, Russian and Algerian ambassadors."

The group rose to its feet as the president gathered up his files.

"We need to rescind the moratorium on the whole animal research thing," he said to his chief of staff.

"General Ferguson, I presume Captain Campbell's team is working on the latest crisis du jour?"

"Yes, Mr. President, they're in the, ah, lab, as we speak."

32

Raines suited up and entered Eileen's garage lab. She was hoping to find a viable culture. Other than the burrowing sounds of rats, the lab was unusually quiet.

She walked out to the chicken coop. All remaining chickens were dead.

Back inside the lab she found the chicken that had been injected with the blood from the infected turkey. It was dead as well.

"Get out here quickly," she said, closing her cell phone frantically.

Camp arrived out of breath a few minutes later. She gave him the quick tour.

"What do you think?" she asked.

"It's not what died; it's what didn't. The rats. Can we grow the virus in them just like we would a human breast cancer tumor? We can grow a vaccine, a treatment that stems the tide for the infection in them. They might be the only subjects we have left."

The sound of a car pulling into the driveway pulled Camp's attention away from virology and vaccine developments. Two men were getting out of the car. They looked familiar.

"Carry on, Colonel."

"Aye-aye, Captain. But you'll need to incinerate some birds when you're back."

Camp walked out to the car. The morning sun didn't have enough juice to illuminate the images well enough, but his hearing was just fine. He recognized the Ukrainian accents.

"Congratulations, Captain Campbell. We understand you have been promoted."

"Borysko, Fedir, what brings my two favorite Berkut Golden Eagles to rural Pennsylvania? Or were you just in the neighborhood looking for a good bowl of borscht?"

"Agent Daniels asked us to brief you about your friend, Chip Smith."

"Is he okay?"

"He's fine. We used an aerial detective and took a thorough look at his father's farm, including the use of hyperspectral imaging," said Borysko.

The technique analyzes a range of visible and infrared wavelengths as its scans terrain from the air. Cameras mounted on a helicopter detect variations in the intensity of light of various wavelengths reflected by vegetation on the ground. The precise pattern of intensities has been found to reflect changes caused by nutrients released into the soil as bodies decompose. "When searching for clandestine graves, we traditionally look for signs of disturbance on the ground or dig small test trenches to identify the most likely area. The images showed some interesting objects buried in the garbage pile behind one of the barns. A quick excavation and, unfortunately, we discovered the bodies of Harvey and Mildred Smith. I'm sorry."

Borysko dropped his head. He did not enjoy bringing bad news to a colleague in arms.

"How'd they die?" asked Camp after a lengthy pause.

"The lady was strangled. Mr. Smith's throat was slashed from ear to ear. The frozen ground kept their bodies fairly well-preserved, but the medical examiner will make the final ruling on the causes of death."

"So no Costa Rica."

"I'm sorry. The crime was committed on American soil. We've turned it over to the FBI, and I'm sure they will bring whoever did this to justice."

"Right. I'm sure."

SEOUL, SOUTH KOREA

Tae Sook Yoo was frantic. His executive secretary was on the telephone talking to Dokwang's director of research at the Ulsan facility down on the coast of the Sea of Japan.

"Mr. Yoo must speak with Mr. Lee immediately. This is urgent."

Two attorneys entered the room as she worked the phone.

"It is time. Everyone is assembled in the conference room."

Tae Sook Yoo stood up from his desk and looked out the window over Seoul. He could see the taxicabs thirty-six floors below and wished he was in one of them and on his way to the airport.

His secretary hung up the telephone. Yoo looked at her waiting for an explanation.

"Mr. Lee knows about this meeting. But they believe he has left the country."

The elevator lobby inside Dokwang, Ltd. was buzzing with activity. A three-person team from the KCIA, Korean Central Intelligence Agency, arrived and was ushered down to the conference room where the chief of NIS, the National Intelligence Service, was already seated with two members of the FBI and an American diplomat from the U.S. Embassy in Seoul, Korea.

Tae Sook Yoo and his two attorneys stepped into the conference room after all had been seated.

For the next hour, the FBI, KCIA, and the NIS laid out their case against Dokwang. Tae Sook Yoo sat at the table stoically and expressionless until Mr. Lee's name was brought up.

"Finally, we have a file in this envelope provided to us by Mr. Lee," said the chief of the Korean National Intelligence Service as he pulled out an envelope and placed it on the table in front of an FBI agent. "In this file, Mr. Lee explains the entire plot. He has provided us with emails and notes from more than seventeen conversations with you where he asked you repeatedly to stop working with Pavel Pahvchik. In fact, the FBI has also provided us with photos of Mr. Lee, who traveled to Moscow in order to persuade Pahvchik to end the plan."

The chief let Tae Sook Yoo see a copy of the photo of Mr. Lee and Pahvchik at the Pushkin café in Moscow.

"But Mr. Lee says that you told him he would be terminated if he did not comply with your wishes. Now this is only an investigation Mr. Yoo. You have not been charged with any crimes yet. But we need to hear your side of the story."

Tae Sook Yoo's eyes were fixed straight ahead. His face was visibly red as anger overcame him.

"Do you wish to add anything to our investigation?"

One of his attorneys spoke first.

"If any criminal charges are filed, we will defend Dok-wang at the appropriate time."

The room was silent. Everyone waited for the next move.

"I have a file, too, a file on Mr. Lee."

Tae Sook Yoo stood and his attorneys stood with him. They whispered in his ear.

"Sit. I will bring it so the entire truth can be known."

The attorneys sat down as Tae Sook Yoo left the conference room. The FBI agent took the envelope from the table and opened the clasp. The envelope was empty. There was no file inside. They were fishing without any real bait as they tried to lure Yoo in.

Yoo entered his office and closed the door. On the credenza behind his desk he allowed himself a slight moment of reflection as he looked at the photos of his parents, his wife, and his only son.

He looked out the window again then pulled the deep file drawer at his desk out just a few inches as he stepped up onto his desk.

The silence in the conference room full of international investigators was broken with the sound of shattering glass. Tae Sook Yoo's secretary ran into his office and let out a blood curdling scream as she saw people gathering around Yoo's body on the sidewalk, thirty-six floors below.

ATLANTA

Dr. Janis Vitter finished her briefing at 1600 Clifton Road. The H5N1 virus was spreading at an alarming pace. Though accurate counts were difficult to come by, authorities believed that more than 2 million birds had already been culled worldwide, the latest being poultry farms in Turkey and Israel.

The World Health Organization reported that out of the 317 confirmed human cases, there had been more than 270 fatalities. The virus was seriously lethal to humans.

Colonel Raines shared her findings from the Lightner Farms lab. She reported that with the help of some independent geneticists they had developed a vaccine prototype that provoked the human body to produce an immunological response to the avian influenza strain that was circulating the globe.

"Are you suggesting that you've already put your vaccine through human clinical trials, beyond animal trials?" asked the head of the FDA.

"No, we are only trying to pass the baton. We had a very limited human clinical trial with four of us who volunteered at Lightner Farms. In each one of us we successfully measured an immunological response. The vaccine prototype was both safe and efficacious, at least for the four of us. Obviously, it is hardly scientific. No double-blinds and no placebos. Given the circumstances, it's the best we could do."

General Ferguson looked over at Camp. The general was a bit surprised. "You say four of you took the prototype?"

"Yes, sir," Raines said. "Clearly, we have no capacity to manufacture the vaccine. But given the urgency of the situation, the emerging threat of a worldwide pandemic capable of killing millions and millions of people within twelve months, I'm sure you can take our findings and work with industry to produce a DNA vaccine expeditiously."

"Well, you've all read the reports from our analysts and scientists here at the CDC. There is general concurrence that this is exactly the vaccine we need," said Director Vitter.

General Ferguson waited in the hallway for Raines and Camp.

"Colonel Raines, Captain Campbell, on behalf of the chairman, I want to extend our sincere appreciation for a job well-done."

"Thank you, sir."

"Captain, I have approved your leave request. Given the situation, please report to the Pentagon in nine days where we'll discuss your next assignment. Colonel Raines, I've transferred you back to San Antonio according to your request."

"Sir, I'm going to take nine days of leave as well before I report, with your permission of course."

"Well, what a timing coincidence between the two of you. Pleasant journeys."

33

GETTYSBURG

Camp carried two small duffel bags down to the front door as Eileen handed Raines fresh blueberry muffins right out of the oven and wrapped in aluminum foil to keep them warm.

"It's just a little something to munch on for the drive to the airport in Philadelphia."

"Thank you, Eileen."

"Will you be coming back after the trip, Leslie?"

"Sometime, eventually, but I plan to fly back directly to San Antonio from there."

"Well, Godspeed, in all you do. I'll miss you."

The two exchanged a long embrace.

"Thank you for the use of your garage," Raines said laughing.

"I'll never look at it the same way again, that's for sure."

After a few more farewells they loaded up the Defender and left for the airport.

SAN JOSE, COSTA RICA

They had no checked baggage so Camp and Raines walked directly outside into the evening warmth and humidity of San Jose's Juan Santa Maria International Airport. They jumped on the Alamo Rental Car shuttle bus where they picked up their Chevy Cobalt.

Camp plugged in the GPS coordinates for Calle 30, Avenida 2 y 4 and sat back to enjoy the drive to the Hotel Grano de Oro just off of Paseo Colon, the central road in San Jose.

A young man greeted their car out front as they walked into the ornate lobby to register.

"Good evening and welcome to the Hotel Grano de Oro. Is this your first time to visit us?"

Raines spoke up as Camp reached for his wallet.

"First time to Costa Rica," she said.

"Marvelous. Disfrute de sus vacaciones."

"Two standard rooms under the last name Campbell."

The smile on the face of Raines strained ever so slightly as the clerk pulled up their reservations.

"Yes, indeed. Please, may I recommend our restaurant for dinner this evening after what I presume was a long flight? Our restaurant Grano de Oro merges Costa Rican tropical with European cuisine under the expertise of our French chef Francois Canal. The gazpacho, tartar de salmon and paté de la casa are simply magnificent."

Camp looked at Raines, who was steadfastly checking out the adjacent restaurant.

"Yes, we'd love to. Perhaps a shower first and then dinner," Camp said as he handed Raines her room key.

An old, red-cherry staircase led to the second floor of the forty-room, Victorian mansion where their rooms were lo-

cated at the end of the hall. The hallways were lined with period photographs and ornate art displayed in the nooks and
crannies like a living museum. The rooms were tiny, with
standard accommodations and wrought iron headboards
over queen mattresses.

Dinner was delightful, as was the bottle of Malbec Finca
Noceti from Argentina.

"So where are you taking me tomorrow, sailor?"

"No plans. No reservations other than tonight. Thought
I'd cash in my traveler's checks at a local bank tomorrow and
we'd take it from there."

The morning sun raised the temperature to a perfect 78
degrees Fahrenheit. May is traditionally the start of the rainy
season in Costa Rica, and the gathering clouds suggested
the travel warnings were probably accurate. Even rainy days
produced five solid hours of sunshine. The rain was more
like Mother Nature's morning drink.

Camp drove the Chevy down several streets. Nothing was
plugged into the GPS as he had no idea where he might find
a bank. Finally he spotted the El Banco Credito Agricola at
Avenida 4.

"Why don't you stay out here and enjoy the sunshine
while it lasts. I'll only be a few minutes."

Raines kicked back in the seat and lowered her window as
Camp went into the bank.

The teller quickly converted $2,000 of American Express
Traveler's Cheques into one million Costa Rican colones.

"Is there anyone here I could speak to about places to visit
in Costa Rica? I'm looking for some ideas."

The teller struggled with her English but sent Camp over
to the new accounts manager.

Raines closed her eyes and let the warm sunshine help

heal her from an ordeal that seemed to visit her anew every night about an hour or so after she fell asleep. She was waking up with the same dream, the same deep thud in her chest, and the sounds of ribs cracking and desperately struggling to breathe until she finally awoke in a sheer panic, completely out of breath.

The driver's door opened and Camp returned with a huge smile.

"Well, Raines, I'm finally a millionaire. One million colones. We struck it big."

"You were gone long enough. I'm surprised you didn't rob the joint and get us ten million."

Camp entered some coordinates into the GPS and pulled away from the curb.

"I guess you know where we're going now."

"I had a nice conversation with one of the managers. She gave me a great recommendation, a 'can't miss' resort on the ocean."

"So where is it? Or is that a surprise?"

"No surprises. It's about a four-hour drive from here. She said Playa del Coco is a pretty little fishing and tourist village where you can find supermarkets, banks, pharmacies, restaurants, stores, bars, nightlife and more."

"Playa del Coco sounds a bit like Playa del Ebola, if you ask me."

"Hadn't thought of it that way," Camp said, laughing as he pulled his Oakleys down over his eyes. "She recommends a four-star resort about five-minutes past Playa del Coco called the Ocotal Beach Resort. It's in Playa Ocotal, Guanacaste Province, on the Northern Pacific coast of Costa Rica."

"Sounds wonderful."

"Here, she gave me a brochure for it."

"She had brochures at the bank?"

"Yep, tourism is everyone's business in Costa Rica."

Raines leafed through the brochure. It was breathtaking. She read it out loud.

"Ocotal is a four-star beachfront resort, a leader among Costa Rica's hotels and resorts, known for its outstanding style, comfort, and service. The property lies along the country's beautiful Northern Pacific coastline and yields breathtaking panoramic views of the Papagayo Gulf,'" she read.

"Now that's what I'm talking about."

"It says Ocotal offers an extensive variety of services, including romantic honeymoon packages, weddings, the best scuba diving in Costa Rica, sport fishing, exciting adventure tours, snorkeling trips, superb cuisine, and comfortable rooms, all set against captivating tropical scenery."

"Romantic honeymoon packages, eh? Did you come here for your honeymoon, Raines?"

She dropped the brochure for a second as the irritation shot through her like a poisoned dart.

"Yes, as a matter of fact, Charlie and I did. We got two rooms with standard beds."

Camp felt the blow to his ego in his gut. Point awarded to Raines.

"No, we did not honeymoon in Costa Rica."

"So his name was Charlie, your ex-husband?"

"Yep."

"That's it? Just 'yep'?"

"What do you want to know, Camp? There's not much to tell."

"How'd you meet? How long were you married? You know, the basic 411."

"Well, after I graduated from Auburn University I was

branch chief at the Navy's marine animal mammal program in Key West, then on to the same assignment at Kaneohe Marine Corps Air Base in Hawaii. Charlie was a Marine."

"Ouch, bad combination from the jump."

"We got married in Hawaii, honeymooned in Hawaii, and thought we could stay on the islands for a few years together and then figure things out."

"And?"

"And he got orders for advanced officer combat leadership school at 29 Palms in California about the same time I was admitted into the Army's Combined Laboratory Animal Residency Program in Maryland. When I offered to reject the assignment and quit the Army to be with him, he told me I should pursue my dreams and that we should take a long look at our marriage."

"Divorce? Were you having problems?"

"Not that I was aware of. He said it was a 'fun ride' and going our separate ways would be best for both of us."

Camp was silent as Raines watched everything but looked at nothing as the Costa Rican countryside passed by.

"*I* thought we were in love. *He* thought I was a Harley, a nice ride. He never thought twice about me after we left the lawyer's office. I cried for six years."

"I'm sorry, Raines."

"After my residency I served as department head at the Naval Medical Research Institute in Bethesda, got my board certification in veterinary preventive medicine and laboratory animal medicine. Blah, blah, blah. You know the rest."

Raines picked up the brochure again, hoping to change the subject.

"Ready for some education?"

"Hit me."

"Costa Rica is bordered by the North Pacific Ocean to the west and the Caribbean Sea to the east. The country was given its name by Christopher Columbus in 1502, who believed it to be abundant in gold. He proclaimed it 'Costa Rica' or the 'Rich Coast.'"

"That boy got around."

"Costa Rica is one of the biologically wealthiest countries in the world, boasting twenty-five national parks, eight biological reserves, forty-nine national wildlife refuges, eleven forest reserves, thirty-one protected areas, fourteen wetlands, two absolute natural reserves and two other protected wildlife areas. It is also home to some 9,000 different kinds of flowering plants, including more than 1,300 species of orchids."

"It is beautiful. We earned this, Raines. We earned some downtime away from cell phones, outbreaks, pandemics and General Ferguson."

Before she could answer the sky opened up like a hydropower dam. The rain hit the windshield with force as steam started to rise from the pavement.

34

Camp knocked on the door to her bungalow hotel room. She clearly had not been up yet.

"So, I thought vacation meant we could sleep in as long as we wanted to?" she said after finally unbolting the lock and opening the door. Camp could see that she was only wearing a man's buttoned-down white dress shirt for sleeping attire.

"Come on, woman, I've already been out for a six-mile run. Get yourself dressed and meet me down at the K-Lamar beach bar for coffee. It's right next to the dive shop and swimming pool."

Raines rolled her eyes in playful disgust and closed the door to her bungalow.

Camp pulled a chair out from the table and positioned it for maximum sun exposure. He pulled off his gray t-shirt and sunned himself in his khakis and flip-flops as the waiter brought him coffee. Camp talked his ear off and asked him countless questions about the resort, Costa Rica, the beach, the little town of Playa del Coco and the international clientele that visits.

The waiter's eyes were distracted as she approached. Camp flipped up his Oakleys as her long legs walked up and sat down. She was stunning in her two-piece white bikini. The flowing white shirt was unbuttoned now and covered her top but couldn't hide a fresh scar on the right side of her chest.

"Colonel, you look, ah, different."

She ignored him.

"May I have some hot tea, please? A splash of milk and a dash of sugar?"

The waiter retreated but stole another look over his shoulder as he walked away.

"You said I should change and we're at a beach, so what did you expect?"

"I don't know if we should push that old, punctured lung with any scuba diving yet, but do you think you're up for snorkeling after the rain?"

"I'd love to."

"The waiter was telling me about all of the cool things to do around here."

"You sure have turned into Mister Chatty Cathy since we got to Costa Rica. Since when do you strike up lengthy conversations with complete strangers? The first three months I knew you the most I could get out of you was mono-syllabic grunts. Now you're auditioning for the Travel Channel."

"It's vacation, Raines, I'm just trying to unwind."

The waiter served her tea as she inhaled the fresh air of the sea.

"He said we should check out the Father Rooster Bar and Grill tonight."

"Who?"

"The waiter. Said it's an old farmhouse turned into a bar, where tourists and residents from Ocotal Beach meet for a very relaxed beach atmosphere and some night life, excellent food, great music, even dancing."

"Sounds great. Oh what, oh what, oh what, pray tell does an Army girl wear when she's clubbing at Father Rooster's?"

"I think you'd be a hit in exactly that."

The rains came on schedule and departed just before three in the afternoon. Camp and Raines enjoyed a few hours of snorkeling before they met at six in the lobby for the quick walk down the sandy beach to Father Rooster's.

They sat at the bar in tall bamboo bar chairs sipping frozen margaritas. Two television sets were tuned to ESPN and CNN respectively. A live, four-person Latin music band, called the Coco Locos, were playing salsa and meringue in one corner of the dance floor. The bartender said the crowd would get larger closer to eight o'clock.

The waiter who had served Camp and Raines in the morning was now running cocktails to the guests seated at the outside tables. He caught Camp's eye, smiled and nodded out towards one of the isolated beach chairs.

Camp looked out and saw one single chair beneath an umbrella table. It was not too far away from an outcropping of huge rocks. It looked like a great place for diving but instant peril for any boats.

"Geez, I left my wallet back in the safety deposit box in my room. I never got it out after we finished snorkeling. Are you good for a few minutes here by yourself?"

"As long as you don't stick me with the tab because I plan to order ten of these drinks tonight, dance until dawn, then sleep until noon."

"Well, then, I won't be long."

Camp walked out of Father Rooster's where the waiter handed him a tray, a fresh Mai Tai cocktail, and put a white service napkin over his forearm.

He looked very official.

He handed the waiter a $50 tip and assured him that his old friend would be thrilled to see him again.

As he walked through the sand holding the drink tray slightly above his shoulder with his right hand, he gently padded his pockets to make sure everything was there.

Camp sat the drink down on the umbrella table. The gentleman never acknowledged his presence.

Camp looked back at Father Rooster's which was almost entirely out of sight hidden behind beach tents and other large rocks on the sand.

Camp stepped to the side and followed through with a quick punch to the man's temple. The man was dazed but not knocked out. With two swift movements he removed nylon rope from his pants pocket and wrapped it around the man's chest before he could respond. The napkin was quickly forced into his gaping mouth just before he started to yell.

Camp knelt down in front of him.

"So you must be old Harvey Smith. What a pleasure it is to finally meet you."

The man started to struggle. Anguish and fear screamed from his eyes.

"I had heard from my parents that you and Mildred sold your farm, cashed out, and retired here in Costa Rica. The good folks at El Banco Credito Agricola in San Jose were kind enough to tell me that you were withdrawing your money at their branch down here in Playa del Coco. And the waiter here at Father Rooster's wants you to know that he has enjoyed serving you your Mai Tais every night before sunset. But he says you're a lousy tipper."

The man's eyes darted from side to side. He was panicked and was looking for help from any beachcombers that might be passing by.

"But now that I get a real good look at you, I'm not so sure you're Harvey Smith after all. In fact, you look a bit more Asian than old Harvey did. Let me guess. You're Korean?"

The man's breathing was rapid and frenzied.

"If I didn't know better I'd bet you were Mr. Lee from Dokwang, Ltd. Tae Sook Yoo and all of your old buddies from Pahvchik's Bratva wanted me to say 'hello' to you if our paths ever crossed."

Camp reached into his pocket and pulled out a knife. The man's eyes focused on the shining steel blade that sparkled against the setting sun over the Pacific.

"Funny thing, Mr. Lee, but after you bought Harvey's farm, he bought the farm, too. They found him and Mrs. Smith buried in the garbage dump. Poor Harvey's throat was slashed ear-to-ear, probably with a blade like this."

Camp stood up and walked behind Mr. Lee. He put his left hand on Lee's shoulder and held the knife under his chin so Lee could feel the cold steel.

"But I'm not here for Harvey Smith. I'm here for Kentucky. He was right. I didn't have the stomach for killing so I spent all my time trying to save people instead. I got the medal, but he was the brave one, not me. He died a horrible, painful, lonely death, Mr. Lee. I'll bet you didn't even know that you killed Kentucky, too. But I want you to think about that as you look out over the ocean."

Camp reached around under Lee's chin and pressed the blade into the skin beneath Lee's left ear. He felt a trickle of blood over his hand.

"Gentle at first, Mr. Lee, I want this to last so you can enjoy every minute of it."

Suddenly, a strong hand clamped fiercely onto Camp's forearm above the hand that was holding the blade. Three sections of the beach sand next to the rolling surf erupted with volcanic speed as three men lunged toward him. Three more divers emerged from various points in and around the rocks.

The voice was familiar.

"Thank you, Captain. We'll take it from here."

The knife was removed from his hand before Camp ever realized what had happened.

"Worm?"

The DEVGRU team removed Lee from the beach with lightning speed and into a submersible raft before Camp could even comprehend what had happened.

"Special Agent Daniels said you'd find Lee. We're much obliged."

Worm pointed back to the beach. Camp turned around in time to see Daniels nod and walk away. By the time Camp turned back, Worm and the team were out to sea and gone.

Raines was on her second frozen margarita when Camp sat down next to her.

"Geez, sailor, you cut yourself."

Camp looked down at the blood on the backside of his hand.

"Yeah, a jagged edge inside the safety deposit box. But I got my wallet," he said as he dipped his finger into his Margarita and washed the blood off his hand.

"Good, because I'm getting hungry."

The bartender brought Camp another drink. Raines could see he was upset but didn't want to push it. The Coco Locos were on a break so they watched CNN.

A feature story was being aired from Southern California.

"The Stadtmueller family adopted this rat from the Newport Bay Spinal Cord Research Center shortly after the scandal broke," the reporter said. "You may remember that this is the same rat whose spinal cord was snipped by the late scientist, Dr. Erol Meisberger."

A little boy named James watched the rat play on his kitchen table.

"Beauregard loves to chase his food when I roll it down his cage. Sometimes he'll play with this red ball, too," said James.

"Can I hold him?" the reporter asked.

"Sure, he loves to be held."

The reporter picked up Beauregard and held him up to the camera then put him down as he scampered around the table. James' mother was next.

"Families all over America should try to adopt these animals that have been tortured and abused in these cruel laboratories. As you can see, Beauregard is well-adjusted and makes a fine pet."

"Mrs. Stadtmueller, this is the same rat that was paralyzed in an experiment, correct? They snipped his spine and then injected him with stem cells?"

"Horrific. How we, as a civilized society, could have allowed animal experimentation to happen like this is beyond me."

"And now this rat is walking?"

"He can even run. He's normal again," interrupted little James with great pride and excitement.

The reporter turned to the camera.

"If you'd like to adopt some of these little guys, or other animals there's an animal adoption agency in just about every county. We were horrified to hear what scientists did to this rat, now we have to wonder if there may be hope for the millions of people with spinal cord injuries. For CNN Special Features, I'm Katie Thompson."

The Coco Locos returned to their instruments and started a slow ballad with a romantic Latin flare.

Raines reached out and grabbed his hand.

"Come on, sailor, this may be your last chance to dance with me tonight. Other men will be lining up shortly."

Raines pulled on a resistant hand and finally dragged a half-smiling Camp to the middle of the floor. They were the only couple dancing.

The hand that only minutes before had held a knife to the throat of another was now draped gently around her back as he held her right hand softly in his.

"That's all I was hoping for, Leslie. To keep Jane alive long enough to see what might happen, to see what breakthrough might be discovered."

"Like Beauregard?" she asked, softly nodding towards the TV in the bar.

"Sure. But how many millions of people just missed the fact that Beauregard is walking again? It worked. The animal research worked, and now the scientist is dead. In my heart of hearts, I truly believe there are cures and treatments out there. We've only begun to uncover the hidden mysteries of disease."

"Fleas and rats can lead us to what's possible, Camp, for both good and evil."

As they danced, Camp pulled closer and looked tenderly into her eyes.

"I guess it's time, isn't it, Les? Time I finally let her go and stop trying to save her."

Camp let go of Leslie's hand and wrapped his arms around her. He held her tightly and passionately. She could feel his tears pouring down her back as the sun finally fell below the horizon on Ocotal Beach.

EPILOGUE

ON JANUARY 20, 2009 Barack Obama was sworn in as the 44th President of the United States. Transition teams, White House movers and decorators were busy in the days leading up to the final transition between President George W. Bush and then President-elect Obama.

Some would say that the entire world was focused on the peaceful transition of power in Washington, DC. Competing for headlines in the newspapers of the world was next to impossible.

But on January 19, 2009 a few news outlets ran an obscure story that never gained much traction in the United States. It was the last full day of the Bush administration. The *Telegraph* headline in London read: *The Black Death has reportedly killed at least forty al-Qaeda operatives in North Africa.* The *Sun*'s headline stated, *Deadliest Weapon So Far...the Plague*, and then when on to lament that anti-terror bosses would be happy because it killed the terrorists themselves. The Homeland Security Newswire went deeper:

Peter Goodspeed writes in the National Post *that the very day Barack Obama was sworn in as president, warning Americans "our nation is at war against a far-reaching network of violence and hatred," there were reports an al-Qaeda affiliate recently abandoned a training camp in Algeria after forty terrorists died from being exposed to the plague during a biological weapons test. The report, which first surfaced in the British tabloid* The Sun, *says members of al-Qaeda in the Land of the Maghreb (AQLIM) hurriedly abandoned their cave hideouts in Tizi Ouzou province, 150 kilometres east of the Algerian capital Algiers, after being exposed to plague bacteria.*

The Homeland Security Newswire wrote:

The newspaper (The Sun) said they apparently became infected while experimenting with biological weapons. Algerian security forces discovered the body of a dead terrorist alongside a road near the abandoned hideout.

U.S. intelligence officials, speaking anonymously with Eli Lake of the Washington Times on Tuesday, could only confirm the sudden base closure after an unconventional weapons test went wrong. The officials said they intercepted an urgent communication in early January between the AQLIM leadership and al-Qaeda's top leaders in the tribal region of Pakistan. The Algerian terrorists said they were abandoning and sealing off a training area after a leak of a chemical or biological substance.

AQLIM, once known as the Salfist Group of Call & Combat, is one of the most radical and violent Islamist groups operating in North Africa. It has ties to Moroccan terrorists who carried out the 2004 Madrid train bombings and bombed the UN headquarters in Algiers in 2007, killing forty-one people.

Plague comes in two types of plague. Bubonic plague, which is spread by bites from infected rat fleas, killed a third of Europe's population in the fourteenth century but can now be treated with antibiotics. Pneumonic plague is less common but more deadly. It is spread, like the flu, by airborne bacteria, and can be inhaled and transmitted between humans without the involvement of animals or fleas.

Goodspeed reports that for years, U.S. Defense Department officials have warned al-Qaeda operatives have been actively pursuing sophisticated biological weapons research.

What do government intelligence agencies choose to tell the people? And what do they decide to keep classified?

And on the day before Barack Obama was sworn in as the 44th President—as the world watched and waited for hope and change—what was perfected in the remote cave hideouts in Tizi Ouzou province, 150 kilometers east of the Algerian capital Algiers?

What was uncaged?

GLOSSARY

AHF	American Humane Fund (fictitious)
ALF	Animal Liberation Front
AQLIM	Al-Qaeda in the Land of the Islamic Maghreb
ASP	Aden Sea Pharmaceuticals
BDU	Battle Dress Uniform
BIOT	British Indian Ocean Territory
CDC	Centers for Disease Control
CMO	Collection Management Officers
DARPA	Defense Advanced Research Projects Agency
DEVGRU	U.S. Navy's Naval Special Warfare Development Group (SEAL Team SIX)
DFAC	Dining Facility
DIC	Disseminated intravascular coagulation
DKW	Dokwang Pharmaceuticals, Ltd (fictitious)
DRS	Departement du Renseignement et de la Securite, Algerian Secret Police

GAPA	Great Ape Protection Act
HFV	Hemorrhagic fever virus
HUMINT	Human Intelligence
H5N1	Influenza A subtype (bird flu)
IED	Improvised Explosive Device
IG	Inspector General
LCAC	Landing Craft Air Cushion
NCS	National Clandestine Service
NIAID	National Institute of Allergy and Infectious Diseases
NIBC	National Interagency BioDefense Campus
NIH	National Institutes of Health
NMT	No More Talking (fictitious)
OMON	Special Purpose Militsiia (Police) Detachment, Ukraine
PCRM	Physicians Committee for Responsible Medicine
REBOV	Reston Ebola Virus
SAS	Special Activities Staff from the CIA
SEAL	Special Operations Forces of the Navy on SEa Air and Land
SECDEF	Secretary of Defense
SIV	Primate version of HIV
SPEC OPS	Special Operations
TOC	Tactical Operations Center
USUHS	Uniformed Services University of the Health Sciences
VLCC	Very Large Crude Carrier ship
XO	Executive Officer

ACKNOWLEDGEMENTS

I'M NEITHER A scientist nor a soldier. As such, I depended heavily on those who are both for subject matter expertise. Everything contained within this work of fiction had to be plausible, if not believable. I'm grateful for the scientific contributions from Michael Conn, Dennis Stark and Mike Streicker. I offer my sincere thanks to my DPS partner and good friend Kent Politsch for his unwavering encouragement to "just write" and to Rebekah Lovorn and Vickie Collins for early draft critiques. Also, I offer many thanks to my staff, colleagues and friends including Nahla al Bassam, Liz Hodge, Cherie Proctor, Michael Stebbins and Misty Ray.

I'm indebted to Frankie Trull for championing the mission of biomedical research for more than thirty years that has allowed researchers to pursue breakthroughs and cures for modern health. Frankie, you have been an incredible friend, mentor and boss.

My life was changed by Col. David W. Sutherland and the U.S. Army's 3rd Brigade Combat Team, 1st Cavalry

Division "Greywolf," for protecting my rear-end and for allowing me to serve beside you during the surge in Operation Iraqi Freedom. I will never forget the sacrifice of SSG Daniel Wagoner and the 109 others who made no greater sacrifice during the deployment.

I consider it an honor and a privilege to serve with America's finest. Many thanks to my friend General David Petraeus who invited me to be part of the civilian surge in Afghanistan for the first six months of 2011 where I filmed KEYSA KAWEL with my new Pashtun friends and trained Public Affairs Officers for the Afghan National Army.

I give my love and appreciation to my wife Debra and my sons Andrew, Ian and Oliver for allowing the old man to keep playing in his sandbox of dreams.

I am proud to note that it was the DEVGRU team that flew through the night and entered a compound in Abbottabad, Pakistan and removed Osama Bin Laden from the FBI's Most Wanted list early in the morning on 2 May 2011.

And finally, to Worm; forgive me for asking who you worked for when we were waiting for our Blackhawks at Balad. Civilians ask stupid questions. You were the most unique warrior I have ever met. Thanks for sharing the stories and, just as I promised, you're in the book. I'd send you a copy but I didn't catch your last name...